American Apocalypse III:

Migration

Also by nova

American Apocalypse: Beginnings
American Apocalypse: Refuge
Gardener Summer

American Apocalypse III:

Migration

by

NOVA

Flying Turtles of Doom Press

Copyright © Steve Campbell 2010

All rights reserved, including the right to reproduce this book, or any portions thereof, in any form.

This novel is a work of fiction. Any references to real people, events, establishments, organizations or locales are intended to give the fiction a sense of reality and authenticity.

First published in 2010 by Flying Turtles of Doom Press. Previously published in unedited form online at http://theamericanapocalypse.blogspot.com.

ISBN-10: 1456406426
ISBN-13: 9781456406424

First Edition: November 2010
Printed in the United States of America

For Marilyn and Elizabeth

Acknowledgements

Thanks as always to Bill McBride of Calculated Risk.
Tanta Vive!

To my readers and especially those who read online as I write and offer suggestions and comments. Thank you very much!

To Chile, the lady who makes my words sound intelligent. Thanks!

THE WAR OF THE GIANTS AND THE GODS

The giants are coming, Fafnir and Fasolt,
Muscle-bound mountains of mountainous flesh,
Builders of castles, drawers of door-bolts,
Armored with steel and gauntlets of mesh

Now they are coming to carry off Freia,
Mistress of apples and joy of the gods,
Light-warmth and sunlight of heedless Valhalla,
That humanoid legend, foil of the Norse

Shrewdness of Loge, hammer of Donner,
O giants, O giants, cunning and low,
No one can save her, not even the clever,
Never by shrewdness or hammer blow

Those are the gods in their castle so high,
Those are the giants of glacier and fire,
By dearth of the apples both races must die
At the end of those eons of hopeless desire

What are those apples, ripening fair
That Freia has plucked in the green orchards of
Those self-centered godlets we nominate Aesir?
Lightness eternal, enjoyment of love

Pride and dishonor have sold and condemned
The apples of joy for a puppetry wealth
As if the gold apples had shrunk to their stems —
Who can reflower a fruit by his stealth?

O giants! O godlets! How stupid you are.
Only a miracle saves what you've lost.
And yet you've condemned all of us to a war.
See what your greed and dishonor have cost

From Here to Babylon September 16, 2010 © Pavel Chichikov

American Apocalypse III:

Migration

CHAPTER ONE

Three Months Later

The bones were the first thing I noticed. I stood inside the shallow cave and kicked someone's head out into the sunlight. A piece of skin fell off as it bounced along the top of the crusted snow. When it rolled to a stop I noticed teeth marks where someone had gnawed on it.

It was cold outside the door. I felt like a woodchuck. If I saw my shadow, would that mean Spring was coming? Or was that if I didn't see my shadow? Maybe I'd ask when I went back inside.

I didn't think seeing the bones meant anything prophetic. Then again, Freya had been telling us it was the dawn of a new age. She had been talking about that a lot lately. According to her, we were on the cusp of a millennial realignment or some such cosmic shit. Sometimes I missed the Freya who kept her mouth shut.

I looked around the cave. There was a fire pit that was still warm and some belongings stacked in the back next to the door I had come through. Nobody was around. I figured they must be out hunting or gathering.

I had wondered if I would meet anyone when I stepped out through Freya's magic door. In one possible scenario I had run in my head, I pictured a couple screwing and me yelling, "Hey! Is that my wife?" Another scenario had featured a herd of cannibals wearing tattered North Face parkas and gnawing on bones. I couldn't think of a good line to shout out for that situation but I still had time to come up with one. Mostly though, I imagined people in animal skins gnawing on the remains of someone who had once been a copier repairman.

Back in the mineshaft, we had talked about what might await us. Cannibals were a distinct possibility. Then again perhaps the Feds had managed to get the situation under control before too many people took to gnawing on their neighbors. We had no way of knowing since being inside a mountain apparently blocked Freya's ability to get an aerial view. We'd had plenty of time to speculate, though.

I walked to the entrance and stood just a foot inside it so that I could see outside without being too exposed. Snow was everywhere, blinding in its brightness. Night's suggestion to take a pair of sunglasses was smart and I was glad I brought them. The light was painful in its intensity. The low light environment we had been living in for months now was making me a little crazy. Well, perhaps more than a little.

When I brought up the idea that perhaps it was time to take a peek outside, I was surprised that no one objected to letting me be the first one to take a look. For all we knew, I could step out into a crowd of crazed zombies. I didn't care. I had to get outside. Depending on what I reported when, and if, I popped back through the door into our world, we would all start coming up for air.

Tracks crossed the snow, packing it into paths in places. It looked like at least one or two people were in the immediate area. I didn't like the small size of some of those bones in the corner of the cave. Then again maybe there were from a big rabbit. I looked forward to meeting the Gnawers. I wasn't going to take any of them home with me. I just wanted to talk, to share, to reach out to them, and then to kill them.

The air I liked. It was clear and clean. God, it smelled good. I drank deeply of it. Living in tunnels and breathing air vented only through a series a cracks in the north tunnel and then filtered through the smell of the dead was not optimal by any means. The air outside was cleaner. Fresher. I had forgotten how good it was to breathe clean air. It was going to be hard to go back inside. Without thinking, I moved out into the sun and the world.

I stepped back into the shadows. It was time to go back. Time to return, no sprig of green to bring back with me though. Our plan was to wait it out until Spring. Based on the snow depth we still had six weeks to go. Suddenly that seemed like an awfully long time.

I stood there hesitating. With every second that passed going back became less appealing. Then I heard the sound of approaching feet, the crunch of snow giving away the fact that someone was trying to sneak up on me.

Two things we gained from tunnel life were freakishly good night vision and excellent hearing. Freya claimed it was her doing, but I was not so sure about that. I also wasn't sure if I liked having enhanced senses. I never knew that Ninja farted as much as he did. However, it was kind of sexy to sit down next to Night and hear her heartbeat speed up as I began caressing her. What was very weird was that Freya had no heartbeat that I could hear. Nor did she fart.

The sound of footsteps was getting closer. There was only one person – someone who was scared. That was good. I wasn't scared. In fact, I was feeling pretty damn good.

Wait. I cocked my head. No, there were two people. The second one was not moving, and had probably sent the one who was sneaking up on me to scout, or as a sacrificial lamb. I moved back against the wall, waited, and listened to the sound of the approaching heartbeat.

I heard the approaching heart go into overdrive a second before the person leapt into the cave, and screamed, "You die!

3

You die!" What landed five feet in front of me was rather unimpressive except for the stink. First impressions are the most important and he failed miserably. Dirty clothes were layered like tree rings over a small body of unknown gender. The eyes were frightened. Grubby mittens clutched a steak knife made of what looked like fairly good steel.

We stared at each other for a couple seconds but it probably seemed like an eternity to the other person. I smiled, raised my finger to my lips, and said, "Sshhh." I motioned for him to lie down. He got most of it right because he dropped to his knees. This was good; I gave him a B+ for his ability to size up a situation. I motioned to him with a quick, choppy hand gesture to lie down. He looked at me blankly, then figured it out, and stretched out on the cave floor. I would have hesitated, too, if it had been me. The floor was rather nasty compared to how it had been months ago.

He lay there looking up at me. His heart was no longer pounding as rapidly in his chest. I winked at him and began yelling and thrashing around inside the cave. I pulled the Ruger, shot a round out the entrance, and then thrashed and yelled some more. I stopped and looked down at him. He raised his head up, screamed a rather thin-sounding victory cry, grinned, and curled up in a ball on the floor.

I waited and listened. I didn't have to wait long. I heard the listener outside bound forward on his way to claim fresh meat. He jumped into the entrance of the cave, pulling the trigger as he did, spraying the wall with a three round burst.

He missed. I heard two rounds ricochet away. Once upon a time, in a virtual world far, far away, we called that tactic "spray and pray." He would have to do his praying in the afterlife. I shot him in the face and watched him drop to the snow.

I kicked the one lying on the floor and told him, "Don't even think about moving." I walked over and picked up the Gnawer's M-16. I recognized it as one from our armory. Gunny had stenciled numbers on each stock in olive green.

I moved to the entrance, crouched, and looked for traffic. I didn't see any but that didn't mean anything.

The dead Gnawer's body was nasty and dirty. He had three months' growth of beard, and I knew it hosted a colony of something that would make me itch. The lack of facial hair on my captive, size, and the quality of the scream made me think it had to be a kid. Male or female, I wasn't sure which yet.

I told my captive, "Get up and strip his body for anything worthwhile."

The dead guy was wearing a small daypack. The kid was going to have to roll him over to get to that. The daypack yielded a blanket, a bowl and a blue chipped Mikasa dinner plate that was once part of a nice set. It was wrapped in a dirty t-shirt.

The Gnawer had on layers of clothes and a sheath knife attached to a belt he wore strapped around the outside of his coat. His feet were wrapped in pieces of nylon, probably over a pair of shoes judging from the outline they made. The nylon was likely cut from someone else's coat.

After the kid got the belt off the nasty body, I told him, "Make a pile of what you find. Skip the clothes."

He nodded. I kept watch on the world outside the entrance as well as on the kid. The pile produced a meager lot of worldly belongings. Some string. A pocketknife. Matches. A handful of loose .223 rounds. Some wadded up paper and a wallet.

Also in the pile was a pair of socks so brown and pathetic-looking that I mistook them for roadkill, and a chunk of meat wrapped in a piece of plastic. The kid threw this out the entrance in disgust.

"Alright. Pack it up," I told him.

He stuffed everything into the daypack.

"Okay. Walk to the wall. Do not move once you reach it." I followed behind him, stopping close enough that all contact with the clean air was now gone.

Freya had given me the magic word to make the door appear. I grinned as I recited, "öppen sesame." Maybe Shorty was getting a sense of humor after all. Then I shoved the kid in the back, hard, and followed him through the door. I shoved him again once we got into the tunnel.

"Hey! Stop! I can't see."

"Just keep going. If we need to stop or make a turn, I will tell you."

I heard him grumble and told him, "Shut the fuck up and walk."

I planned on surprising Max. He did not believe I knew how to take prisoners. Plus, a little live entertainment would be a nice break in our boring lives. I was curious about was going on out there in the world. Hearing about that would be a nice change from listening to Freya talk about her grand plans for changing the world.

Shelli ate up everything Freya said and licked the spoon clean to get more. Night, I could tell, was becoming a believer. Well, actually I think she was one, but I was really hoping she would stop there, and not move on to becoming a fanatic like Shelli had. Max? I had no clue. Ninja? He was ready to rumble for her. He wanted to be her crusader and smite the evil ones. Me? I really didn't care one way or the other as long as she didn't interfere with my sex life or expect me to change.

After we had been in the Bubble for a couple of days, Freya performed a ceremony. At least I think it was after a few days. My time sense was severely handicapped without the sun. Since I took Night's word on how long we had been there, she could have told me two years and I probably would have believed her.

The little ceremony Freya performed had changed the belief equation a bit. She had each of us come and sit in front of her while she touched our eyes and ears. That was a little strange. Fortunately I handled strange pretty well. It was boring that I had a problem with.

6

The ceremony would have had more impact if there had been a light show and billowing clouds of smoke, maybe with some music by Epica playing in the background. I spent a few days afterward designing sets for it in my head.

Instead, Freya gathered Max, Ninja, and me together, and told us she had a gift for us. Night and Shelli were gathered behind her like backup singers. The vibe was a little strange, but they were smiling and I was bored. Max got to go first. He wasn't asked; he was invited. Freya was sitting in a chair facing an empty one and acting as if someone had shoved a "Queen for a day" stick up her ass.

She had Max sit down, then she stood up and told us, "I am Freya reborn. All of you will come to realize this in time. Some of you will take longer than others." She looked at me, and I grinned. "I owe you, and I will now grant you a gift. You are warriors. This gift is given in recognition of your past valor and to assist you in what is to come."

She stepped forward and told Max to close his eyes. She lightly pressed a thumb over each eye and said:

"mörker blir ljus. distans i halva"

Then she lightly touched his ears and said:

"hörseln av en uggla"

Afterward, I noticed him studying her when she was not looking. She repeated it with Ninja and I. Then she spoke a little bit more, which I ignored. Ninja fawned over her after the ceremony.

I wasn't sure I liked the changes in my senses. It took awhile to readjust the filters in my head. The better night vision was good. It was dark in the mine and a couple of times I had come close to stepping on someone else's pile when I went to take a dump.

I wasn't the only one who had problems adjusting but the enhanced hearing seemed to bother me the most. A drop of water sounded like a handclap. At one point I told Ninja if he didn't learn to speak more softly I was going to pistol-whip him into pudding. Night got up and took me down one of the side tunnels where we spent the rest of the day. It helped.

The tunnel I pushed my captive down was a rather long mineshaft. It in turn led to another shaft that led to the "Bubble" where we lived. There were more tunnels and smaller bubbles. I had explored them all after we had stumbled in here. It was nice at the time, but I was ready to move on. We were living in what had been a working coal mine for years until the coal ran out or was too high in sulfur content to burn anymore.

The main bubble was almost completely collapsed. Until about four months ago there had been enough room to back a train into it. In the past, all that extra room had been handy for loading coal. Later, about a year and a half ago, it was used as a staging area for a coup that never happened. Four months ago, that changed.

As best as we could determine, based on Freya's information, and what we found lying around, there had been a Burner/Army renegade operation based here. The Burners had needed the Army and the Army had needed the Burners. Or, at least one ambitious General thought he did. The Burners controlled or were very influential throughout a large and still productive part of America. They could have delivered legitimacy to the General. If the coup succeeded, the new administration would have legitimized the Burners in exchange. This was important, as the Burners were not faring well with the current administration whose policy echoed an earlier policy regarding the American Indians. In other words, "The only good Burner is a dead Burner."

The mine complex had become the storage facility designed to provide logistics to the Army strike force. Their plan, we think, was to build a temporary holding area for an armored battalion. They could use the railroad to move them and their hardware to Manassas, Virginia. There, they planned to offload and roll into Washington, DC, to secure their objectives.

8

Supposedly there was an infantry component as well, but we never found out who, what, and where they were, or what happened to them.

The army had sprayed a lot of the mine walls with white foam that hardened into a soft concrete of some sort. Coal dust is nasty stuff. We had quickly learned to stay out of areas where they had not sprayed.

A Burner contingent had also been living here. What happened to them was also a mystery. Freya's mother was supposed to be here but we found no sign of her. We were living in the same place where the Burners had lived. I found runes carved in the rock but when I brought Freya to look at them, they were gone. She didn't seem too disturbed by their disappearance.

About four months ago, the Feds found out about the operation. Max could not find any sign of Armor ever having been here, so they were probably caught out in the open on their way here and toasted. Then the Feds had hit the complex with some kind of bio weapon and sealed the entrance with a B-52 strike. We argued whether or not the grid going down had something to do with all of this. We didn't know and probably never would.

We had a problem with the bodies left by the Feds' attack. They were all shriveled up as if someone had drained the juice out of them, but that didn't stop them from having an unpleasant smell. All of the bodies also had one thing in common - they were grinning. Max called it "rictus." If I had been a dentist, it might have been interesting but as one of the people dragging them to a side tunnel it got old. I drug them face down after we searched and stripped them.

CHAPTER TWO

I came back to the here and now and told my captive, "Okay, stop. Now make a left."

"I can't see anything!" he wailed. I heard a hint of panic in that wail. It was dark, even for me. I knew that once we made the turn and headed into our Bubble, we - or at least I - would see an increase in illumination.

"Look. If I wanted to kill you then you would already be dead."

He stopped walking. "What are you? Some kind of freaking bat person?"

I laughed. "I thought I wanted to be one once upon a time but now I am just an owl."

He sniffed. "This is sooo freaking weird."

"Look. I am sure we will have plenty of time later for you to share your thoughts, but if you don't start walking I am going kick you in the ass until you do."

"Jesus. Why you got to be like this?" He started moving. I was pretty sure by now that he was a she. The wail and the ability to get in the last word pretty much convinced me. I thought about asking for a name and decided to wait until later. Nameless and genderless was better at this point.

We were about a third of the way down the tunnel when I told him to stop. I saw a shape pressed against the wall ahead of me.

"Hey, Ninj. I brought us a guest for dinner." Even someone as socially impaired as myself could figure out by the sudden tensing in my captive that my greeting had been misinterpreted. I reassured him. "No. We don't eat people...yet."

"Hey, G. Took you awhile." I could tell he wanted to ask me a million questions. I hadn't realized that would be part of the price of being the first out the door. I was very glad I had brought someone back alive. He could entertain them.

"Where's Max?" I asked.

I saw the flash of Ninja's teeth as he grinned, and turned around. The sound of a K-Bar sliding back into its sheath confirmed what I suspected. Max was behind me.

"You know, Max, someday you are going to get hurt pulling that shit."

He laughed, a low guttural sound. "Yeah. Keep dreaming. Let's go introduce him to the family."

I shoved the kid. "You heard the man. Keep walking."

"Okay. Okay."

We moved forward. Two minutes later I saw a flicker of light ahead and told the captive, "Move toward the light. It will welcome you."

"You call that light? By the way, I saw that show. I always thought it was stupid. What kind of ..."

I cut him off. "Spare me your review. It was a joke."

"It was? I don't think you understand my viewpoint of the current..."

"Just shut up." I heard a mutter but ignored it in order to preserve my last word status.

We came out of the tunnel into the Bubble where Freya, Night and Shelli met us. I noticed that Night was the only one with a weapon ready. The other two were just standing there, watching us approach. Ninja and Max fell in behind the captive and me.

The situation struck me as serious B movie material. *The loyal guard presents the captive to the Queen of the Bubble as*

11

the acolytes and loyal retainers stand ready to hear her judgment. So I went with it.

"Hark! Princess Freya. I bring to you the captive..." I was stuck here, as I had no idea what his name was. "... Gnawer. He brings knowledge of the outer world." Then I smacked him on the back of the head and told him to kneel.

"Ouch! You could have just asked. By the way, I am a girl not a guy." She settled down awkwardly on her knees. "Damn, it's dark in here. Like, do you have any candles?"

"Jesus. Just shut up." Instead of being exasperated I found this funny, probably because we'd been in the tunnels for too long. Then again, the clueless and absurd situations life keeps handing out have always tickled me.

Freya said, "Thank you, Gardener. Night, please question this person for our edification." I looked over at Night who rolled her eyes in acknowledgment. Maybe she hadn't drunk too deeply of the Freya Kool-aid after all.

"What's your name?" Night asked.

"Kathy Lynn Frisbee. I don't have to tell you more. I mean, isn't it just name, rank, and social security or something like that?"

Night told her very quietly, "Listen, you little dipshit. You will answer what I ask you, when I ask you, or I will personally strip you down, smear you with BBQ sauce, and throw you out the front door. Do you understand me?"

"Yes," she muttered.

"What?"

"Yes!" This had a little more heart in it. I pictured her answering her mom the same way a handful of months ago.

Night was starting to get pissed. "Good. Because right now I don't see much reason to keep you alive." Night moved right up into her face.

Kathy wouldn't meet her stare. She dropped her head. "Yes, Ma'am."

12

"Now, start at the beginning. That would be when you left your house. I want to hear where you left from, who decided you would leave, and how you got here. Now start!" The last part was hissed more than spoken.

"Like, I don't know where to start!" Oh, she was a whiner. She was also a woofer. She went, "Woof," when Night kicked her in the stomach. She fell over moaning and clutching her stomach.

Night said, "I don't think you understood me. You have information that could make the difference between life and death for my family and me. Now you can tell me what you know or I will cut your eyelids off. Then you will be able to see my lips move better when I ask you questions, you little Zone bitch."

"Wow!" I was impressed. My honey was not fucking around. The girl lay there sobbing.

Night told her, "Get up and start talking."

The girl pushed herself up, rubbed her stomach, opened her mouth to say something and changed her mind. She shut her mouth, opened it again, took a deep breath, and said, "My father sent me out. There was a group of us. We were headed to some fancy resort in West Virginia where we would be safe. I doubt if you've heard of it." She paused. When she started again, her malice was obvious. "It's called the Greenbrier."

Night said calmly, "I've heard of it. Go on." That surprised Kathy.

It seemed easier for her to talk about it now. "My dad wanted to fly us there but it was too late. He said the administration did not want any families leaving because it sent the wrong message. After the White House was overrun, though, he said that the writing was on the wall. So he made some calls. He was good at that."

"Why, and when, was the White House overrun?"

"Oh, a couple months ago. I didn't see it. I was at Quantico. But I heard it was really bloody. The President authorized air strikes or something. Whatever he did I heard someone tell my dad the body count was in the tens of thousands." The delight Kathy took in the last statement was obvious.

"Why was it overrun?"

"What?" She said incredulously, "You people been on another planet?"

Night didn't say anything. She just shifted her weight a little so she could whip another kick into the girl's midsection. Kathy didn't miss this potential for more pain heading her way.

"Duh. You were under the planet." She laughed nervously. "I mean they lost power and no one had food and people could not get out of the city and they blamed the President which really wasn't fair, you know, and ..." The last part just spewed out of the girl. If I were writing it I wouldn't use punctuation because she never paused. It just blew out of her mouth.

Night told her, "Shut up and take a deep breath."

The girl nodded and said, "I'm okay."

Night replied dryly, "That's nice." The girl, of course, missed the irony. "So tell me, Kathy Lynn Frisbee, you must have been pretty hungry yourself then?" So calm, so reasonable, even a shade of sympathy colored the bait Night threw out to her.

"Oh no! We never went hungry because we ..." She was not totally stupid. She knew that she had said something wrong. She recovered pretty quickly though. "Oh, but I have been hungry since. That horrid man I was with..."

"Kathy." This was Night. "Shut up." Kathy shut up.

"So, tell us how you got out of DC."

"Well, actually it was Quantico. That's kind of the same," she added hurriedly. "Dad got a convoy together. We had some kind of cool military vehicles. Strykers and Bumblebees, I think." Her voice turned nasty. "Our drivers were assholes. They were not allowed to evacuate their families so when they got down the road a bit they dumped us and went back. My dad is going to be so pissed."

"I bet that was rough," Night said.

14

"You aren't kidding! We were dumped near some little shithole - I think it was called Stephens City. Casey knew about it. He told us his dad owned the place." She laughed. "Casey was a little wrong about that." There was a moment of silence that went as deep as some of the mineshafts we never entered.

I grinned. I always appreciated good news. I looked over at Max and got nothing that anyone else would see and everything I needed to know.

"So," Night continued, "is the President dead?"

Kathy laughed. "You got to be kidding. He went out the tunnel to the Capitol and was up and gone before things really got going. Last I heard he is in Colorado somewhere planning his comeback."

I guess that was important news but I didn't really care. He could have been hung from a lamppost and somebody else would take his place. It did bother me a bit that the shit had gotten so out of hand and that stuff such as this was happening. It just wasn't right somehow.

I thought back to the time at the farmhouse when Night had recited the Constitution, or was it the Bill of Rights? Whatever, this was a long way from those words. The world they represented seemed so long ago that I wasn't sure if I was imagining it. Was there ever an America like that?

Night interrupted my musing by telling her, "Fine. Continue."

"Well, I was really pissed. I had not planned on getting stuck somewhere. Like, if I had known, I would have brought different clothes. There were all those people. I felt as if I was at a really bad concert. We all had guns, so I wasn't scared at first." She paused, and looked serious. "Then it got scary."

"How many of you were there?" Night asked.

She looked up; she was no math whiz, I could see her lips moving as she mentally counted. "Well, there were a lot. I think over twenty. Plus, some of our private security stayed with us. Most of them left with the Marines. My creepo bodyguard stayed with me." She shuddered. "Just because I blew him once in awhile he thought I loved him." She shook her head.

"Then we had a big fight about who was in charge. Casey thought he should be because of who his dad is. Some girl thought she should be because her dad is an Admiral. One of the security guys thought he should be because he was the oldest. Boy, he got pissed when we told him he couldn't be in charge."

Night asked, curious I suppose, "Why couldn't he be in charge?"

The girl looked at her as if she was an idiot. A look I noticed she had perfected. "Because he was staff. He worked for us." She was shaking her head at our stupidity when Night kicked her again. This time she got her in the sweet spot. We had to wait for to quit throwing up, crying, and gasping for air.

Night asked solicitously, "Are you feeling okay?"

"No," she gasped. She was still sucking wind. Night casually stomped the hand she was using to hold herself up while she used the other to wipe her mouth off. "You fucking evil bitch!" Kathy screamed in pain and disbelief.

Night stood over her and looked down. "You really are a stupid bitch, aren't you." It was not a question. It was a statement.

Kathy looked around, searching for a sign that someone gave a shit. She didn't see it. "Okay. Okay. I'm sorry. Please don't hurt me anymore. I will do anything you want." She was looking up at Night when she said the last, but it was obvious to all of us what she was really saying.

"Sorry, honey. I wouldn't fuck you with Ninja's dick." I laughed. Behind me I heard him say indignantly, "Hey!"

"Shall we continue?" Night asked.

Kathy nodded her head. "Well, there was not much left in the town. That was for sure. I stayed with Casey. He had hooked up with the security guy who seemed to know what he was doing." She grimaced. "He certainly was doing Casey. The funny thing was Casey kept asking about some guy named Gardener. I think he had a crush on him or something. The security guy, Malcolm, beat the shit out of Casey one night after he told him Gardener could kick his ass." She shook her head. "Casey was a really stupid bitch."

She sighed. "It was crazy. People killing each over the silliest shit. No food. We stayed in the police station. It had already been cleaned out like the town. It was cold, too."

"So how did you feed yourself?"

She didn't say anything at first. Night reached down and tugged on her hair. I made a mental note to make sure she washed her hand later.

She continued. "Okay! I was thinking. We robbed people! They just kept coming. The only problem was they kept coming but they had less and less. Plus, they were meaner. It got harder and harder and we started losing people." Her voice was getting quieter now. She was cradling her injured hand and I noticed she was beginning to rock back and forth.

"It was bad...really bad. So Lonny told me we could make it if we got far away from all the people. I told him my dad would come for me but Lonny just laughed when I told him that. I tried calling him with cell phones from the people we robbed but I couldn't get him." She was crying for real now. "I know he will come. I know it."

"Hey!" Night snapped. Kathy looked up. She had been rather grimy-looking before. The snot flowing out of her nose now did not improve her looks. Night spoke to her again a little less harshly. "Don't worry. I am sure you will see your dad soon enough."

"You think so?"

"Sure. So did you hear anything about a farm that was nearby? One with walls?"

Sniff. "Yes." Sniff.

"What did you hear, Kathy?" Even my patience was starting to run out. Night was showing signs of wanting to rip her head off.

17

Then Shelli decided she couldn't keep her mouth shut any longer. "What about a diner? Did you hear anything about that?"

Kathy wiped her nose on her sleeve. "It didn't have any food in it."

Night glared at Shelli. Shelli ignored it, and was on the edge of asking for more information when Freya told her, "Silence." She shut up.

"Kathy, the farm. Tell us about it."

"I don't know. It's a bad place. It's why I left with Lonny, my creepo security guy. They..." She swallowed hard. "They keep the...they call it the 'Farm' because it's where they keep the other white meat." She swallowed hard. "That was supposed to be funny. They are probably gone now. They were going to make a slave pen there, too. That was Casey's plan at least. I know you probably think I am not a nice person but eating people...ewww. I mean it doesn't taste like chicken." She stopped short. "I mean that's what I was told."

We just stared at her.

"What! What the fuck are you staring at? You were safe in here. You probably have a microwave, real food and ketchup! So don't fucking judge me! I did what I had to do!"

I'd had enough. "Kathy. Behind you." She turned around. "Did you eat any kids?" She just stared at me. Her eyes told me the answer.

"That's what I thought." I might have let her slide for munching on a insurance agent or tech support person. I couldn't give her a pass for eating kids. Not knowingly.

She screamed, "Fuck you! Fuck all of you!"

"Hey...it's okay." I held out my hands and, using the best soothing voice I had, I said, "It's okay. We understand. " I kept moving toward her, whispering, "It's okay. It's okay." I held out my arms to hug her, inviting her to come to me so I could hold her close.

18

She came to me, hesitantly, but she came. I pulled her close with one arm and drove the bayonet into her back at an angle. She looked at me in surprise.

I whispered, "It's okay. Daddy is waiting," and held her until she died. Then I let her drop to the floor.

The aftermath of quiet was broken by Max, who said, "She would have been nothing but a boil on our collective ass." A less than thrilling graphic I thought. He continued, "G, you impressed me. You took a prisoner. I like personal growth like that in a brother. Now you get to drag her to the tomb tunnel."

I sighed and grabbed her feet. As I was dragging her away Max yelled to me, "Check her pockets!" I heard him laughing as I dragged her out of the Bubble and down the tunnel corridor. Damn, she was leaving a trail.

CHAPTER THREE

When I came back Night was holding the crumpled piece of paper from Lonny's pack. "G, come check out this flyer."

Citizens of the United States!
DO NOT DESPAIR!

You have not been forgotten!
These flyers were dropped with a pallet of food
as part of your government's plan to assist you.
The power has been restored to numerous areas.
Relief supplies are being marshaled and order restored!
Please return to your homes and help us rebuild America!
Residents of the Washington DC Metro area, please report
to the receiving centers closest to you.
The following locations will provide you with assistance!
Haymarket   Winchester   Centerville   Sterling

Please have ID ready.
NO WEAPONS ALLOWED INSIDE THE CENTERS!
LOOTERS WILL BE SHOT!
MARTIAL LAW IS NOW IN EFFECT!

version 1.b HS rel 1, DC area drop

Night handed it to me. "It was probably dropped by air."

I read it out loud and said, "Well, that's nice. I knew they had it under control all along." I handed it back to Night.

Max snorted. "Right. Notice it doesn't say who is President."

Night laughed. "As if it matters."

I added, "I wonder why Lonny bothered saving it. I doubt if he would have received much of a welcome."

Shelli answered for me. "Hope?"

I shrugged. "Or toilet paper?"

"So, do we have a plan?" I asked Max.

Before he could reply Freya spoke. "Yes. I need to go to the door. I need to see."

I was okay with that. Being outside made the tunnels and the Bubble seem even more confining. Plus, the air quality really sucked. From the way everyone responded so eagerly, I think they all felt the need for a little fresh air themselves.

"When, Freya?" I asked.

"Why not now?"

The rest were a little giddy about going outside, except Max. His response to the idea was, "No one is going anywhere until they get geared up first. That includes you, Shelli." It dawned on me that it had been awhile since I'd heard her moans coming from their sleeping area. Oh well, Max was a big boy. They would either work it out or not.

As soon as we were geared up, everybody followed me back to the door. Max and I went out first. I went right and he went left. Being left-handed that worked very nicely for me. Once we cleared the magic door Max froze the rest of them in place with a hand signal. We did a high/low at the cave entrance. It was clear. We stayed in place while the others came out.

I watched them out of the corner of my eye. They sucked up that fresh air like emphysema patients who had been away from the oxygen tube too long. I checked out Max. I think I saw his

21

nostrils flare twice. That was a pretty heavy-duty reaction from Mr. Stoneface to the fresh air.

Freya came up to where we were watching and stood in between us. Max had his binoculars out and was scanning the trees so he missed them coming. One minute there was nothing in the evening sky, and then there were crows. Lots of crows.

I heard Freya whisper, *Gott... Komma min barnen, komma.*" The crows landed in the trees about fifty yards from us.

Landed is not really the right word. *Settled* would be more descriptive but not still quite accurate. I don't think there is the fitting word in English. Crows are talkative birds. They have a surprisingly complex language, as I was to learn later. These crows didn't talk. They stared at us. Well, at Freya actually. I looked over at Max who replied with a tiny shrug - more of a twitch really.

"Freya, what happened to the hawks?"

"We need more eyes to see, more wings to fly," she answered. It was my turn to shrug and mentally reply, *Whatever.*

We stood there watching the crows stare at Freya for a couple minutes. Then the murder rose as one, circled once, and on the second pass the tight group shattered as each bird flew off in a different direction.

There was a moment of silence. I broke it by asking Night, "Want to build a snowman?"

She grinned in delight, answering, "Sure!"

Max stayed on watch while we built a snowman, then Ninja and I threw snowballs at each other and Night. Shelli stood by herself watching. A few minutes into it, she bent over, packed some snow in a ball, and hit Ninja in the back of the head with it when he wasn't looking. It was war.

After about fifteen minutes I went over to Max and asked if he wanted to be relieved. Much to my surprise he did. He promptly hit Shelli with a nicely packed snowball. I watched everyone laughing and trying to kill each other. Alliances formed and dissolved in seconds. Curses were uttered and retaliations threatened. For one of the few times since she had joined us Freya actually looked her age.

Then we heard the boom of a high caliber rifle somewhere nearby. Max sprinted in leaps that covered yards to where he had left his M 16. Ninja was right behind him. Night picked up Freya, catching her in mid-snowball throw and bolted toward the cave entrance. Shelli belatedly followed. She was slow. Too slow. Even if she had lots of training she would never be in our league.

I didn't see anything but that didn't mean squat. I was aware of how much we stood out against the snow. Everything we had available to wear was designed for a season that was gone. Max motioned for Ninja to back into the cave entrance. Then I followed him in.

"Okay, one at time through the door. Ninja first. Set up when you get through." Ninja nodded. He understood. Max wanted him to set security inside the door in case we were rushed.

Freya said, "I can't go."

"Why?"

"Because, Max, I have to wait for a crow to return."

"How long?"

She closed her eyes for a few seconds. "We are fine. There is a small band moving north of here. In the east about two miles is another band. They are encamped. Another band is about one mile below us and to the east in the wreckage of the town. They fired the shot. It was a lone traveler. No one has a visual on us. The crows will return just before sundown and roost here."

"Fine. Gardener and I will stay up top. Night, take Shelli down. Tell Ninja what's up." She nodded, took Shelli by the elbow and went through the door. As soon as they were gone we went back to being as still as a rock wall.

We waited. We were getting very good at waiting. No one spoke. We just watched the woods, the sky, and the location of the sun. Right as the sun was about to set, a single crow returned. It flew in a circle above us, made a pass at the trees, found one it liked, and landed. It stared at Freya and she at it for about five minutes. I watched Freya when I wasn't watching the treeline.

She stood there, eyes closed, her face to the setting sun and not the crow. When she opened her eyes the crow cawed once and took off. She said softly as it flew away, *"Väl gjort bror gala."*

I looked at Max. "Take down the snowman?"

"Yep."

It may seem like what we did - the playing in the snow - was dumb, but we needed it. The only problem was that being outside made being inside feel even more oppressive. The air quality really sucked.

What did our world inside look like? It was not just a tunnel carved into the side of a mountain. Coal had been extracted from inside this mountain for over eighty years. It had been a good mine, maybe even the Comstock Lode of local coal mines. What had been a shaft in the side of the mountain grew to be a hollow cavern at the entrance.

A rail spur had been built here, probably in World War II, so a train could back its coal cars right into the cavern for loading. The coal was brought up from the interior of the mine on a narrow gauge track and carried in little mini coal bins. The coal was dumped into a funnel that could be closed or opened as needed. That in turn fed the train's coal cars.

Around this main cavern, or "bubble," were a number of smaller bubbles that had been used to store bins and machinery. One bubble had a set of showers and a locker room for incoming and outgoing shifts. Unfortunately the showers no longer worked. Venting on this level, and as far as I could tell on the next two, was a mix of old style ventilation shafts and fans. Below that it was all mechanical. I had tried to go deeper into the mine but gave up. The air was noxious, and I had a bad feeling about whether it was structurally safe.

Water came from the lowest level we were able to access. It was not plentiful, and getting to it was like diving without air tanks. Go down, get the water, and come back up quickly. The water had begun to flow with a little more volume in the last month or so. We had already noticed an increase in the dampness on our level. Max thought it was because of the snow melting. The water was definitely cold enough to be snowmelt.

The army had blown some kind of coating on the walls and floors to cut down on the dust. One part had been converted to very Spartan living quarters where Freya had lived with the Burner contingent. There were a number of cots stored away with blankets. Those came in handy.

The Army had also pre-positioned food as the armor brigade was probably to have spent a day or two waiting for the signal to roll. We got the food. Unfortunately, the MREs were the only worthwhile item we found in any quantity inside the mountain. It would have been nice if the complex had been a mother lode of weapons and other goodies, but it wasn't. If it ever had been, the cave-in at the main entrance had buried most of it.

When it came to eating the MREs, no one bitched much anymore. Not since we now knew what other people were eating. I thought they were fine, especially the stew, which I liked best. The meals were better than what I had spent most of my life eating.

Early on I caught Freya going through the MREs. She was opening them and eating the desserts. Since the reason I caught her was that I had entered the storeroom in hopes of finding a few cinnabars or anything with sugar to snack on for myself, I wasn't too hard on her.

While we gorged on the desserts, I asked Freya how she had ended up in such a shit hole.

"My Mother brought me."

"Yeah, but why?"

"Because."

"Really? So where did you come from? The North Pole?"

She stopped to swallow and cocked her head. "That's just silly. Nobody lives there."

She never did give me a good answer. All she told me was that she had been "invoked."

I asked, "So did it hurt?" She just rolled her eyes.

Mostly we talked about what our favorite desserts were. Sometimes we would argue over the trade value of the desserts we each found. I would trade the ones I didn't like for the ones I did. The problem was she liked them all.

We got busted a couple days later for it and were royally chewed out by Max in public, and then I had to listen to Night in private. Freya and I were supposed to forfeit our desserts for a month. I had to, but I know Shelli was giving Freya her desserts. It took almost two weeks for Night to forgive me and let me have a bite of hers.

It was obvious that being outside had changed us. We wanted out! The question was what to do next. While we worked that out Max put us through a training program. Our days became tightly scheduled.

Max started training us in basic self-defense moves, such as what to do if faced with an assailant with a knife. Or how to hurt someone badly if pinned by an assailant and how to take someone down if you were on the ground and they were standing. We learned six ways to hurt someone badly with our hands, and how to stab someone correctly.

They were simple moves, and we practiced them over and over for a week. Only Freya was excused from the training program. I called Max on that after a few days.

"Max, she may be a Shorty but she needs to know how to do this stuff, too." I looked at her. She sat on the sidelines doing something with the sticks she had collected from God knows where. She would toss them in the air, and then stare, sometimes for hours, at the patterns they made. It looked like a pretty boring way to amuse oneself. She looked up when she heard her name.

Max looked at me and grinned. "She is fine, G. Trust me."

"Max, I would and have trusted you with my life. It's not about trust. It's about making sure Shorty doesn't end up in a stew pot, or in some asshole's harem."

He sighed. "G, really. You know she doesn't have a heartbeat. Doesn't that tell you something?"

"That she's a member of the undead? Or that she has a really slow heartbeat? She is a kid, Max." I emphasized the last. More to myself than anyone else I mumbled, "She is not going to get hurt." Then stronger, "I will not allow it, Max. She will not get hurt!"

I felt Night stir behind me. I realized my posture had changed. I told myself, *Relax. Relax. It's Max. It's okay.* The switch had been flipped, though, and I felt the momentum of the change begin to pick up.

I said again, "She will not be hurt, Max!" Even I heard the change in my voice.

A far away, tiny voice way back in the corner of my head whispered, "Max, do something. Please stop this." He did.

He smiled. "It's cool, G. Go ahead. Teach her." He stepped back slowly. "It's okay, G. No one will hurt her. She's okay."

Night was behind me now. "Honey...it's okay. Come sit with me. Okay?" I felt her light touch on my arm and I shrugged it off.

"No. Freya, come on, it's time you learned this. Past time."

Freya smiled and said, "Okay." She swept her sticks back in her bag and dropped them inside her shirt. She stood up and walked over to where I stood. "It's okay," she told Max.

I felt Night move away and watched as Max did the same.

"Gardener," she said quietly, "we understand and appreciate." Then she spun in the air and took my head off at the shoulders.

Not literally. It just felt that way. I even reached up to make sure it was still attached.

I shook my head a little and said, "That was interesting, Shorty," and then I drew on her. I felt my fingers touch the wood of the butt of the Ruger for a millisecond, and then a spear went through my heart leaving me doubled over in pain. I managed to gasp, "Jesus. Shorty, that hurt."

I forced my bent-over body to straighten up and found that she was gone. I looked around for her. She was sitting cross-legged again on the sidelines and was pulling her bag out. She looked up at me and smiled.

I smiled; well, I moved my face muscles back at her and looked over at Max. "Yeah, I guess she can sit this one out." Then I blacked out.

I came to about a minute later. The first face I saw was Freya's. She said, "I'm sorry. I am growing stronger and I didn't compensate."

I looked at her grave face and blue eyes and said, "You pull that shit on me again, Shorty, and I am going to jack you up." I grinned. So did she.

I sat up, and carefully got to my feet. "Okay. Damn it, I'm fine." It was embarrassing having everyone staring at me as if I was going to keel over and die.

"Night, really, I'm fine."

We went back to practicing, without Freya.

I felt a little strange after my encounter with Freya. No one looked at me any differently. The only one whose behavior changed, and that was temporary, was Night. She was very gentle with me before we went to sleep.

A few more long days went by. Freya was sitting off to one side away from everyone else. I joined her as Max demonstrated the correct way to draw a pistol to the others. She began lamenting the fact that Ninja had eaten the last cinnamon dessert the day before. I had been thinking about her and something she had said once, and decided now was the time to ask about it.

"So what is this about needing people to believe in you? I thought goddess types came fully charged and ready to zap the crap out of people."

She didn't answer right away so I asked again.

She replied somewhat peevishly, "I heard you the first time. I am trying to figure out how to say it." A minute passed by.

Then she told me, "Think of a line or wall between two worlds. In that wall there is a tiny opening. The 'Me' that exists threads itself through that tiny opening, with a part of me in one world and another part in this world. Each part of me is governed by a cycle. I am at the part of the cycle where I have shrunk to almost nothing in this world. The time has come where I need to grow again here. As I do, I gain more and more power here until I am almost all-powerful. A true Goddess. Yet once I reach that stage I begin to die again. I don't really die, not the way you think, because nothing can grow forever."

I nodded my head. So far I was following this.

"So my power from this side, after a certain point, is drained off to feed the me on the other side, which in turn has become almost nothing during this turn of the cycle. This renews that world. For a short time period - short from my point of view, everything is in equilibrium. This is what you call a 'Golden Age.' It doesn't last. Nothing lasts forever except the cycle." She said this with a note of regret.

I had to agree. If I knew anything at all about life, it was that nothing lasted.

"So you are a battery that has only charged a little bit?"

She nodded her head. "Yes. I am like the talkie-walkies you had in the station. I think you would see one green bar on my readout right now."

"What happens if I start believing in you? Does that help?"

She smiled. "More than you have any idea."

29

"Okay. I will. But this doesn't mean you get all the desserts we find."

She laughed, replying, "Finders keepers, losers weepers."

CHAPTER FOUR

Without any discussion about it, we went back to the practice of eating dinner together and talking afterward.

Max told us, "Based on what Freya says about the weather changing, we have about two weeks before we can move. It'll be pushing it but the snow will be almost completely gone by then. We will still stick out but we can make up for it by moving at night."

He started arranging MRE wrappings and torn pieces of cardboard on the floor in front of him. "The way I see it is this. We leave here and go back to see if we can find any of the others. We strip the place of everything we can get our hands on while we are there. Then it is time to move on. Gardener and I talked once about what it was going to be for us - farmers or the Golden Horde. I say 'Golden Horde.'"

Everyone nodded their heads.

He continued. "We get away from the Zones and the Feds. We take what we need, and we go elsewhere and build a true Golden Horde. Then we begin to take back what is ours in the name of the people. We burn away the bullshit. We stop the insanity of raping the world that we and our children to come will live in. We make things right again."

We were all nodding our heads. Then I realized something. Nobody had said where we were going. "Max. Ummm....where are we going?"

Freya answered for him. "Montana."

"Montana? You got to be kidding me. That's where all the nut jobs go. It's like the holy land or something for them."

"Yeah, but when we get done, G, they will either be our nut jobs or they will be dead," Max replied.

The day we left was a cold one outside. A freak snowstorm had held us back two extra weeks. Now the snow was almost gone and the air smelled of Spring. The smell of dirt and leaves was better than a bouquet of flowers to my nose and soul.

Max and I took over watch positions, and let Freya commune with her birdbrains. That's what I called them, as in "what do Freya's little birdbrains see for us now?" She sketched a map in the dirt of what they saw. I asked her why we couldn't do the flyover thing and see for ourselves.

She bit her lip, looked away for a few seconds, then looked at me and said, "I can't sustain that kind of connection for long periods without becoming drained. At least not yet." I nodded. It made sense based on what she had told me earlier.

And so the great migration began. That's how I thought of it. I had no idea if we were going to walk all the way to Montana, or if we would even get out of the state. I didn't really care. It was just nice to be moving again. It was almost sundown and I could feel the temperature change. I doubted the cold would bother anyone. The weight we were carrying would keep us warm enough. We were thin on all our supplies except ammo. We had burned almost none of that in the past few months.

We had talked about how we wanted to do this after dinner almost every night for the past week. The big question was whether to avoid contact with others or to seek it out. Did we want to take the risk of one of us getting hurt? Would we alert others? Was it worth it?

32

The problem was that we had to get supplies and there weren't exactly any stores left where we could stock up. Our only choice was to take from others. We decided to only take on groups we could devour. No mercy to the survivors allowed if they showed they had taken what they had from others. Especially if they had snacked on them afterward.

Max told us, "Anyone still out here is guilty of something. Don't sweat it."

There were a couple of small bands working the area between our town and us. The great population movement had dried up at least a month ago as best as we could tell. Power was even on again in some places, although not many. From what Freya's little birdbrains showed her, the power was on sporadically inside the Zones with more lights visible closer toward the core area. She patched me in the night before we left. It was not pretty out there. Crows being what they are, I got a closer look than I needed at what they were eating out there. I guess dead humans were just another form of roadkill to them.

I asked if she could see inside the Zones and into Washington DC itself. That was out of her range. The only reason she knew about the lights increasing deeper into the Zone was from a bird that flew high enough on the border of to see deeply into the area. I asked whether it was a hawk. She told me it was. She didn't understand why I thought it was funny that we were flying our own predators.

Despite all the talk of us being the second coming of the Golden Horde led by the Max Khan himself, we skirted the first band in our path. There were twenty of them; of that at least fifteen were males who were fairly well-armed. They were moving away from us and probably headed into Ohio. We had three solid warriors, plus one woman who had certainly shown she was hard-core enough. Shelli was an unknown; personally, I thought she was more of a liability than an asset. And we had Freya. Another unknown, but one I think was able to safely stand on the sidelines and take care of herself should the need

33

arise. I wanted to go for it but Max said there was no need at this point.

We kept moving. Max and I agreed that Freya should send periodic updates to whoever was walking point. He emphasized to us not to rely on them completely.

"Just because the bird doesn't see anything bad doesn't mean there isn't somebody waiting for you. I want to use them for terrain checks and large movements. That's it." I had watched enough birds to know that they could be fooled. Max had the killer closer line. He told us, "If birds are so fucking smart then nobody would bother to go duck hunting." It made a lot of sense once you thought of it that way.

Three days later we were sitting with our backs to a gray stone outcropping. We stopped about an hour early as Max thought it was the best place we were going to find to shelter in. It was damp and uncomfortable, and I slept like a baby.

We were moving at night instead of during the day. Our eyes were good enough to do it now and it was safer. As usual Night and I had separate watches. In the evening we popped the heaters and ate hot food. What would have been dinner was now breakfast and we could cook because we would be moving on. Once again I sent thanks to the inventor of MREs. Whoever thought of these things was a good person. They had included coffee.

After we finished eating and just before we moved we were briefed. This next band was going to be our first action since leaving the cave. Based on the birdbrains, it looked like they were working the road and about a half mile on either side of it. They were about eight miles from our old town. This was just about the distance people might cover in an afternoon on foot if they were moving quickly. They would be tired and easier prey by then.

We each received a thirty-second feed of the area. The little birdbrains saw things a lot differently than a human eye did.

They were best at distance viewing. Up close they tended to focus on nothing for more than a second, and then they usually were interested in things that were of no interest to us. Bright and shiny objects fascinated them. Since we were not trash collectors this was rather useless from our point of view.

The camp for this band of brigands looked like a standard Tree People camp minus most of the blue tarps. They had the strewn trash and unburied human shit part down pat. The big difference was the Tree People might have eaten a squirrel or two. They may have even had a pure breed dog fresh from someone's backyard over for BBQ. They did not, as a rule, eat people. Nor did they decorate the fire pit with skulls. Then again, some Tree People encampments did contain an element that might have thought that kind of decoration was an awesome idea.

The band slept inside their shelters and even posted a sentry. By now most of the dumb asses were either dead or back in the Zones. The smart ones probably had a town they thought they could hold. My guess was the military would be pacifying little towns and the surrounding countryside for the next couple of years. At some point the government would start a resettlement project, probably sooner than later. They had no choice; the big city model had failed considering the state of the current infrastructure. Plus, they needed functioning farms and safe roads.

Somehow the thought of living in a resettlement town was about as unappealing as a Tent City. Most Tent City inhabitants would likely see them as an improvement though, just because they would probably be run a little looser and people might be able to have gardens.

Max cleared leaves from a patch of dirt and laid out our plan of attack with a stick from an oak tree. Nothing subtle or fancy. No heroics. Just slaughter them, loot, and keep going. We were going to move on them around 03:00 in the morning.

They were living in three dome tents camouflaged a while ago with pine branches and chopped up bushes. I don't think it had worked as well as they had hoped. The branches were dead and had dropped their needles, so now they were just a dead skeletal overlay of camo gone bad. The tents were pitched in an arc facing the fire pit. There was a clump of pine trees, Christmas tree size - if you didn't mind spindly, about thirty feet away. That was where the women went to take a dump. The men probably went anywhere.

As usual, a ring of trash surrounded the encampment. What was unusual was what the trash consisted of. There was luggage - enough to pack a tour bus, toys, some kids' backpacks, a flat screen television, five bikes, and a bunch of plastic bins. Good scavenging was in store for whatever band came along after us.

The plan was for Max to take out the sentry and cover the front of the tent area from the side. Ninja, Night, and I would come up behind the tents, hose them, and then move. Night would stay on Max's side while Ninja and I took the other. Shelli would stay with Freya at a distance and watch our backs. I liked how Max phrased that. It mollified Shelli in case she felt slighted, and kept Freya out of the way. We had M-16s and one M-14. I had the M-14.

We moved into position. Once Max gave the signal we were going to rush the remaining yards to our spots. We didn't want to make any noise crunching leaves near them. That was another problem with my improved hearing. We sounded like elephants moving. We were not really that loud; it just sounded that way to me. We got into position and Max took off to kill the sentry.

He could move amazingly quietly. I knew that from past experience and listening for his movement now only confirmed it. I wasn't sure if I heard him approach the sentry or not. I did hear the sound of fabric rustling and the impact of the knife into his kidney, followed by the sound of a gasped breath. Then nothing. Max had to wave at us twice. He had changed his position so quietly that I didn't pick up his movement and signal the first time.

We made our move. I had the shortest distance to cover. I had just braced myself when Night, who had the longest distance to cover, hit her mark. All three of us froze for second, locked eyes, nodded, and began firing. I don't know about the others but it felt as if I was shooting into a bag of cats. The tent bulged and rippled as the people inside tried to get out of their beds and away from the hail of bullets. Mewing sounds and groans emanated from inside. I dumped the magazine, after trying to space the shots in a pattern that covered the fabric. I inserted a new one, and moved to our new position, slapping Ninja on the shoulder as I went past to remind him to move with me.

I was the only one to have someone make it out of his tent. That was irritating. He made it about seven feet and collapsed. Max moved in and kicked away his handgun and then moved back. We were still hearing moans and groans coming from inside the tents.

Max kept watch while we closed in on one tent at a time. Night and I worked the same side of the tent together. I jammed my bayonet in, and made a foot long slit. Then I grabbed the tent fabric, stuck the blade in above the previous cut and peeled it back. Cutting open the tents was like popping the top on a can of stink. These people reeked of old roadkill and poorly wiped asses.

The opening I made gave Ninja a window into the inside in case anyone was still feeling frisky enough to be hostile. As soon as he saw a body, he shot it just to be on the safe side. Max must have seen or heard movement in the tent next to us because he pumped a three-round burst into it. I heard that, sheathed my bayonet, and drew looking for movement. Nothing. I holstered the Ruger, pulled the bayonet again, and moved on to repeat the procedure on the next tent.

We finished all three tents without incident. Ninja and Night were using my standard method of checking for possible possums. That is, with a kick in the head. I don't know how they felt about doing it, but I found it very satisfying.

I heard Ninja's rifle fire once. Someone must have twitched. I realized as I kicked my kills that a bayonet might come in real handy attached to the end of the M-14. Besides looking wicked, it would be perfect for people poking. My bayonet was built for a Mauser so I didn't think it would work on this rifle but I was definitely going to look into it.

I finished up and walked over to where Night was working. She was done and just standing there, shaking her head.

"What's up?" I asked her.

"Damn, I don't look forward to searching these vermin-infested, rancid, pieces of dog shit."

"No kidding," agreed Ninja. He kicked someone. Probably just out of irritation with their smelly, wormy ass.

Max gave a barely audible whistle, just enough to get our attention. He was standing over the guy who had made it of the tent. We drifted over to check him out. He was still alive but unhappy with how it felt. I didn't blame him. I had shot him in the stomach.

What caught our attention was his necklace. It was truly a unique bit of handiwork. On a leather thong around his neck were tied a number of strands of leather. Each strand went through a wedding ring that was wrapped once to hold it in place and then continued another inch where it ended with a wrapped and knotted finger bone, presumably from the hand that once wore the ring.

He was looking up at us and was not seeing any love. "The necklace...pant...moan...was my girlfriend's...not mine...help me...hurts."

He was from my tent so he was my responsibility. Not that any of the others would hesitate to kill him. That was obvious.

I looked down at him. "Stomach wound?"

"Yes...hurts."

"Want me to fix you up?"

38

He nodded his head and whispered, "Please... I am sorry for what I did."

I pulled the bayonet from its sheath and watched his eyes widen as I did. "Don't worry." I cut the leather thong. I pulled the ends together and tossed it over by where Max had kicked his pistol.

"I bet saying 'I'm sorry' and 'please' smoothed over a lot of shit in the old days."

He didn't say anything.

"Yep. Well, let me fix that stomach wound for you." I drove the bayonet into his right eye. "Okay. All better now." I pulled it out, wiped it off on his shirt, and began searching his corpse while it was warm enough to keep the bugs from jumping ship.

After we dragged the bodies off to the side Max had us take our knives and probe the ground where the tents had been. I hit something right away - a coffee can with a mix of gold and silver coins and more jewelry. Night got lucky, too, but hers was mostly watches. Rolex watches were nice, but not worth even pennies on the dollar compared to what their original owners had paid for them.

"All right!" Hearing this told me Ninja had also hit the jackpot.

While we were doing this Max went through the weapons. We kept the quality handguns only. Anything else we left behind after pulling the bolts and breaking the firing pins. We had changed the rules on the dividing of spoils by mutual agreement. Everything was divided and given to Night. She kept track of payouts and shares. Personal combat kills still went to the victor, but I told her the Gnawer's necklace could go into the common bank. I almost said "pot" but that seemed a little tasteless, even to me. I chuckled to myself about how it would be "tasteless" anyway once we'd removed the rings and chucked the bones.

We were loading up our packs when Max came up to me and said, "Burn everything that's left."

I shrugged, "Yeah, well, I am already getting antsy about being here."

"I know." He spat in the direction of one of the Gnawer bodies. "Well, time for us to find a place to hole up."

CHAPTER FIVE

We were still a day, maybe half a day if we pushed it, from our town. We weren't moving fast since our goal was to move without anyone knowing we had been there. Max didn't want us to just show up and kick in doors. The first stop would be the farm. I didn't expect to find anyone alive. Yet it was something that had to be done.

"Then," and he emphasized this to me in private, "only if it is doable will we go into town. I know you. You want to just charge in there, find Casey, and kill him. We are not going to do business that way. Not if we want to survive, let alone grow. There will be plenty of Caseys in the world for you to kill."

I wasn't thrilled but he had a point. Not one I liked, but one I understood.

The trail we were following had seen some heavy traffic since the last time we were on it. We spotted a few graves but the rotting corpses uncovered by the melting snow outnumbered them. Corpses and trash. You could have stepped from one to another and never touched earth for the last three miles before town. Of course stepping on corpses would have been messy and potentially a source for broken ankles but I liked the analogy.

Did it stink? Yes. Did we get used to the smell? No. Was it a health hazard? Most definitely.

We had to swing out away from the town in order to come up on the farm from behind. There was a hill near it where we planned on setting up an observation post. We would camp on the other side of it so we could not be seen by anyone in town. We ran into feral dog packs twice along the way. They were wary rather than afraid. They were not starving so they backed off, not by much but they did give way. That was a good thing, as we didn't want to shoot them. Shots would be far too noisy this close to town.

We made the hill by the farm a few hours before daylight. We cold camped. No need to send the smell of coffee wafting over the countryside. Somebody might smell meat cooking and decide it wasn't worth expending too much energy checking it out. Not unless you went in a group, otherwise you might end up being open pit BBQ yourself. Coffee, though, that was different. That smelled like civilization and somebody with quality supplies. That would draw Starbucks zombies and God knows what else.

Everyone went up to take a look at the farm. Max went up first and stayed up there as each of us went up. Shelli took about twenty minutes longer than everyone else. That didn't go unnoticed, but it did pass without comment. She didn't say anything when she came back. The flushed face and faint smile spoke for her. I went up last, crouched, moved next to Max, and lay flat. He didn't say anything, he just handed me the glasses.

I had a feeling it was bad when Night came back and was really quiet. She just shook her head in response to my look of inquiry and turned away.

It was bad. Someone had been crucified on top of the berm by the gate. Not just crucified; it looked as if they had jammed a pipe up his ass. The house had been burned down, and so had the mobile home.

I started doing slow sweeps back and forth with the binoculars. It looked like there were bones in the ashes of the house near the garden. The outbuildings were still there, as was the garage. The garage doors were open and someone had tagged the inside. Damn graffiti artists were like cockroaches. They survived no matter what happened.

I handed the glasses back to Max and asked, "Tonight?" He shook his head yes.

We went back down and joined the others. Might as well. There was not a lot to observe up there. The mood was quiet. At sundown I began getting ready. Ninja wanted to go with us.

Max told him, "You saw those dog packs. I need you here with Night. It is going to take you and her both to shut them down if they come sniffing around."

Freya was getting ready to say something when Max shot her a look that made her close her mouth. Max was not big on talking when we were in the field. With him, it was silence, awareness, and readiness. Since he trained us, it was the only way we knew.

Shelli didn't have the training. She started to tell him, "But Freya said..."

Without any hesitation, and as cold as the ground the corpses around us slept on, he told her, "Shut up, Shelli." She shut up but it was obvious that she was pissed.

Something was happening here that I was not getting. I looked over at Night and all I got was a sad smile. I mentally shrugged. Once Max and I stepped off none of this would take up space in my head. Max and I blacked our faces and hands. Night did mine. Max did his own. At the last minute I left the M-14 behind. Max watched me hand it to Night but didn't say anything. I slid my bayonet in and out of my sheath three times for luck. Then I jumped up and down to see if I jingled. I didn't.

Night came over and gave me a goodbye hug, which was very unusual. Then she reached up, drew her finger down my cheek and turned away. I had gone through most of my life feeling as if everyone, except for me, had been issued the "How to be a Member of the Human Race" handbook. I hadn't felt that way for a couple of years now. I did now, and I didn't like it.

I looked over at Max. He nodded, and we went over the top and down the hill. It was eerie approaching the farm this way. The ruined farmhouse and blackened trailer were reminders of what once was and what might have been. We went in from behind. After we hit the outbuilding we moved in bursts covering each other. We had discussed how we were going to do it before we went over the hill. It only took three seconds: a couple hand signs from Max and a nod that I understood. The plan was to make a circuit of the area behind the berm to make sure it was clear. Then we would focus on looking for any sign of our friends.

We hit the garage first. Nothing but a couple of decaying nude bodies missing their legs. Their asses looked gnawed on, too. There was some scattered trash in the corners. I didn't see anything worthwhile but Max saw something that caught his eye. He motioned for me to keep watch and moved in to fetch the treasure that caught his eye. It was a five-gallon plastic gas can. Empty, of course. We moved on.

The outbuildings, which we had used to store garden tools and junk that Tommy could not seem to part with, were still the same. Some of the tools were gone, the pointy and sharp ones. The rest of the stuff was still there. The other shed was larger. It held the lawnmowers, the Bobcat, and wheelbarrows. They were all still there.

The new additions were the bones and skulls. Little skulls. One was missing a tooth in the same place that a little boy I once knew had one missing. The side of the head had been caved in. I froze in place.

I don't know how long I stood there. I do know that I went empty inside. Empty except for a cold wind that blew through me. In the far dark recesses of that emptiness I heard the clank of gears grinding and metallic shrieks as machinery moved for the first time in years. The doors were opening to rooms I had locked away years ago and the gibbering demons of my childhood were once again loose. I stood there on an empty plain of grayness and waited for them. Sharp of teeth and filled with fury, they raced toward me and I opened my arms to embrace them.

I came back to Max's voice. He was saying something to me. I don't know what and it didn't matter. It was soothing. I turned to look at him and snarled. He didn't flinch. He stared back at me.

"I know. I need the fuel from the lawnmowers and Bobcat. Meet me at the berm by the gate."

I grinned, at least I think it was a grin. "I am going into town, Max."

"I know. We both are."

I stood on the top of the berm. The town was a couple miles away and dark. Reckless? Yes. Did I care? No.

Next to me was Tommy. I hadn't recognized him from up on the hill. Or I hadn't wanted to. They had propped him up on a steel frame shaped like an A. There was no crossbar to it. Instead, the pipe they had hammered into his ass helped prop him up. He smelled like a rotting corpse. I took a deep breath, held it, blew it out softly, and grinned.

"Well, Tommy, don't you worry. Payback time has come."

I wondered for a brief moment if I was crazy. *Probably,* I thought, but I didn't really care.

I whispered to him, "Tommy, I am going to hurt some people tonight." Then I laughed. Well, in my head it was a laugh. What actually came out sounded more like a howl. It felt good. Very good. Better than all the times before, but far more uncomfortable. I felt coiled, like a spring being tightened. There was no looseness or slack. No feeling of being light and free. Just a dull, throbbing need that was more cousin to lust and no friend to forgiveness.

Light blossomed behind me. Firelight. Max was setting fire to everything left that could burn. It smelled good when the night wind shifted. He jogged up to me, the gas can stuffed inside his pack sloshing with each step.

"I see you found Tommy."

"Yeah. We've been shooting the breeze."

"Good. I was going to take him down, but I think we will leave him up so he can watch."

I was tired of talking. Words meant nothing to me. I just stared at Max. He grinned, uttered a guttural "Yeah," then he jumped off the side of the berm and hit the ground running. I was half a second behind him.

We loped across the fields. I am not a runner, especially not a distance runner. I was now. It felt good. I needed to move.

Ahead of us was movement. A dog pack. I sped up so Max and I could go back to back. We stopped twenty feet short of them. The dogs spread out. This was a "Big Dog" pack. No little dogs allowed. There were six of them. Not a real problem, just an inconvenience. They were all at least ninety pounds, and a few were growling. Deep growls that sounded like a Harley idling.

The leader was not the biggest, which meant he must be the smartest and the meanest. He moved away from the pack and stopped. A long scar crossed his shoulder and ran up his back. He wagged his tail.

I said, "Hi, Woof. Found some friends?"

A Rottweiler stepped forward, growling and showing us his fine set of teeth. Woof turned and snapped at him; he eased back.

Woof barked twice at me. Sharp, reproachful barks.

"I know. They didn't want to come."

We stood there and stared at each other for a minute. "We're going to go, Woof. Come by after we are done. You should have enough to feed all your friends."

Woof barked, turned, and was gone. We started moving again.

We came into town from the good residential side. We went from house to house, pouring and lighting, until we ran out of gas. We didn't have time to burn the entire town down but we could try. Max tossed the can aside and stuffed his Zippo back into his pocket. His eyes were glowing red from the flames that were beginning to catch behind us.

Some of the people who still lived there were light enough sleepers to wake up and wander outside to see what the hell was going on. They gathered in a little knot in the street.

We ran up to them yelling, "Fire! Fire!" They stopped talking to watch us run toward them. We shot them all down and kept going. Max zigged through a backyard, taking the fence in stride like an Olympic hurdler.

The good feeling was coming back to me. The feeling that everything was good, and I could do no wrong, make no false move, and miss no target. I saw a burly, bearded man stick his head out the window as we cut through another yard. He opened his mouth to yell something at us and fell backwards. Max had shot him in the face with his M-16. A clean snap shot while moving. I wasn't the only one who was running pure and right.

We cut through a yard and crossed into the business district. It was a mess. Burned and abandoned cars packed the main road. Trash was strewn everywhere. The businesses themselves had shattered windows and were stripped inside of anything worth something to someone somewhere. We stopped long enough in front of a row of shop fronts so Max could put his Zippo to work.

I stepped into a shop through a shattered display window to keep watch. I thought about posing as a mannequin but decided not to. Max had just dashed inside the third shop down from me when I heard footsteps running down the sidewalk toward us.

Just one man from the sound of it. One who wasn't used to running based on the noise his labored breathing was making.

I waited. Just as he drew even with me, I swung my arm out and clotheslined him. He went down hard on his ass, losing his grip on the M-16 he had been carrying in the process. I stepped out of the window and kicked him in the balls. Then I dropped on him as if he was a horse and I was a cowboy stunt man. Thank God for knee pads.

"Hi," I said to him. He was too busy listening to his nuts scream to answer right away. I looked up and down the street. Nobody. Cool. I gave him a long minute to recover while I studied him. He was wearing eyeliner, lip-gloss, metal studs in his nose, and industrial earrings. He was hot.

"Hey, big boy. Your eyeliner does not match your lip gloss."

"Fuck you."

"I thought you might say something like that." I pulled the K98 bayonet from its sheath, smiled at him, and cut the tip of his nose off and tossed it over my shoulder.

"Awwgghh!" He started to scream. I reversed the bayonet and jammed the pommel into his mouth.

"I need you to answer one question when I pull this out. Where is Casey?" He nodded his head that he understood. I pulled it out.

"Oh man...the fucking jail."

"Thanks." Then I flipped it up in the air, instead of catching it I let it sink into his right eye. I wondered if I was getting into a rut with the eyeball thing. *Nope. I don't see it happening,* I told myself and laughed.

Max was standing next to me. I looked up at him. There were no flames near us yet but his eyes glowed red. *Cool.* I hoped mine did too. He grabbed the M-16 from the sidewalk and tossed it through the broken window into the shop. We headed for the jail.

We pounded down the alleyway past pools of water, trash, and graffiti-tagged walls. If Casey was the Mayor then he was going to be vulnerable in the next election to a "clean up the town" candidate. Then again, I planned on making that position vacant in the next ten minutes, so I didn't think he had anything to worry about.

Just as we were almost through the alley two men came around the corner running straight at us. Using his Sarge voice, Max bellowed, "Where the hell is Casey?" All of us came to an abrupt stop. "God Damnit! Report!"

The "Where the hell is Casey?" had confused them, but the "Report!" must have been out of character for what they were used to. They tried to swing the barrels of their M-16s up. They were too slow. Max stripped their magazines and stuffed them into his pants pockets. Then we were moving again.

CHAPTER SIX

I suppose if this was a movie we would have stopped right there. Made a quick plan. Had a "Bro, I love you" moment. Then I would have run out in front of the station and screamed "Casey!" as rain streaked the charcoal on my face and mist rose up from the parking lot. Instead, as we hit the street in front of the station, I went left and headed for the back door while Max took the front.

It seemed like just yesterday I was going out this door, and here I was going back in. I took the back corner of the building as sharp as I could. I wanted to run toward the back door with my right shoulder brushing the wall. That way I cut what I had to watch to a 180-degree arc. The local equivalent of Max in the role of "The Sarge" was standing next to the back door haranguing two men about getting their shit together. One was still putting on his vest.

The Sarge had his shit together, as did the bored-looking one. They both tried to shoot me instead of talk to me. They were not fast enough. The bored one managed to get off a shot that only missed by a foot or two. It probably would have helped him if I had stopped. I didn't.

I hit the guy trying to put on his vest at full speed. That was a good thing. It kept me from continuing on past the back door. The bad thing was I expected him to go flying on his ass. He didn't. He just staggered back a bit, and then, instead of going for a weapon, he decided to hug me. That was nice of him, but I really wished he had brushed his teeth first. Or scraped his tongue. Or had all his teeth pulled. Or all of the above.

He had his arms around me, with his face in mine, and he was growling like a bear. I smiled at him and stomped his instep, twice. The second time he loosened up a little. Then I head-butted him. These were moves Max had us go over and over just a week ago. They worked and he died. I took a deep breath. That hurt a bit. He had been strong, probably thanks to the high protein diet he had been living on.

I grabbed the door handle and swung it open while staying to one side. That was a wise choice. The boom of a shotgun and a lot of metal went through it. Somewhere inside a quick burst from an M-16 sounded, and I heard Max's voice.

"You can quit fucking around out there, G." I walked into a slaughterhouse. I was impressed.

"You find that little shit Casey?"

"No. But I think I know where he is."

"Cell block?"

"Yep."

We headed toward the door leading to the cell block. I stayed about six feet back and low while Max flung it open and moved back. I shot the guy waiting for us just as he shot through the open door. If I had been standing up I probably would have been dead or at least seriously pissed off. Being fast was good. Being smart and fast was better. Living long enough to learn both was an option most of the people who went through this town in the past few months never had a chance to do.

"All right, Casey. Come out with your hands up," Max yelled through the door. I was back on my feet and waiting. I heard someone stirring out of sight.

I yelled, "Casey, sweetheart. Come out and let's talk." I was picking up a lot of background noise from people inside the actual cells. The augmented hearing thing was nice, but I was going to have to look into earplugs. My ears were ringing from the guns and my head was starting to throb.

"Is that you, Gardener?" So he was in there after all, the crafty little rascal.

"Yep. It's me. You coming out? Or am I going to have to burn you out?"

There was a pause. "Just don't shoot me. I can help you. You know that, right?"

"Hurry up, Casey. We need to move."

He scuttled into view, stood there, and smiled at me. "I thought about you a lot, Gardener."

That much was obvious. He had cloned my weapons, and was dressed like I was the last time he had seen me.

"Hey, Casey." I nodded at his gun belt. "Vaquero?"

He actually had the grace to look embarrassed. "No. Dad refused to buy me a Single Action. I did get a real bayonet." He turned a little so I could see it.

"Nice, Casey. Let's see how well you remember our time together." I told him, "Look me in the eyes."

He swallowed and nodded.

"I don't care if you are Gay."

He nodded his head. "Truth."

"I think your copying my look is cute in a twisted way."

"Truth."

"I think you killed my friends."

"Truth... Wait, Gardener! I wasn't the only one!"

"I think you ate people. My people."

"Stop! I'm sorry about that. I was hungry!" He held up his hands. "Please. Gardener. Please. Don't do it."

"I'm a heart breaker, Casey."

I drew and shot him in the heart. He actually looked surprised that I did it.

Max looked at him, then at me, and grinned, "Congratulations. You just killed Mini Me."

After I saw what was in the cells, I wished I had kneecapped him. The first tip-off was the muted cheer that greeted Casey's demise. The second was the smell.

I went in first with Max watching my back. I took one look and just stopped. The cells were full of people who were scared shitless. They were cowering in fear, pressed against the back wall. One woman had her child tucked behind her. She looked at me with such intense hatred that for a second I considered shooting her in psychic self-defense.

I told her, "Relax, lady. I don't eat people." A whoosh of relief, both mental and verbal, washed over me.

She said, "Then get me the fuck out of here, cowboy."

"Max," I yelled, "unlock the cells."

He pulled the manual levers that disengaged the locking mechanism. "Hurry up, G. We've got to move."

I bent over to pull off Casey's gun belt and search his skinny little self and was almost knocked over by the rush of people. I stood back up and began smacking and yelling at them, "Get the fuck off me and stay away!" I heard a burst of M-16 fire, which I hoped was Max. The people from the cells froze.

An old guy, probably sixty at least, pushed some young and still plump girl aside and said, "I know how to use that Colt you got there, son."

"Fine." I handed Casey's weapon to him. "Let's go." I moved up to the door and looked back at my crowd. "What's your name?" I asked the old guy.

"Jefferson. Retired Virginia State Police." I nodded and thought, *We'll see.*

I looked at the people and yelled, "All right! Out the door! Now!" The woman with the kid was hurrying to be the second one out except that I hit her with a forearm and knocked her back against the wall. She glared at me until the burst of an M-16 and a shotgun splattered parts of the ones who were in such a rush back against the wall. Well, that worked. Visitors had arrived while I was caring and sharing with Mini Me.

I leaped through the door, somersaulted twice, and came up behind my old desk. I jumped straight up, pulled the Ruger and the Navy Colt and screamed. I don't know where the scream came from but it sure felt good.

Acquire and shoot. There were three of them. I shot the man with the shotgun, and the woman by the door first. The one closest to me had been caught looking back toward the door, which fatally slowed his reaction time. Jefferson blew his head off. Damn if that Colt Python wasn't loud. Where the hell was Max?

Without turning around I yelled, "Move them out the back!" as I moved deeper into our old office space. Shit. There he was. He was down on the floor and laid out on his back. Sonofabitch! I dropped down next to him.

His eyes were open and he was breathing heavily. The front of his shirt was torn up and he was bleeding from one arm.

"Jesus, that hurt," he told me.

"Come on, Max." I stood up and extended my hand. He gripped it and came to his feet. The freaking Python boomed again. Jefferson was on the job and doing what I should have been doing, watching the front door.

Jefferson grinned at me and said, "Time to go, men." Then he dropped like a stone as the man coming through the door shot him in the head. I returned the favor.

I handed Max his M-16 and asked, "You can do this?"

"Hell ya. Let's go."

We headed out the back. I scooped the Python up from the floor as I passed Jefferson.

Max was moving, but it looked as if he was having trouble breathing. God Bless body armor. I didn't know what was up with the wound but it wasn't pumping blood. We came out the back door to a crowd. It looked as if everyone we had sprung from the cells was waiting for us. I was getting ready to yell, "Shooo!" I didn't get the chance.

54

Max cut me off by yelling, "You want to come with us? No weapon by the time we leave town means no admittance."

The woman with the kid told the woman standing next to her, "Watch her. I will be right back." She disappeared inside the station, and was quickly followed by a young guy of about twenty. I handed the plump girl who still had meat on her bones the Python; she took it as if I had just handed her a fresh turd.

"Don't point it anybody unless you plan on shooting them," I told her. She just stared at the gun.

One of the women in the group turned to Max. "That's not fair!"

He looked at her as if she was a total idiot, which she was, and told her, "Fuck off." Not very snappy but it got his point across. She, and two others, decided to run inside. The mom came back out toting the M-16 followed by the young guy carrying the shotgun.

I figured it was time to move. I moved out a bit, away from the group, as did Max. We both heard feet running. Max hit them with a burst as soon as they came around the corner. It was the waitress from the diner and she had not been armed. Now she was dead. I heard Max mutter, "Fuck!' but he didn't go to her, and neither did I. She never liked me anyway.

Max cocked his head. I didn't hear anything unusual. Then it dawned on me that whenever I see a crow fly overhead, Freya TV must be back on the air. I was thinking that my antenna must be broken or I was behind on my payments because Shorty wasn't beaming anything to me, when I received a quick burst of video on the area around us. The business area, and some of the residential area, was on fire quite nicely.

Max cut off his sleeve, and I went over to help him. He handed me his medic kit, but his eyes never stayed on me for more than a second. They were always scanning. The wound was not bad. It was really the underside of his arm that had been gouged by the passage of a bullet.

"What about under the armor?" I asked him as I stuffed some gauze over it and wrapped it up.

"Hit at an angle," he told me. While I finished up he said, "Back the same way. Arc around the residential area. Clump them in the middle. I've got point."

I wanted to say "What the hell?" except this wasn't the time and place. *Shit,* I thought, *Protect and serve.* Well, it wasn't all bad since it only applied to the ones with weapons.

We were moving now. About half of them had weapons. The other half had looks of fear and confusion.

The guy with the shotgun waited for me, and asked, "How do I use this?"

I replied, "You don't. Just move with Max. " We picked up a few more weapons as we headed back to the farm. The greatest concentration of people left alive in town was in the residential area. We were going to bypass that area. By the time we hit the town limits we had four people still without weapons.

Max stopped, looked at them, and said, "You heard me. No gun. No go."

"This is not right! I don't like guns!" wailed one woman.

"I couldn't find one," said another.

"Yeah! He took mine before I could get to it!" whined a guy who, despite what he had been through, looked like a Hollywood action star.

"Fine," Max told them. "Follow us and I will shoot you. Probably in the knee." He looked at the others. "Move!" Then he stepped off at fast stride toward the farm. Our new group followed. I had drag so I waited and looked at the ones left behind.

"Go back. Look for weapons and food while there is no one to stop you." Then I followed our group across the field. Out of the corner of my eye I saw a dog pack watching them.

We skirted the residential area and headed back to the hill where we had left everyone. Freya must have told them that

56

company was coming. Max told our people to load up, we were moving.

This was going to be interesting. We could see in the dark, but the new people couldn't. They had amply proven this already, as they stumbled their way across the fields to get here. Silent and deadly was no longer how I would describe us. I was glad I was behind them. Max had stopped them about a mile outside of town and individually inspected each weapon and put the safety on. I would have also stripped the magazines.

One of the new people complained about moving again. Max stopped what he was doing and turned to them.

"Listen up. I will tell you this once, and once only. You do not belong to this family. You are nothing to me. At best you are cannon fodder that eats. If..." and he emphasized that, "you can hack it, you will be accepted as a member. We will feed you and train you until then. You will have to do the rest."

"And if we don't?" asked a woman defiantly and with an underlying contempt. Max drew his .45 and shot her. He let the boom of the gun and the shock of what had just happened dissipate.

"I am not fucking around. My people will not die as a result of your failure to obey. You stay with us, and not only will you survive, no one in their right mind will fuck with you, let alone eat you for breakfast."

That hit home. I was surprised at how dense people could still be. Some of them still didn't get it.

"I will give you one chance. You can take your weapon and walk away now. If you stay...the only way out is feet first." He waited. No one took him up on the offer. Somehow I was not surprised. "All right. You will keep up or be left behind. You will not bitch. You will do what you're told, when you're told. Or I will kill you and strip your body."

CHAPTER SEVEN

We moved on after Max stripped the body of the woman he had just shot. I didn't have but a few minutes with Night before she left. She was assigned interpreter duties to the new people.

I heard her telling them, "You will not talk. If you fall, you will fall silently. You get one warning, and then I will stick my knife in you and leave you for the dogs." She paused to make sure they understood. "Watch me. When I stop, you stop. When I kneel, you kneel. Let's go."

Max took point. He had Freya right behind him. Then came Shelli and the cattle guided by Night. Ninja took the left flank and I had the right.

We moved about six miles that night. We arrived with same number of people we started with, which surprised me. I would have put a loaf of bread on Night gutting one, but it was not to be. We fed everyone, and told the new people to sleep while they could. Since we didn't have blankets they had to cuddle. I noticed the pairing off had already started.

Max took the first watch. Ninja and Shelli had the second. Night and I actually were assigned the same watch. A first for the year!

I was puzzled by our movements earlier. We had never been more than a couple of miles from the town. We just circled it. Later Night told me what was going on. We hadn't gone far from the town because we still needed it. We were going back into it in the daytime. No one would get a lot of sleep.

Max had us up and ready early. Before we went back into town, he gave a short speech to the assembled multitude of New People. If we had bread, and a basket to put it in, I would have handed it to him. I doubt he would have appreciated the symbolism. Then again, the other half of our team would probably not have "gotten" it either. Damn heathen furriners.

He began by asking, "How many of you know how to handle the weapons you are holding?"

Out of the twelve people, I saw three hands go up. I knew at least one them had to be bullshitting.

"Okay, when I get done I want you three to show Ninja - that's him there," he pointed him out, "what you know. The rest of you can hold onto your weapons but I am unloading them. You can carry the ammo. If I find out that you have loaded it without permission I will be very unhappy. We will teach you how to handle a weapon.

Now is not the time however. Today we are going back into town. You will look for everything that can be used to survive in the woods. This includes necessities for yourself. Think of it as going shopping for the gear we all need. Food and ammo are the first priority. We will all go in together. While you shop, we will protect you. Together we will survive and prosper as a people!" A couple of them actually clapped.

Three passed the Ninja certification test and Max assigned them to him. I laughed when I saw his face after he heard that. I quit laughing when he assigned the rest to me.

Night was going to be in charge of my group while they looted. I was going with her to provide security inside. Ninja and his crew were going to cover the outside. Max, Freya, and Shelli were going to scout the next target as we worked. It sounded good. I noticed Max didn't ask for questions after his speech.

We moved right away. Everyone was tired but, as Max pointed out, we were not going to be the only ones taking advantage of the change in the balance of power inside the town. Plus, there had to be a few Gnawers and general lowlifes still floating around. Maybe, if the town had really gone bad, a Catholic priest or two. There was also the chance that we would find some of our friends. I had already written them off, but people liked to hear you say shit like that.

The town was still burning when we filed back in. The plan was to work the high-end residential area, such as it was, that had not burned down. Then hit the station, food bank, and diner. Shelli also wanted to go by her house. Ninja and I did the entry at the first house after Max and crew scouted it. It was empty, and it was trashed. Stupid trashed. Trashed for the hell of it kind of trash.

Night herded the new people into what was once the great room. She told them, "Listen up. We need forks, knives, plates, clothes, blankets. If you have a question, ask me. Bring what you find here to me. Look for bags, packs, whatever. Move!" She looked at me and grinned.

"Yep" was all I said. I didn't like this. I was uneasy about coming back here. I understood the need. I just didn't like it. I paced inside the house. I stopped at the windows and looked out. I watched Max and his little group enter the house across the street. He was in and out fairly quickly. I saw a crow sitting on the next house over and for some reason a shiver ran down my back.

I went downstairs; the new people were racing back and forth on their Easter egg survival hunt. Like squirrels they piled their tawdry finds in front of Night who was going through them. They had found an old style piece of luggage, the kind without wheels. She was going through the crap and putting what passed her quality control into the luggage.

She was sitting, balanced on her haunches, something she could do for hours I think, when she caught me looking at her.

"What?"

"Nothing," I told her. What I was thinking was, *Is this is it? Rifling looted houses for used toothbrushes and steak knives? This is freaking survival? And we were going to bring a kid into this?* I stood there, pretending to look out the window, in reality lost in my thoughts.

"Okay, G, we're ready," she said. I pulled my head back into the game and tried to banish the shitty feeling I was sinking into.

"Good. I'll move the others." Ninja was covering the front door with one of the new guys. I gave him the hand sign, and he tapped his new guy to go around back and tell the other two to move to the next house. Then we covered while Night and her crew moved to the next house. Ninja went in with me, and we did a quick sweep. Max and crew might have checked it, but I wasn't trusting Night's life on how good a job they might have done.

We were starting get it down as we continued working the block. We were moving more smoothly because people had a better idea of what they were supposed to be doing. On their own they had split into basement, first floor, and second floor crews as needed.

I was on the first floor with Night when I heard the boom of Max's .45. They were five houses down from us by then. I was just getting ready to send one of the new people to tell him to slow down. The gap was getting too big. Now I could do it in person.

I went out the front door, stopping long enough to tell Ninja, "Pull your people in and go defensive. Make sure no dumb ass shoots me when I come back." He nodded and signaled that he understood, I slapped his shoulder, drew both my pistols and started sprinting toward the house. I heard a short burst of an M-16, and then Max's .45 firing steadily.

Whoever it was they were having a problem with in the back of the house was out of sight. I veered across the street and went around back. My plan was to go down one more, then go inside the house next to them and see what I could see.

As I came around the corner I heard Max yell, "Clear!" I changed direction, cut through a weedy yard and came out in front of the house they were in. Five concrete steps led up to the open door. As I went up the steps I heard Shelli scream. Not just any scream. It was a high-pitched wail of despair, horror, and a cry for help to the gods.

Her scream came from downstairs, and I was through the door when I spotted the stairs leading to the basement. Max was upstairs, and I heard his boots hit the staircase leading down to the floor I was on. By then I was already two-thirds of the way down the basement stairs. I hit the bottom landing and froze.

The basement had been dry-walled, but that was about it. There was a green felt pool table; well, it had been green once, now it was mostly red; red because it had been used as an operating table. Each pocket in the felt had a five-gallon paint bucket underneath it to collect run off. On top of the pool table were a couple of hacksaws, pliers, and other Craftsman quality tools. It struck me how shiny they were still.

Shelli was holding Freya's hand, bent over sobbing between dry retches. Freya looked at me, her eyes as big as saucers, and her face white and frozen as snow. In the background I heard meowing, and cries of pain that were muted in volume, unclear what was being spoken, except the intensity of pain. I turned around slowly and saw them.

It was a meat locker of living and dead children. They had been tied to bolts that had been driven into the studs behind the drywall. They had been evenly spaced. Some were still living, because only small pieces of flesh had been carved from their bodies so far. Eyes glazed with pain unimaginable, muted in the expression because they no longer had tongues or were too withdrawn into the horror to make a sound.

My heart and my head exploded. Memories of my own youth splashed forth. Rage and blackness most vile ran like acid through my soul.

I shattered. I ran. I ran as if the hounds of hell were pursuing me, and they were. Not only did they pursue me, they were inside me, which only made it worse. I screamed, and I kept running, running into the wilderness. The wilderness of my insanity.

I ran, and I ran some more. I ran until I fell down. Then I got back up and ran some more. I ran past one group that was traveling. I was on them, and then past them so fast that I triggered no reaction. At least no bullets whizzed by. I just kept going. My side felt as if a knife had pierced it.

The last time I fell down I crawled off the path and into some bushes. Then I cried. Not tears, but sobs. Snot running, bottom of my heart, toxic waste vomit from my soul sobs. Somewhere during all this I went to sleep, but not for long. If I thought what I had seen with my eyes open was bad, I was wrong. Mr. Nightmare convinced me how wrong I was. I wanted to scratch my eyes out, to reach inside my head and rip all my wiring out.

I stood up and started running again. My brain had shut down. I was incapable of rational thought. Instead I had fragmentary loops playing in my head. I liked the "Run! Run! Go! Run! Go!" the best. I could deal with that. The other one was a whisper: "Children...Children...come here." That one was not good. The images that accompanied it were even worse.

Inside my head the dark monsters of the past were busy, each jostling each other as they clamored for my attention. They so wanted to talk to me and tell me tales of yesteryear. They smiled at me with rotted teeth and said it would be okay but I knew better. I knew how they lied. So I ran. And I ran some more.

I didn't eat because I had nothing to eat. I drank from streams like an animal, and pissed as I ran. I didn't care. I fell hard at least once. I remember one time realizing the loop had changed to "Loser, Die!" Over and over it played.

The next time I stopped, I sat down on a fallen tree and pulled the Ruger out of the holster. It was so beautiful. I unloaded it, and spun the cylinder. I looked at the bullets I had dropped to the ground. Each one in its brass jacket, all dressed for a party, and all I had to do was send the invitation.

I reloaded and thought about it, at least as much as I could. That wasn't very much. I couldn't break through the loop. So I staggered to my feet and ran some more.

I was getting hungry. I lay there, somewhere in the woods and watched a squirrel watch me. I imagined shooting him. I knew I could hit the branch he was on. The concussion would drop him undamaged to the ground. Then I pictured him after he was skinned and I threw up. I rolled away from the small puddle, wiped my mouth, and fell asleep.

CHAPTER EIGHT

I don't know how long I slept. Maybe five minutes. Maybe five hours. Regardless I was still asleep when they found me. They were not Good Samaritans. I woke up to a boot in my side, and heard a voice say, "Damn if he doesn't stink." Another voice said, "Nice weapons though... if you want to play Cowboys and Indians." I felt someone strip me of my gun belt, and then I heard the second voice say, "He's young. He can work. Just needs a little TLC first." I heard laughter as I passed out.

I woke up to pain. Someone had a hold of my hair and was using that to lift my head. I growled. I heard the voice laugh, and tell someone, "Yep, I thought he was still with us." Then he let my head drop. It bounced off the ground.

"C'mon, sunshine. Time to sit up and eat."

I sat up. Damn if my head didn't hurt. I opened my eyes and focused. The first thing that caught my eye was the bowl in front of my face. I smelled corn. A dirty hand that led to a burly white male with a gray-streaked brown beard was holding it.

I took the bowl and stuffed my face. No spoon. Just my fingers. It was dried corn that had been boiled in water to make mush. It was good. I knew better than to ask for more.

"So you hungry, buddy?" Burly asked.

"I was. Thanks."

"No problemo," he replied. He nudged the man next to him. "He's got manners. I like that." The guy he nudged was white, thin, had black hair, and was semi clean-shaven.

"Yeah, not a lot of that going around these days." He grinned at me. "My name is Don, and the big guy, that's Roger." He held out his hand. I hesitated, and then I shook it.

"So...you going to tell us your name, cowboy?"

"Gardener."

They looked at each, then back at me.

Roger said, "Yeah, that's what we thought."

Don added, "But we weren't sure. You do have some awesome nightmares. That's for freaking sure."

Roger added, "A lot of whackos are running around in these woods."

"So what are ya'll doing in these woods?" I asked them pointedly.

"We're bounty hunters," Don replied. Roger nodded his head.

"Can I have my guns and bayonet back?" This was the big moment. They were both armed but they had not cuffed me. If they didn't give them back then I was going to see how fast they really were. Once again, they both looked at each other and came to an agreement.

"So where is that guy you hang with? You know, the famous 'Max Pain'?"

I just stared at them. "My guns."

Roger reached behind him and opened a plastic trash bag. He pulled them out and handed them to me. "Freaking single action revolvers." He shook his head. "Word is that they might as well be automatics in your hands."

I stood up and strapped them on. What a difference. I felt better already. He handed me the K98 and I slipped it into its sheath. Then I pulled it out three times. Now I was really okay.

"You got anymore of that corn mush?"

Both of them laughed. I noticed a hint of relief in the laughter. "Sure."

While Roger ladled it into my bowl I asked, "What's going on in the world? What's up with the bounty hunter gig?"

"Damn, Gardener," Roger replied, "That's a few hours worth right there. You want the short or the long version?"

In between mouthfuls I said, "Your choice."

He shrugged. "Okay. We have time to do this. Which one you want to do, Don?"

"I'll do the short version. You tell a better story, so you can tell him about the rest of the shit."

Roger sighed and settled in. "Damn, I don't know where to start. What do you know, Gardener?"

I told him, "Not much. Not since the White House was overrun by the hordes."

His eyebrow arched. "Damn. You have been out of touch for a while. No wonder you look like shit. You been living in a hole in the ground or something?"

"Nope, the bat cave. Go on. I'm listening."

"Well, I don't know everything. You know, the big picture stuff. What I do know, well, I am not sure how much is truth and how much is bullshit. "

I nodded.

"You know the lights went out big time?"

"Yep." Damn, this guy took forever to get rolling.

"Yeah." He visibly shuddered and looked away for a couple seconds. "You're lucky you were in the bat cave because the shit that happened then was extreme."

Don chimed in. "Ain't no way I want to go through that again."

Roger said, "You know people were eating each other, Gardener?" I nodded my head.

"Hell, Roger. They still are," Don added.

"Yeah. That's the civilized ones. You don't want to know what some of the assholes were up to." I just stared at them.

"Yeah, I know. I'm wandering. Anywho, the military took over with General Rupert J. Jones in command. He declared

Martial Law and started kicking ass. It's supposed to be temporary. At this point he can hang around as long as he wants as far as I'm concerned."

Don agreed. "Yeah. He gets stuff done. If you can't cut it, he gets someone else in."

Roger continued. "No shit. God help you if you get caught stealing or profiteering." They both laughed. "Yep. Those Wall Street people, they thought they were so slick. Flying away to their estates in helicopters and planes when the lights went out. They thought they could go back to doing business as usual once the power came back on. After the General hung a few in Times Square they got the message."

"Whoo man! That Goldman Sachs guy. What was his name, Roger?"

He shrugged, "Damn, I don't remember."

"Anyway, he was crying and carrying on something fierce."

"Didn't help him none, He died anyway." The satisfaction in Roger's voice was obvious.

"Yeah. Well, the country is getting organized. I mean there are some loose ends..."

Don laughed. "Yeah, Roger. Like about a third of the country."

"Well, damn. We've got lifetime employment then."

I looked at them. "What third?"

"Well, California, and most of the West Coast is a little unsettled."

Don rolled his eyes. "Let me translate Roger Speak for you. They went nuts when the terrorists dropped the grid. I mean a lot of mellow got permanently harshed." He quit grinning. "I have relatives out there. I haven't heard from them. Preliminary reports are that the LA area population is about 50 percent lower than it was a couple months ago."

"I told you before, Don. They are probably in Mexico."

"Right." All of a sudden Don looked glum.

I asked them, "What terrorists?"

Don answered me. "Who the hell knows. The General says Arabs. Others say Burners. A few say it was at the breaking point already. Don't really fucking matter to me anymore."

"Yeah. I guess not." There was moment of silent while we all revisited memories. I did not want to go down that road. I was still getting flashes of images that I would rather not focus on. My temporary insanity seemed to have passed, broken like a fever dream in my sleep.

"So what's up with the Bounty Hunter thing?" They both looked relieved to change the subject.

"Yeah. Well, we got lucky. Been lucky and stayed that way. Me and Don here, we were contractors at Fort A.P. Hill when the power went out. We didn't have any family close by. So we stayed to help out."

"Damn smart decision on our part," Don added. "Anyway, part of the 10th Mountain Division was there training. They, and everyone and everything else handy, we just circled our wagons."

"Yeah. Then the people came...and came...and came."

Don hastily broke Roger's little loop there. "Yeah. We did what we had to do!" he said defiantly, as if I was going to judge him.

I had a pretty good idea of what had happened. Their barrels must have glowed white-hot. I told them both, "Yeah, I know. We all did shit. But we didn't eat anyone." They both vehemently agreed with that.

"So we're all good except for California?" I found that a little hard to believe.

Roger said, "No. Not even close. New York was even uglier than LA. Those bridges... Plus, they say there are still bodies coming ashore in Jersey. Well, let's just say no one is going to want to go swimming there anytime soon."

Don added, "Or eat lobsters or crabs."

"The Baltimore to Richmond corridor. Shit, you probably can guess at that one. I suppose what really pissed me off was the

UN air dropping food. That, and the Asians on the West Coast with their relief shipments. It was like we were freaking Somalia."

"So, you guys are pretty well informed for a couple of bounty hunters out here in the ass end of nowhere." I didn't add that they were also pretty well equipped. They also moved as if they knew what they were doing.

"Yeah, well, we were briefed before we came."

Don added, "Plus, I like to surf the net." We both looked at him. He shrugged, held his hands, palms up, and added, "Really."

"So who are you looking for?" I asked. Before they could answer a crow settled on a branch about ten feet above our heads, cawed, cocked its head, and stared at me. "Soon!" I yelled at it. It nodded and took flight. That was a bit of a conversation stopper.

After a long moment Roger asked me, "So, you talk to crows a lot?"

"Yeah. Squirrels, too. Deer sometimes. But you have to have a lot of dough to get them to pay attention." I waited for a response. They didn't get it so I said, "You were telling me who you were looking for?"

Everything had been okay up until now. All of a sudden the vibe changed. I noticed Roger take another look at his watch. What? Did he have a dental appointment? Way off, at the edge of my hearing, I heard movement. Someone, no more than one person, was coming. Approaching very quietly, too.

"Gardener, it's like this. We were hired to find a lost kid."

"A kid?" I really didn't want to talk about kids. "What about kids? What's wrong with the kids?"

"No. Not kids. A kid." He added very quietly, "We think you might know her."

I don't know how I would have reacted a few days ago. I will never know. My mind heard them, but it wasn't processing the

70

incoming words correctly. Images were starting to spew forth inside my brain again.

"Kids?" I must have sounded like an idiot to them.

Roger let a little irritation creep into his voice. "No. A kid." At the same time the movement in the woods was getting louder. Someone was coming.

I was starting to lose it again. My brain was whispering, "They're in the woods. They want the kids. Badness in the woods! Badness in the woods!"

"Why?" I whispered.

Roger replied, "We need to talk to her."

Don laughed. "More like stick her in a deep basement somewhere."

"That was the wrong answer, Don." I think the flatness with which I replied tipped them off.

It didn't matter. They were sitting on the trunk of an oak that had fallen to the forest floor. I was facing them, sitting with my back against a maple, my ass on the ground. My legs were drawn up in front of me. I was planning to move anyway because the ground was cold. Now I just needed to move a little faster.

I leaned forward and pushed off with my legs. This launched me forward like a rocket. My head drove into Don's face and I heard his nose break. That probably hurt, but not as much as my bayonet punching through the squashed tissue of nose a second later. I am sure of that.

Roger was drawing his weapon from his fancy "operator's" rig and turning so he could shoot me. That would have hurt; not that I cared at this point.

I wasn't thinking at all. If I'd had fangs, I would have ripped Roger's throat out. I had the bayonet out already so instead of drawing my Ruger, I snapped forward from the waist and grabbed him. Then I yanked, and dragged him off the log to me. Like Don, he was wearing body armor, and I needed him close enough to punch the blade through an unprotected body part.

71

I had no idea if he was wearing plates, or whether it was the high dollar, almost knife-proof, super armor. A long time ago, Max told me, "Don't mess around, G. Just cut his throat, or jam it into his kidney."

When I yanked Roger down he fell on top of me. His sternum was flattening my nose, but I hardly felt it. All he needed to do was get the barrel of his weapon pointed at me and pull the trigger.

It would have worked, except that as he fell, I embraced him and drove the blade into his kidney. Max had told me that the pain was so intense that the person you knifed would be unable to move or utter a word as they died. He did not mention that they would also lose control of their bladder. Not that it really mattered considering the punishment my clothes had taken.

These two were taken care of, but their friends were still coming to take care of me. I shoved the body off me, rolled to my left and jumped up.

They were coming fast through the woods, running in a staggered line. I didn't have any problems seeing them. Even wearing camo, we all stood out since it was early Spring. The only real cover was a clump of pines that led to an even bigger bunch about fifty yards to my right. I started running toward them. They had rifles, M-4s from the looks of them. I needed to close the distance. They didn't.

They knew that too. "Fuck 'em" went through my head. "Fuck them all." The front two sent a burst toward me. I grinned at them. Then I went flying through the air.

CHAPTER NINE

"Son of a bitch!" My foot had struck a root I was sure wasn't there a second ago. It was just as well I was airborne though. I felt one round pluck at my shirt, then it was time for tuck and roll. I hit the ground and rolled. I would like to say it went perfectly, but it didn't. I came up off balance and stumbled for a couple of feet before I caught my balance. Plus, my right shoulder was talking to me. Then the world got weird.

I managed to take down the one on my left but my shot at the guy on the right was off. I didn't miss. I just hit him low in the chest just as Freya and the dogs showed up.

It was Freya, but not the Freya I knew. This was a taller Freya dressed in white from head to toe. Her hair was loose and gleamed golden in the light.

She didn't even look at me. She just raised her arms and screamed an undulating cry that ended in:

Döda dem alla!

I felt the hair all over my body stand up. I screamed the same words back to her and the world.

Woof raced past her. He and all his buddies. They split into two packs and swarmed the two guys in the back. The guys didn't have a chance. I heard one of them sucking wind through a throat that had been ripped open before he went under. That left me with the remaining soldier. He was wearing a helmet but all it did was keep his head from exploding when I shot him.

I raised my arms and screamed:

Döda! Döda! Döda dem alla!

It echoed back to me and I felt good. Really good.

I kicked the body lying in front of me. For no reason, it just felt good. Sometimes I wished I could stay in this space forever. Living one endless battle after another. Well, maybe not endless. I would like some quality time with Night every once in awhile. Thinking about her brought with it a palpable sense of longing.

I kicked him again and thought, *Assholes like you are always getting in my way.*

Woof, and part of his crew, padded their way over. They stopped in front of me, and looked at me, the cooling corpse, and then back at me. All of them were licking their chops, wet with the blood of the fallen soldiers they had just feasted on.

"Don't get any ideas, guys. I will put you on a spit before you can bark twice." The littlest one, a new addition to the pack, I thought, whined. She was probably seventy pounds of muscle. I ignored her.

"Hey, Woof. Thanks for coming by. You're looking good." Woof barked. I guess he agreed with my assessment. The long scar he had running across his shoulder and then up his back was a healthy pink. "Okay. Well, go ahead and dig in." I laughed and walked over to where Freya stood watching us. As I did I heard a bone crunch and two dogs growling at each other. I didn't bother to turn around to look.

I stopped about four feet away from her and looked her over. She did the same. She was taller.

"Hey, Shorty. Looks like you grew a few inches."

"Hey, Gardener." She smiled. "Looks like you lost a few pounds."

74

"Yeah. I suppose so." I paused. We stared at each other. I don't know for how long. I looked away first. I had to. There was a depth there that I wasn't sure I could come back from if I stared any longer.

"So...what brings you to the neighborhood?"

She looked at me with an amused look that said *you are dense,* and replied, "The dogs needed the exercise." There wasn't much I could say to that.

"Thanks. I'm glad you did. How far away are they?"

"Not far. C'mon. I will help you strip the bodies. Then we'll go. Night is waiting for you."

We started with the two in the back first. The other two were still getting chewed on. It was messy.

"You think Woof would understand if we told him to wait on the serious chewing next time until we were done stripping the bodies?" I asked Freya.

"I doubt it. It's not as if they are going to chew on anything we want," she said as she was picking up an M-4 and shaking the blood off of it. "Plus, I think it would take the fun out of it for them."

"Yeah. I suppose that's true." I looked over my shoulder at a German Shepherd and a Rottweiler having a tug of war over the left arm of the first soldier I had shot. The Rottweiler won. "Don't want to do that."

I was surprised the blood and miscellaneous guts did not faze her. "So, Freya...this doesn't bother you?" I indicated the bodies.

She laughed and said, "I have walked battlefields where the only reason there was mud was because so much blood had been spilled. Swords and axes will do that." I thought about that as I undid his helmet. It was a small. I tossed it next to his weapon.

"Okay. So you are Freya. I don't understand what you are doing here when you could be up in the sky riding cool horses. And, why were these guys looking for you? They were looking for you, right?"

She sighed. "Yes, they were." Then she laughed. "That's not me on the horses. They work for me so I suppose I could ride one if I wanted." She stood up after wiping her hands on the corpse's pants.

"I am not a priestess, but I suppose I am going to have to play one this time around. That's the role the Burners wanted me to play. You know, the charismatic figurehead who can work miracles. They wanted to ride what they called into existence all the way to the White House. I was supposed to be a photogenic puppet and spiritual leader."

She laughed. "I am not a spiritual leader. Those will come after me perhaps. That is not for me to know. I am here to bring change. Old style change." I looked at her. Her eyes were glittering. "You do understand what kind of change I bring, don't you, Gardener?"

"Yeah, I think so. Is that why they are looking so hard for you?"

"Yes."

While we talked I looked for ID. I found it, too. They were active duty military but I could not tell what branch. The military IDs gave very few clues about their owners. Everything was on the chip. The second soldier had some kind of high tech cell phone. I remembered that high-end soldiers were, at least before the crash, wired to a network. Some were even monitored for health stats and vital signs. If that were still true, then there were a lot of flat lines showing up somewhere. It was time to move.

It was weird. Once upon a time I thought of myself as a geek. I did corporate tech support and lived on the Net. While that seemed like a million years ago now a few things had stuck with me. What was weird about it was that I no longer saw this stuff as "tech." Rather, it was more akin to black magic. To me, Freya was normal. These dead soldiers were the ones who were the alien beings.

I was getting a bad feeling about hanging around, having learned to have a healthy respect for drones and helicopters. I grabbed and stuffed as much gear as I could handle in one of the light packs. Freya was matching me move for move. The only helmet that looked as if it would fit me was the one from the guy whose head I had exploded. I pulled it off what was left of his head and dumped the rest of his head out of it. Then I shook it hard and dropped it in the pack. I was going to give Night the small one.

"Ready?" Freya nodded. "Let's go." I scooped up the super duper cell phone looking thing and led off at a quick trot. Freya was right behind me. I went about fifteen yards and stopped. "Freya. You got anything up high? Maybe a hawk or an eagle?"

She shook her head no. Then asked why.

"Because that is where trouble might come from." I looked over at Woof and his buddies and yelled, "Woof! Get the hell out of here!" I doubt if he had any idea what I was saying, but I felt I owed it to him. "Which way, Freya?"

"Follow me." I shrugged and followed her. It felt a little strange. I noticed she was carrying one of the M-4s. She had always moved quietly. Very quietly, as quietly as Max. Now she moved faster, too. It took me a minute to figure it out. Her stride was longer. We ran in silence for almost a mile. I was sweating it the entire way.

I was glad when we splashed through a shallow stream. It was Spring, and the water was running as high as it would probably get this year. I stopped. Freya pulled up within seconds of me stopping. She went into overwatch without hesitation. Someone had been paying attention during our training sessions in the park and while we were moving.

I scurried around looking for the right size piece of wood. Once I found it, I cut off a piece of my shirt and bound the cell phone to the wood. Then I launched it into the stream and watched as it sailed away. I was pretty sure the phone was waterproof. Hell, knowing the US government, it was probably bullet proof, rust proof, and cost four million in old dollars. Hopefully it would fool them long enough for us to put some distance between them and us.

I realized as we pounded along underneath the trees that if I was going to choose a movie that best represented this phase of my life, it would be *Terminator 3*. Then again *Braveheart* might work. I also realized I was going to need some new boots soon. I should have checked the soldier boys for foot size.

We were running in the dark now. I could hear other things moving in the woods. An occasional deer. Once I was sure I heard a bear. In the background for at least the last hour was the sound of a dog pack moving. Woof was pacing us. Occasionally I caught a glimpse of them. They were good at moving fast and blending in. It was a comforting feeling having them out there.

Freya was slowing down. I doubt it was because she was tired. She dropped to a walking pace to let us, or least me, adjust and cool down. Then she held up her fist, signaling me to stop. We stood there for a minute while I listened to the person on watch move from where they were standing. I recognized him from his silhouette, the sounds he made, and how he moved. It was Ninja. I was home again

God, I was glad to see him. "Hey brother!"

We hugged. "Missed you, G."

"Yeah."

"C'mon. Let's go see the rest. I think someone hasn't slept since you left." That someone came out of nowhere and was in my arms.

Damn, she smelled and felt good, even wearing body armor. She had her head pressed up against my chest and was muttering in Chinese. She looked up at me. I could see the tears in her eyes. I know I felt them in mine.

"Don't you ever, ever leave me again." She was beating on my chest with one hand while holding me tight with her other arm. "Oh God!" Then she went back to holding me tight.

I looked up to see Max standing there. "Hey, Max."

"Hey, G. I see you brought back some toys for the troops." He stuck out his hand. Night let go of me enough that I could shake it. He pulled Night and me in close. It was only for a second or two. Then he released us, and stepped back. "Good job, G. See me when Night gets done with you."

A muffled voice from my chest said, "That won't be until tomorrow."

He laughed. "I would be disappointed if it wasn't."

Night was looking up at me and then I was kissing her. No armor on those lips.

When I came up for air we were alone. She looked around, and then said, "About time. C'mon." She took me by the hand and led me to a spot a little ways away from the camp. It was already set up for two.

"How did you know?" I asked her.

"I knew." The last full sentence I heard from her that night pierced me deep inside. So deep that it may not have fixed everything but it diminished it. She told me, "I will have your children and you will be a good father."

The next morning I met the kids. They had taken three alive out of the basement. One had died within hours. The other two were in fair to good shape. They had not been gnawed on or had their tongues cut out so their bodies were okay. The one that died had been.

Both were white girls. One was nine and the other seven. Freya had become their new mother. Rather they chose Freya, and she had accepted them. They were not talkers. It was a little weird meeting them. I could feel everyone's behavior change as they casually tried not to pay too much attention to how I was going to react. It was pretty much a non-event as far as I was concerned.

I spent more time talking to Max than anyone else other than Night. He had Freya and I describe how the soldiers attacked us. He wanted to know what the two Good Samaritans had said. He was also very interested in the cell phone. His conclusion matched ours. It was time to move, and move quickly. Freya was being hunted, which meant we were being hunted.

Freya still had the M-4 she had taken from the dead soldier. Max asked her, "You know how to use that weapon?"

She looked at him and said with a completely straight face, "There is not a weapon made that I do not know how to use."

I waited for her to grin. She didn't.

Max nodded his head and said, "I'm sure you do. Now strip it and put it back together for me."

She looked somewhat taken aback, and then proceeded to do it - quickly. As she did, she chanted in singsong fashion, "The M-4/M-4A Carbine is a 5.56 mm lightweight, gas operated, air cooled, magazine fed with a selective firing rate that can be sighted from the shoulder." She continued on, finishing as she reinserted the magazine and presented it for inspection.

Max gravely looked it over and handed it back to her. "Well done." The city people we had rescued were watching. A couple of them clapped.

"Thank you. It's what I do," she replied without a hint of irony.

The two kids, who had been sitting almost on top of her while she worked, both clamored, "Let me try!" The older one, Valerie, told Mist, the younger one, "No! You sing. I touch the metal."

Staring directly at Max, Freya handed her the weapon without even pulling the magazine. I started to reach for it, but Max gave me a minute shake of his head no. Valerie stripped it, and put it back together almost as fast as Freya, while Mist chanted the specs in the background.

Once again Max inspected it and told them, "Good job." He looked at Freya. "Can they use them?"

"Yes."

"Arm them. Let's get it together, people. We've got miles to go."

CHAPTER TEN

So it began. We were a motley crew. I had drag so I got to see them move out. Max was point. Behind him was Freya. Ninja and Night had the flanks. Shelli led the new people, and kept an eye on Valerie and Mist. They wore daypacks with less weight in them than what they were probably used to carrying to school. I noticed they carried their M-4s like professionals. Short professionals. It was going to be interesting to see how long they could keep up the pace.

The new people were not in good physical shape and were even less skilled with their weapons. They were bigger, but I had questions about their stamina. The woman with the girl was a possible keeper. The kid she had with her was trying. They both stayed to themselves. The guy with the shotgun was also a probable. He was buzzing around her and fell in line behind her. I didn't blame him. She wasn't bad-looking. The rest were a mixed bag. Some were in their forties, a little too old for this kind of life. They all seemed determined though. As long as they gave it 100 percent, I was inclined to cut them some slack.

Before we started moving out Max told everyone we needed to put some distance between the town and us. We were going to push hard for a couple of days and then lighten up for training. He would then create squads, and we would move, and live, with the squad we were assigned. We were headed west and would be moving on foot for quite awhile. Later we would look for vehicles. I noticed a couple of unhappy faces about moving on foot. I marked them so I could keep an eye on them. I knew why I was on drag without having to be told by Max. Stragglers would not be catching up to the main group later.

So we marched. Much to my surprise everyone kept up. It helped that Max, for all his talk about putting miles between the town and us, was not pushing us hard. On the third day out I got one squad and Ninja got the other. We talked about squad names. I knew Ninja wanted "Raven" so I let him have it. I could tell he was surprised.

"You earned it," I told him. "Besides I have a name I want to use."

"What's that, G?"

"I'm thinking 'Sword.'" This was the first time I had said it out loud. It felt, and sounded, right.

He nodded. "Yeah. That works. You're going to need a flag. Patches, too."

"Yeah." I grinned. "You think you can do me a flag?"

"Sure. You know I still have our flag from the farm?"

"I figured as much."

While we were talking, Night, Max, and Freya joined us. It was time to decide who was going to be in each squad.

Max said, "Okay. I'm going line them up and count them off. G, you get evens and Ninj gets the odds. The woman with the kid; they count as one. Night is going to be in your squad."

We grinned at each other. "Yeah, I know."

"She is going to be in your squad for mess and sleeping, but I am going to use her as my intelligence officer. Shelli is going to handle logistics and I am giving her the oldest ones to help her." It all made sense to me except we were missing someone.

Ninja asked, "What is Freya going to be doing?" Everyone turned to look at her.

She grinned. "I'm the communications officer."

Max lined the others up and counted them off. I got four of them. Of course Ninja had ended up with the ones I thought were the keepers. I was going to ask Night later if Max had shuffled them before he got them to count off.

I took my four aside and told them to dump their packs and let me see what they had. I also wanted their weapons and bare feet out and ready for inspection. While they did that Night and I watched them. We would compare notes later.

I watched them unpack. I was not inspired. Not by their gear, or by their appearance. They were either too young or too old. *Oh well,* I thought. *Life is a bitch but I might as well start getting to know them.* That was something I had avoided up until now.

I started at the left end of the line. My first new guy was Josh. Like most people, he told me his last name, but I forget last names before people finish saying them. Maybe if these guys survived, and I was bored, I might learn them. As it was, I didn't envision having to fill out any paperwork that required them. Plus, I knew I could always ask Night. She forgot nothing.

Josh was white, six foot tall, and weighed, maybe, one hundred sixty pounds wet. He looked to be twenty years old at best.

"Where you from, Josh?"

"Bethesda, MD."

"What did you do before?"

"Ah, nothing. I wanted to go to school but..."

I held up my hand. "Thanks. That's enough for now."

Josh had out a typical load for my squad, which meant he didn't have much of anything. They all had something they had picked up along the way that was totally useless. If it didn't take up a lot of space or weight I overlooked it.

He had only one change of clothes, including socks, which was not good. He had a Concept One daypack with a Dallas Cowboys logo on the front. It was old and stained. It was probably purchased at Target or Wal-Mart back when they were still in business and sold Chinese crap.

"You a Cowboys fan?"

"No, Sir."

"Don't call me Sir. Call me Gardener."

He also had a towel, four bars of Ivory soap, a half-used tube of toothpaste, a toothbrush that looked moldy, and a comb with a couple of broken teeth.

"You brush your teeth?"

"Yes, Sir...Gardener."

"Let me see." I looked at them. It looked as if it had been awhile.

I told everyone, "Listen up. Brush your freaking teeth. You see any dentists around here? The only dentist you're going to see is me with a pair of pliers." The only response I received was wide-eyed stares.

"Okay, Josh. Give two of those bars of soap to those two." I pointed at the two people at the end of our little line. I didn't see any soap amongst their pitiful store of items. "Set the other one aside. We'll see if Raven needs it."

"Hey man! I found them so..." He didn't get to finish the sentence before I had the end of the Ruger's barrel resting between his eyes.

"Don't do that," I told him.

He whispered, "What?"

"Look at me cross-eyed. They might stay that way permanently."

"Okay..." He was still looking at the barrel cross-eyed but I let it go. You can't say I didn't warn him.

"All right. This is how it is. We share. Anyone who does not share is a thief. The penalty for thievery inside our group is death. Is everyone clear on that?" They all nodded, said yes, or did both.

I slipped the Ruger back into its holster. "Let's see what else you got." He had an M-16 as his weapon. He had no spare magazines or ammo, but he did have a nice steak knife in a cardboard and duct tape sheath.

"You fire this weapon yet?"

He shook his head no.

"You have any experience with it?"

"Does online count?"

"For very little, Josh."

"That's what I thought."

I laughed, and then I looked at his feet. "Okay, everyone. When we get done here I want everyone to wash your feet and socks. You will wash your socks and change them for a clean pair every day. You do not want blisters. Blisters will cause you to fall behind and end up left behind. Then you get to deal with whatever is waiting in the woods by yourself." I saw the shudders and fear cross their faces. They knew what I was saying. "Oh, and wash them downstream from where we get our water."

I took a look at the next guy. While I did, Night questioned Josh about DC. She wanted to know what kinds of policies were in effect, whether he'd heard any news on the way out, and if he'd heard any news since.

Like Josh all of the others were white. I would have been happier to have Juan and Jose. They understood that life was a bitch, and they knew how to work. Gym muscles were not work muscles. Juan and Jose could usually work the ass off the Joshes of the world. The Josh types would harden up eventually, but I didn't have a year to wait for it. I wouldn't care if Juan and Jose only spoke Spanish. Hell, we could get by on a fifty-word vocabulary quite well. Too bad they weren't around. Instead I had to work with what I had, not with what I wanted.

I asked the next person, "So, what's your name?"

"Ben." Good. He wasn't taxing my memory with a last name. Ben was in his late thirties or early forties. He looked fit. He seemed calm.

"What did you do before?"

He sighed. "I was an architect."

"Residential or commercial?" He looked a little surprised. His type usually was when it came to me.

"Commercial." He paused. Then, almost under his breath, he said, "Strip malls."

I just looked at him. At least three wise-ass remarks came to mind. I decided to go with, "Cool. Any experience with that M-16?"

"No. Never cared much for guns."

"Well, that's going to change," I told him. I looked over his stuff. He had three pairs of socks, a bowl, and eating utensils. The rest was pretty much the same as Josh. He did have an extra magazine for his M-16.

The other two, Dalton and Shane, were the same equipment wise. Dalton had a Glock and a shotgun. He also had a pocket full of shells. He was the oldest of the four. I could see streaks of gray in his hair. Both had a rudimentary cook set, and Shane had a small first aid kit. He was also easily pushing forty. Both had once worked construction. They were already teamed up.

I thought I could work with them. Both had experience. Dalton had spent four years in the Army. Shane had once worked "security." Shane didn't have any M-16 experience. I considered telling him to switch weapons with Dalton but didn't. My reasoning was they both knew what I knew. If Dalton was hanging onto the shotgun there was probably a good reason. Until he proved me wrong, it was his. I was also going to watch him closely.

When I was done looking them over Dalton asked, "What are your qualifications, Gardener, you know, to lead us?" He grinned an easy grin, but I knew what he was really asking.

"Okay, fine," I told him. "Stand up. C'mon. Stand up."

His easy grin started to slip. He raised his hands and said, "Hey, chill. I'm just asking." He looked around at the others, grinning all the while to show how he meant nothing. He was also showing them how cool he was and how I was the one overreacting. It was pissing me off. Out of the corner of my eye I saw Night stop talking and step around so she could come up behind him.

"Look at me," I said. "What do you see?"

He tried to laugh. "Gardener, relax. I didn't mean anything by it, I swear."

I told him, "If you had stood up with that shotgun in your hand I would have killed you. I still might. Why am I in charge? Because I know how to survive. I don't end up in a cell waiting for the BBQ sauce to be poured. If you have a problem with me or with my leadership, then you better be ready to kill me. If I think you are a threat to me or to my people, then I will kill you without hesitation. Does that answer your question?"

He gulped. "Look, I was..."

"Shut the fuck up and sit down."

We were not the only ones moving around out here. The roads were in use sporadically. The US Army ran patrols occasionally on the smaller main roads, and maintained a presence on the Interstates. Most of their efforts seemed to be concentrated on burials and pushing vehicles out of the way to clear the roads.

We saw only fragmented glimpses, never the big picture. For us, a big picture was a hundred mile radius of where we were on any given day. We had no real idea of what was happening in the United States, let alone the world. This bothered Night, and, to a far lesser extent, Max. I personally didn't care that much. Actually, I didn't care at all. My world revolved around Night and the rest. The only thing I cared about were threats to us.

Freya was our biggest source of information but it was limited. We were able to avoid roving bands and possible ambushes thanks to her. She was also able to push deer our way so we could eat them. The problem was there weren't many left to push. This area had seen a lot of hungry people move through. We were reminded daily that a lot of them didn't make it. It helped keep everyone alert and motivated.

We didn't do much corpse scrounging. The smell of most of the bodies was starting to fade a little but not enough to make it pleasant. We also did not find anything worthwhile the few times we tried. We were the fifth wave of scavengers at best. The first had been the killers, then whoever had come after they had moved on. Next were the buzzards and dog packs. On top of that, it had snowed, and then rained, on the bodies.

Sometimes we found worthwhile stuff in the luggage and packs that people had discarded in order to move more quickly. At first, every piece of luggage was an unopened book for me. I would look inside and try to read the back story. I quit doing that after a while. It became too depressing. It did allow us to outfit everyone decently in clothes and personal items though.

We weren't finding what we really needed. That was ammo and magazines for it. Everyone had a weapon but we didn't have enough ammo to train them to an acceptable level using live fire. We couldn't afford mixing it up with any of the bands or hit the fortified compounds for that reason. Meanwhile we kept moving and did training: patrolling, house clearing, an ambush. They learned how to clean weapons and dry fire.

One day when we were taking a lunch break, Max called me aside. He told me, "G, we need to go into a town. We need to buy supplies, and find a house we can squat in for a few days. We need information, and we need to focus on the next phase."

"Mostly we got to get away from all these freaking dead people," I interrupted him, "before we get sick or someone cracks up."

"Yeah, I know. We aren't far from a middling-sized town. Freya has flown it. It looks okay. I think we need to go in and see what they have. If it's cool, we can spend a couple days gearing up. Plus, we need to see if we can find a shortwave or any kind of radio."

"Okay. Who is going in to look around first?"

"You and Night," he told me.

"She'll like that. Maybe they will have the Washington Post."

Two days later we were there. We went back and forth about what we should say if questioned by anyone in town and how we should act if we were stopped by law enforcement. The only law enforcement presence we could see was a squad of Army MPs. There were some other government-looking types wandering around but we had no idea what they were doing. They were all working out of the same building, a Ramada Inn, so there had to be some kind of connection. Night thought they might be FEMA since they looked like bureaucrats.

I finally said, "Why do we need a cover story? Look. I am not James Bond. We tell them the truth, sort of. We left town when it was overrun, found a cave, and pulled the door shut behind us. Now we are back out in the world wondering what's up."

Nobody could think of any reason why that shouldn't work. So that's what we went with. I still had my police credentials, such as they were, from before. They might carry some weight but I didn't really count on it.

I went back to the squad and told them the plan. They liked the idea of stopping in a town. Visions of fast food and hot showers ran rampant. I left them to babble about what might be waiting until it was time to move out.

The next morning Night and I started down the path that should lead us to a secondary road we could follow into town. From there we would walk into town and see what was up. Max told me we had until nightfall. If we were not back by then he was going to come to look for us.

"Damn, Max. You make that sound like a threat."

He laughed. "No. You're a trouble magnet. That's why I'm sending Night with you. I know she'll get you back on time."

Freya, he, and Shelli were there to see us off. As we walked away Freya yelled, "Remember!"

Ten minutes later, after we were out of earshot, Night asked me, "Remember what?"

I grinned. "She wants me to look for apple pies."

CHAPTER ELEVEN

It was a beautiful spring day. The leaves were coming back and the air smelled clean and fresh most of the time. Once the bushes leafed out it would be a lot harder to see all the trash and occasional pile of bones in the woods. It was going to be years, if ever, before everyone who died out here was accounted for.

We found the road and began walking along it. Sometimes we had to detour from the shoulder onto the actual road because of abandoned cars.

"You see these piles, G?"

"Yeah."

"You know what I think happened?"

"The Army cleaning up?"

"No. Notice how more of them have been toasted." She was right. There were also more than a few bullet-riddled ones. "The ones, like that one," she pointed to a four-wheel drive truck that was upside down and a lot farther off the road than most of them, "they said 'screw it' and tried to off-road it." There were a couple of burned-out cars not far from the truck. "And those probably tried to follow."

I started picturing it in my head. The panic. Guns going off. Collisions. Mass insanity, especially when it got dark. Screams. It almost sounded like fun.

We walked along the roadside and talked about nothing and everything. It was nice. Few were the times like this for us. It was almost normal, except that we both were constantly scanning our perimeter for threats. That had become so much a part of our life that it was as natural as breathing. I had a flashback to when I first became homeless and sold my iPod. How strange it was those first few days going through life without a soundtrack, followed by the realization of how much it had been a barrier to being in tune with my surroundings.

Out of the corner of my eye I noticed a used condom lying wilted on the shoulder of the road. Who had traveled through here, amidst all the insanity, prepared to have sex? Had it been consensual? Or just a way to pass the time in what must have been the traffic jam from Hell?

I had seen something earlier as we walked that was nagging at me in the back of my head. It was trying hard to come to the surface and make me pay attention to it. I saw a flash of silver between two cars and stopped dead.

Out loud I said, "That's it!"

"That's what?" Night asked.

"Look!" I pointed to a bike that was jammed into the wreckage of cars. "C'mon." With a rising sense of excitement I went over to get a better look at it.

"It's a bike, G." She wasn't getting it.

"Night, remember how I used to go everywhere on my bike when we first met?"

"Yeah." She grinned. Then I saw the realization of what I was thinking dawn on her. "Oh my God! Of course!" We both tried to pull the bike out of the wreckage. It wasn't going to happen. The rear wheel had a Chevy Suburban on top of it.

I told her, "You know. This isn't the only one I've seen. I saw one out of the corner of my eye in the weeds when we first came out onto the road."

We started talking about the possibilities of using bikes instead of feet. She told me about China and how, as a little kid, she had seen bikes move as much cargo as a small pickup truck. We were still talking about it as we approached what had to be a checkpoint.

Funny, the birds had not seen this. Max was right. Depending solely on what Freya's wildlife saw was not friendly to our long-term survival. We both fell silent. I thought to myself, *Actually, this is good. If we are going to have a problem then here away from a lot of people is the place to have it.*

The checkpoint was a sandbagged SUV that was missing the front doors and all of its windows. The roof had an antenna on top. I had no idea whether it was decoration, a lightening rod, or connected to something functional. If I was going to bet our lives, I was going to assume it was functional. The woman running the checkpoint had a helmet on. She was black and was scoping us with a pair of binoculars. I was surprised to see her out here alone. I was also surprised to see a wide smile break open on her face.

Night and I looked at each other at the same time, both with the same expression that said, *What's that all about?* I looked just to make sure the pizza delivery guy wasn't behind us. That, other than Night, would be the only thing that could get me to smile like that. There was no one behind us. It had to be us.

I was thinking, *Well, we are an attractive couple,* when I heard Night mutter, "I know her. I'm sure of it."

I looked at the woman. Night was right. She did look familiar. That's when she stepped out of the guard house and began waving, grinning, and calling out, "Night! Night! Gardener! Hey guys!"

Night called back, "Hey, Shayla!" and she started walking faster. They met about twenty paces from the guardhouse, hugged and both of them began talking at once. They laughed some more and Night asked her how she was doing and whether anyone else made it out.

I was running the name and came up with: Shayla. Toll Booth. Good with weapons. Good Attitude. I started smiling. I didn't grin. I don't do grinning. We hugged and then she turned back to Night. She and Night had a lot more contact back then, and besides, Night had good people skills when she wanted to. I didn't. I just stood to the side, smiled a little when one of them looked my way, and watched our perimeter.

Eventually they wound down and said their good-byes. Shayla said she would call ahead and let them know we were okay. She also told us there was nothing in town worth getting excited about.

Actually she told Night, "Girl, we don't have nothin' happening. As soon as I can travel I'm headed into one of the Zones. This country living is getting on my nerves. I need me some music! Some party time!" She and Night said a few more things and I started moving away hoping Night would get the hint. She did and after a final hug, she joined me.

Once we were out of range I asked, "Find out anything?"

"No. Other than it was ugly. Ugly enough that she didn't want to talk about it."

"Yeah." Nothing unusual in that reaction.

Night said, "She's changed."

"How so?"

Night thought for a couple of steps, and then said, "Brittle. Very brittle."

"Yeah. It happens." I had no real idea but my guess is that there were a lot of people running around who had survived but were never going to be quite right again.

As we walked down the road, scattered houses began to appear on each side of it. I began to comprehend how bad it must have been. I know, I had seen enough bodies, but that was out in the woods. Here, in civilization, a small outpost of it at least, was an entirely different version of devastation. This was Katrina, except the flood had been people.

We walked past a white two-story house with a porch. The yard had a chain link fence, maybe three-and-a-half feet high around it - just enough to keep Rover from wandering. Spray-painted on the wall, partly obliterated by smoke damage, was "NO FOOD HERE!"

Every house had some kind of damage. One had plywood on its windows. A skull and crossbones had been spray-painted above the word *DON'T*. That was it. Just *DON'T*. Smoke was coming from the fireplace, so someone was in there. Just looking at the place gave me the chills. We saw trash, personal belongings, and a couple of kitchen appliances scattered in the yards. We passed one house where an elderly black man sat on the steps, a shotgun across his lap. I waved at him. He didn't respond. He was looking at us, but I am not sure if he saw us.

Night muttered to me, "I thought the woods were bad. This is downright creepy."

I agreed. Several minutes later a Ford F-250 appeared at the far end of the street rolling our way. I knew they were coming for us. It didn't surprise me. If I were running security here I would have someone on the way to check us out by now, too. Night looked at me, and then swung out a little more to give us both space if we needed it.

The front windshield was missing so it was easy to see the driver and his passenger. Both were black males. The driver was in his early fifties, the passenger in his twenties. Funny, it crossed my mind that when I was younger, riding in the passenger seat up front was called "riding shotgun." Nowadays this is what it really meant.

Night and I stopped walking and waited. They did not roll by us and check us out through the nonexistent window. Instead they also stopped, and got out of the truck about fifteen feet from us. The passenger opened his door and stood behind it. He covered us with a sawed off shotgun through his open window while the driver slowly came around. He stopped just short of the end of the hood and greeted us over it.

"You two Gardener and Night?"

"Yes. You Chief Rogers?"

"Yeah."

We stared at each for a few seconds. Then he told us, "Go ahead and get in up front, Gardener. The lady can ride in the back with Junior." I wasn't thrilled with it, but I understood.

He had the kind of radio up front that I had seen in State Police patrol cars. His must have been the cheaper version. I was hearing the tone bursts that indicated someone was transmitting encrypted. It was not good enough to decrypt them, which told me a couple of things. Someone around here was mobile and had good equipment. It also told me that whoever it was didn't see him as important enough to hear what they were saying. That meant it had to be the Feds.

He was looking me over without trying to be obvious about it.

"So where we going, Chief?"

"Taking you to the station. My niece reached out to me. Said you were 'good people'."

I thought, *Bet she said more than that.* Instead I said, "She's right."

He chuckled. "I heard about you. Those guns look right, but I thought you would be taller."

"Yeah. Funny how people get that wrong all the time. So why we going to the station?"

"Cause it's my town and that's how I run it." He softened it by adding, "You wouldn't believe the trash we've had to take out."

There wasn't much I could say to that. "Yeah. I can imagine."

"Think of it as professional courtesy. You want me to address you as 'Chief'? You were one not all that long ago. You and your running buddy."

"Naw. Well, only if there are Feds around." Junior in the backseat laughed at that.

Chief shook his head. "Fucking Feds. I suppose I should like them considering all they've done." He sighed. "The thing is they are such assholes." We all laughed.

He hit his turn signal. I hadn't seen a car on the road but old habits die hard. He pulled into the station. It was an old school brick building that was pockmarked with bullet holes. The lower floor windows were covered with pieces of metal that had been welded together. Someone had cut crude gun ports in the shape of a T in them. One section of the wall was blackened where a Molotov had burst.

"Ya'll had a good time," I said flatly. I knew it must have been insane.

He replied, "Yeah. Fun." He spit into one of the numerous potholes. "Shit. It was touch and go for most of it." Out of the corner of my eye I saw Junior nod gravely. "Fucking Eaters, nut jobs, end of the world wingnuts, and generally crazed citizens. Yep. A good time was had by all alright."

The lobby area where the Desk Sergeant would sit was gone, as well as the double doors where we entered and part of the wall that framed them. The best description for the interior would be "shot to hell." It had been sandbagged at some point. It must have been early on because there was fine grit on the floor from the holes that had been punched in the bags. Outside, the area around where the doors had been was also sandy.

He stopped for a minute so we could take it in. "Had a .50 here. Junior had to bust out part of the wall to improve the position." He looked at Junior who standing there, his face impassive. "Going to have to fix that someday."

Junior looked at where the doors had been as if it was the first time he had seen them. He replied in a monotone, "Yep. That's right." Well, now I knew he could talk. The more I saw of him, the more I realized he wasn't right.

There was a soldier on duty, sitting behind one of those folding tables that you find in church basements. When we came in, he barely looked up from an old "Guns and Ammo" magazine. The Chief looked over at him and said, "Don't bother getting up, Jimmy. I got it." Jimmy looked up briefly, nodded his head, and went back to reading.

He told his son, "You can go on now, Junior. I'll be all right."

Junior stared at us for a second, then replied, "Okay," and left. I saw the sadness in his father's eyes as they followed him out.

He told us, "C'mon back. I'll make a pot of coffee." I was suddenly in a much better mood. As we followed him, he said over his shoulder, "I don't have any cream or sugar, and the coffee is old. Got it from the Feds the source of all that is good."

We followed him into his office. It was dim, and had a dank smell.

"Sorry, the power may be on officially around here, but that doesn't mean it works everywhere."

His office walls, even in the low light, showed white rectangles where plaques and pictures used to hang. A bookshelf still had some books and knickknacks on it.

He noticed me looking, and said, "Amazing what will survive a shit storm, and what won't." His coffee pot was sitting on top of a Sterno stove. He poured water from a plastic jug into it, then measured out the coffee from a Tupperware container. He said, "You know, part of the reason we survived, if you want to call it that, was because of you all."

We were standing there. He had three chairs. One was obviously his. The other two were filled with cleaning fluids, dirty shirts, and much to my delight, a couple boxes of ammo. "Oh, yeah." He emptied the chairs by piling or dumping the contents on the floor. With a flourish he offered the one with the cleanest seat to Night. "There you go, Ma'am,"

"Why, thank you," she replied graciously. We sat down as he went behind his desk and settled into his ancient leather covered office chair.

"Well, I have been running my mouth pretty steady. I bet you got a million questions, and I got a few of my own. You go ahead and ask them while I keep an eye on this coffee."

I looked over at Night. She gave me a barely perceptible nod so I led off. "How did we help you survive? What happened here?"

"Well, you saw my niece. She bugged out ahead of most of the crowds and headed back here. She told us what she had seen. We were already seeing trickles, so we decided to get ready."

"How did you manage not to be overrun?" I asked him.

"You mean like you?" He must have seen my face change. "I'm not insulting you or belittling what you did. From what I heard you did pretty damn good for being so close to DC." He paused. "You never been here, have you?"

"No," Night and I said simultaneously.

"Yeah." He continued on, sounding more like he was talking to himself. "Didn't show you the rest of town..." He refocused. "We have a National Guard Armory here. About 55 percent of them reported for duty with their families." Now he really lost focus. We sat there for a few minutes in silence while he stared off at something only he could see.

Then he began speaking in a whisper. "We blocked the highways and posted people at them. That didn't last. It stopped some, maybe even a lot, but they still kept coming. We tried doing disaster relief and managing the situation. That didn't last long either. The Major that was in command, Hollister, he was a good man with a good heart. He blew his brains out a couple weeks into it. The Captain, Scyuler, he... he took over." He paused again.

When he started again his voice was softer. If our hearing wasn't so good now I am not sure we would have heard him. Night reached out to hold my hand. "Well, they say he is on the fast track now. Made Major off of what he did here. Probably even got a Bronze Star." He laughed bitterly. "You ever seen what one of them fancy chain guns can do to a bunch of people packed together?"

We both shook our heads.

"I didn't think so. You have a rep as a stone killer, Gardener, but I don't peg you as a butcher of your own people." He stopped, turned to the wall for a second, got up, and poured our coffee with his back to us. He stood there for a minute blowing on his cup. Then he turned to us. We pretended not to notice that his eyes were wet. "Hang on. Let me go get another clean cup. He walked out of the room.

I looked at Night and said, "Jesus. Why do I have a feeling the best is yet to come?" She nodded sadly.

When he came back in the room he was much more composed. He poured our coffee silently. As soon as he was done pouring mine, I took the cup, held it under my nose, and breathed in the fragrance. I did like coffee.

He noticed me making love to the cup. "Been awhile?"

"Yeah," I told him.

Night laughed. "More like less than a week."

We all laughed. Then Night told him, "You know you don't have to tell us the rest. We're more interested in what's going on now." I heard that and wanted to choke her. I wanted to hear it.

He smiled, and replied, "Thank you but I think I should. You need to know this, and perhaps I need to say it." I breathed an internal sigh of relief.

"Where was I? Oh yes, Captain Scyuler. What a piece of work." He shook his head. "He is good. Real good. He got us organized, and had us pull back into a defensive perimeter. This building here was on the far side of most of the action. Most of what happened was over by the armory and the school. He had patrols go out and put some heads on stakes. Below them he put signs telling people not to bother coming this way."

I nodded. *Nothing wrong with him so far,* I thought.

"The problem was we had a lot of people Major Hollister had already let in. We had people in the school. We had people in tents camping out in the football field. We had them in cars. They were everywhere."

He told us, "We, well, actually Scyuler was still in touch with the Army. They have one of those generators on a truck. Some kind of field generator or something. I think some of them went along just because he had the light and the food. Anyway... Say, you do know we had a coup in DC, don't you?"

Night answered, "Yeah. There is a General running things now, right?"

"Oh yeah. The same one that gave the okay for the air strike when the White House was overrun. Then the President, the one we elected, declared Martial Law, and put him in command of Homeland Security. I bet you can't guess what happened after that?"

I knew the answer to this one. "Airplane crash?"

"Yep. Vice president was also on board. That was about the same time that multiple terrorist strikes took out an amazing number of Senators and Congressman who were not thrilled with how things were going."

I thought, *Slick. That's how I would do it.*

Night asked him, "So where is he now?"

He laughed. "I don't have a clue. Somewhere that's a double secret safe place I suppose."

CHAPTER TWELVE

The Chief told us, "In the meantime, Scyuler had taken over here. He met with his officers and NCOs only. He had to spread it out over a few days, as they were a little busy. After the meetings about seven of them decided to go out 'on patrol.' They never came back by the way. Then he had a meeting with us."

Night interrupted him with a question. "Who is 'us'?"

"Us?" He looked off in the distance. "Let's see. There was me, a few of the local big wigs, a couple of pastors and whatnot. He told us that there was no way he could feed and protect anyone but his troops, their families, and any locals that wanted to join him." Somehow I knew where this was going.

He took a deep breath and let it out slowly. Then looked away from us. "He told us it was about 'national survival' and he was authorized to take whatever actions he deemed necessary to do that. We all wanted to survive. We knew that we would not survive out there. Hell, we were already getting reports of cannibalism. So we agreed to back him up."

Here he paused, shook his head and said, "I am going to burn in hell for going along I suppose." He looked directly at us. "He gathered all those other people up and split them into two bunches. He had the males over sixteen and under sixty-five in one group. Everybody else in the second group. The second

101

group was herded over to the school to hear a lecture on personal hygiene. The men were told that they needed to dig a couple of big holes for disposal of refuse. It all made sense. We had shit, trash, and dead people coming out of our ears.

So we dug the holes while some of his soldier boys watched and provided 'perimeter security'. Then they cut them down." Now he was crying. "We had to watch. It was part of the deal. He told us. 'No one is going to get away thinking they didn't have a part in this.' Then they marched the rest of them out of the school and chopped them up with their fancy machine guns."

Tears were pouring down his face. He stopped talking, and then he slammed his fist down on his desk and yelled, "THEY HAD NO FUCKING RIGHT! GODDAMN THEM!" The slamming of his fist echoed in the silence that followed.

I looked him in the eyes and said, "So what are you going to do about it...Chief?"

We stared at each other. He and I. No one spoke. I waited. He sighed, "You don't get it. You're too young."

"What don't I get? That they took your balls in that football field along with your peoples' lives?"

The blood drained from his face. He stood up. He was wearing a Glock in one of those Darth Vader black plastic holsters. I always thought they looked like they were designed for ray guns.

I stood up. I looked at him and said, "It doesn't have to be this way. You can help us. Hell, you can come with us." I stared at him. I saw no flicker of fear. I liked that, especially since I didn't really want to kill him. I would; as soon as I saw his eyes narrow, he was dead.

Instead he relaxed. He ran his hand over his face. "Shit. Sit down." I waited until he began to sit down. Even then I moved slow enough that I was only halfway down when his ass touched down on the cracked leather seat. It didn't pass unnoticed. He smiled faintly.

"Okay. We need to talk," he said.

Night, who had sat quietly without moving during our little bit of death foreplay, said, "No. I want to hear about what is going on in the world!" I knew that tone. We were going to talk about what was going on in the world.

The Chief grinned. "You two married?"

It was my turn to sigh. "Soon." Night shot me *the look*.

"She's right. I did say I would. I probably don't know a third of what is happening just around here, let alone in the world, but I'll tell you what I know and what I think I know."

Night smiled and said, "Thanks, Chief!"

She is such a data junkie, I thought affectionately. I could tell she was on her way to charming him. She was good at that. We were definitely opposites. I noticed he was already starting to lighten up and focus.

"Well, let's see. Let me start with what's going on in town. I think we are seeing on a micro scale what is happening everywhere. Everywhere being where the Fed has boots on the ground." He laughed. "I love saying that." He said it again just to prove his point. "You remember how they were saying that all the time? Didn't work out so well. This country has been run by idiots since forever."

Damn. I don't want to sit through another 'What's wrong with America' rant. Thankfully he veered back on topic.

"Yeah, so we have the Feds here. The armory attracted them like bees to honey. We are a regional headquarters, or rather will be soon. They are still getting their shit together. We have a graves registration group on the other side. They are going to be busy for quite awhile. We have an army battalion staff. No battalion yet. Most of the troops, which is about a company, are out with the freshly promoted Major Scyuler pacifying the area."

I interrupted him. "We need to know the army stuff. We just don't need to know it now. We have someone who knows that kind of stuff better than us." Out of the corner of my eye I saw

103

Night nodding her head. Just for her I added, "What's up in the world?"

"You mean Sergeant Max Whelan, don't you?"

Cautiously, I answered him. "Yeah."

"I knew he had to be close by. It fits with everything I've heard about you two. You probably have others, too?" He was looking at me with what passed for a shrewd and penetrating stare around here. I thought, *What do we got to do? Nail him to the topic?*

"Yeah," I replied.

He liked that. "Good. We'll need them." That did not pass unnoticed by Night or I. "The USA is still fifty states I think. At least on paper. I doubt if Alaska is, except in name only. Hawaii probably still is. The navy will make sure of that. There are a couple civil wars going on. That's probably why the troop presence is so light here. Let's see..." He was staring off in the distance, probably checking his mental map. "There is the Burner/Mex v. the Feds in the Southwest. The Alabama Militia is trying to ride again down south. Oh yeah, Montana declared their independence. Come to think of it I think Utah is saying they are 'neutral' for now. There are some cities that are still pretty ugly and a lot of areas that need pacifying. I think the main problem is finding the people that actually make everything work and convincing them it's safe to come back."

"If they are still alive," I added.

"Yeah." We all could agree to that. If this were a cartoon, we would all have balloons over our heads saying the same thing: "FAT CHANCE."

Night asked, "Chief, what are they telling the people? Are they even saying anything?"

"You know, if I hadn't seen them massacre all those people, and heard a few stories, I would think the General was the best thing that could happen to us. The army has a flat screen and speakers they bring out. They set it up once a week for his 'Status Report America' broadcast. We are all invited to watch

104

it. It's a big deal around here now. Kinda like going to the movies. Heck, once they even had free Kool-aid for everyone. With sugar in it," he added. "They didn't last time." The disappointment in his voice was obvious.

"So what does he say?" Night asked. I thought, *Thank you, honey.* This was starting to feel like a meeting to me and I hate meetings.

"He tells us how the country is healing and that steps are being taken to accelerate it. He says that he cares, and is working to make sure the 'Pigmen' and criminals are caught and punished. He explained to us that a terrorist isn't always some Middle Easterner. They could be the person next door. Anyone who is not helping the people survive this great crisis or who is working against the 'Great Healing' is an enemy of the community."

"So who defines what and who is 'helping the community'?" Night asked him.

He looked at her, then at me, and said, "You got yourself a smart one here. Who defines it? The Feds, of course." He jerked his head to the right. "Down that street a couple of blocks and out at the motel. That's who defines it. They already think I'm not getting with the program."

He paused. "Actually, I never thought about this before, but almost all of the people who saw what happened at the football field and disagreed with it are gone. Then again there are a few that have done some serious ass kissing since then. They're doing pretty good." He trailed off here, lost in thought.

"So how long do you think it will be before you go away and never come back?" I asked him.

He stared at Night and me and didn't have an answer.

"You know what I mean don't you?" I asked him.

He snapped back at me, "Of course I know what you mean." He drummed his fingers on the desk for a minute while we sat there and listened to the beat. "Okay, my guess is you're here for re-supply. I can tell you that isn't going to happen. The people you have in the woods; keep them there. This is not a town you want to wander around in. They won't be missing anything. We don't have squat open for business anyway."

He looked at Night. "Let me make a guess. You do the logistics."

She smiled at him. "How did you know?"

He laughed, "Well, Gardener here is no diplomat. That's for damn sure. Yet you're with him, and Max is out there somewhere keeping an eye on the troops. You're here for re-supply. That means you must be the logistics brain." He sat back looking pleased with himself.

"Why, thank you, Chief." Then her tone changed. "So, can you help us with that?"

"Yeah, probably. Depends on what you want and how much." He looked at me. "You're not much of a meeting guy, are you?"

"Nope," I replied.

"I have known a couple of guys like you over the years. They weren't much for it either." He fished in his pocket and pulled out a key ring. "The one with the red sticker on it will open up the armory door for the station. It's the black steel one. Go down the hall, it will be the second on your left. Don't worry. Your woman will be fine with me." He didn't have to tell me that. I already knew. He wouldn't stand a chance against her. He was making a mistake, all too common. A petite Asian woman does not equal a lack of viciousness and speed.

She gave my hand a squeeze and let go of it.

"Thanks, Chief."

As I left, he yelled, "Don't lose those keys."

I walked down the hallway. For a police station this place was dead. Then again, so were a lot of people. I found the door and opened it. I automatically felt for the light switch and was surprised when the lights came on. That was weird.

I didn't waste any time wondering about it. I had entered black plastic gun heaven. For a small town police office, Chief sure had a lot of ordinance. It had to have been left over from when they were using the building as an outpost on the defensive perimeter.

Scyuler and his men had probably left soon after the threat of getting overrun had passed in order to run their pacification mission. He didn't seem to be the type to forget stuff like this, so he probably intended on collecting it when they returned. Or, if I were him, having a second stash of arms off the books might make me feel better, especially if there was another administration change - one that frowned on massacring civilians. This led me to the next revelation. If the people running the country were doing this crap as a part of officially sanctioned policy then they were not going to leave office gracefully. They couldn't.

I looked around. A lot of the weapons were in boxes with numbers stenciled on them. These weren't police weapons; these were army weapons. Too bad I really didn't know what a lot of this was without ripping open the crates. I started memorizing numbers. I would tell Max what I had seen. He would know. I recognized the M-16s/AR-15s in a rack. I also now knew where the .50 had gone that had been in the doorway.

What surprised me were two big bins full of pistols of all different kinds and makes. Just about everything ever made was there. They must have been confiscated afterward or picked up. The same thing for another bin full of hunting rifles and shotguns with long hunting barrels that looked as if they had just been dumped in there. Some of them looked rusted. I looked closer and realized it was dried blood.

I started picking through the handguns. There were some nice guns in here, at least by my standards. The bin was noticeably lacking in black plastic. They were there, just not in the quantity I would have expected. Then it dawned on me. These probably came from the people from the football field. I thought about it for a minute and shrugged. They wouldn't be needing them anymore.

107

A lot of them had been tossed in the bin, holsters and all. I started going through them, and found that most of them were still loaded. *Very cool!* I started dumping cylinders and magazines into my hand, and then transferring them to a pocket in my cargo pants. I put .45 in one pocket, .38 and .357 in another. The 9mm and everything else ended up going into the same pocket. Somebody else could sort them later.

I usually carried a lightweight daypack in one of my pockets. Failing that, I tried to carry a plastic bag. I learned to do that not long after I became homeless. You never knew what you might run across, and being able to carry it off instantly could make the difference. Why? Because anything good that you might find was usually gone by the time you turned your back. I stuffed a couple of handguns in the daypack while I sorted through them.

I found a nice .380 Walther PPK that I set aside for Night. If she didn't want it, we could always sell or trade it somewhere along the line. I also set aside a Ruger Single Six. It would be even better than the PPK for her, and good for training. Plus, .22 ammo would be - should be - easy to find.

Then I saw it. The match to the Vaquero I wore. It was still in a stained holster, and had the leather cartridge belt, which still had rounds in the loops. I pulled it out of the holster and looked at the serial number. It must have come off the line in Rugerland just days after mine. I opened the loading latch and dumped it. Out of the six rounds, two had been fired. Whoever had owned it had loaded them with Corbon hollow points. Others had probably laughed at the 'old school' rig but that didn't mean he was an old fool. I hoped he'd had the chance to explode someone's head before they tossed him into the pit. I fished two .357 rounds from my pocket, checked the barrel, and reloaded it.

I stood up and strapped it on. *Yeah. Hell yeah!* I was going to have to make some adjustments but it was definitely right. I tried carrying a Blackhawk before, but it just didn't work. I was standing there thinking, *Damn, I wish I had a mirror to see how awesome it looks*, when the door opened. It was the Chief, and behind him was Night. I spun, drew both guns, and watched his mouth drop open. Night silently took a step back away from him.

"You should knock," I told him.

"Next time I will," he replied

"I see you found the ghost guns." I looked at him quizzically. He looked a little embarrassed. "The bin, it holds weapons taken from ..." I could tell he didn't want to finish the sentence.

"Yeah, I hope you don't mind. I helped myself to a couple."

"No. That's why I gave you the key. I enjoyed talking to your fiancé. I am going to be joining your group." He added hesitantly, "I've got one hell of a dowry if that helps, and I have a couple other people that may want to come."

I nodded noncommittally.

He continued. "Night mentioned you are looking for bikes. I'm going to take you for a ride. I think we can do this, but we are going to have to move fast."

Night said, "Gardener, I have some ideas. The Chief thinks we should be ready to move by tomorrow morning. We can talk about the plan later."

"Hey, Chief. Those green cans. They really have M-16 ammo in them?"

"Yeah. Go ahead and take a couple."

I slung my backpack over my shoulder, grabbed a couple cans, and said, "Ready when you are."

As we headed back down the hallway, me following him with Night in the middle, he asked, "You never were in the military, were you, Gardener?"

"Nope. Why?"

"No reason."

He had me curious. I had been down this road before. The people who brought it up were always trying to stake a claim to some kind of perceived skill gap. One that I had, and they didn't, because, of course, they had been in the military.

"There had to be a reason you asked, Chief. Let me guess. You were."

He stopped suddenly and turned around. "Look, Gardener. Quit believing I'm trying to belittle you. I'm just trying to figure you out." He looked at the twin Rugers in their holsters. "Hell, you're too young to have ridden with the 7th Calvary back in the day." He turned around and continued walking again. Over his shoulder he said, "God knows I think we are headed back to those days. I just can't figure out who is going to be the cowboys and who is going to be the Indians this time around."

"I don't know about all that," I told him. "I think it's going to be more like 'the quick and the dead' for awhile."

CHAPTER THIRTEEN

We headed out to the Chief's truck. Jimmy wasn't at his post. I don't know if he had to take a leak, or just decided to wander off. I didn't ask. I noticed that the Chief paused for a second, shook his head, and continued on. We got in the truck.

I settled in, and then asked him, "Where you getting the diesel to run the truck, Chief? The army fueling you?"

"No. They probably would, but there would be strings attached. I've been siphoning gas from the wrecks. This truck will run on damn near anything I've been told. I just haven't wanted to try it yet. I don't actually go much of anywhere in it anyway. There's nowhere to go. I don't feel like driving past the people down by the Armory, so I'm going to head away from town, and then come back around to what I want to show you."

He paused, concentrated on driving, then told me, "Don't think poorly of Jimmy back there. He is a good man. He didn't crack when some of the others did. He hung in there and did his job. When it was over, well, he just kind of shut down. Lost his family, lost most of his friends, lost just about everything. He saw too much that was too ugly. So I think he is just...oh, I don't know. Best word I can think of is drifting. It's as if something came loose inside, and he can't - or won't - bolt it back down. I don't know if you're following me."

I nodded my head. "Yeah, Chief. I am. More than you think."

111

"I thought you might." He didn't say anything after that. We sat in the cab and looked at what had once been a small town. Maybe it would be again some day. If the army maintained a presence here it probably would. One with a different character I'm sure. Any time there was a concentration of horny young men who got paid regularly, there would be a town that focused on fulfilling certain needs.

What we saw was not surprising. How anything had escaped unscathed was surprising. This was outside the defensive perimeter, so who knows how many had passed through here, left some trash, took a dump, stole something from someone else, and moved on. I could guess what the insides of the houses looked like based on their outsides. If the army didn't stick around, then this town was going to be a village, at best.

I asked the Chief, "Who did the house-to-house cleanup afterward?"

"Army did. I did. My officers, those that were left, did. That's what I do now. Watch empty houses and businesses and make sure they stay that way. Nobody here is keen on strangers, especially drifters."

"Going house to house is not real fun." I was interested in what he had to say.

He laughed. "Damn, Gardener. You see all these burned-out houses? They had people in them. We tried warning them to get out but they shot at us. So we came in heavy, used a loudspeaker to tell them one more time to move. If we knew someone was in there and not moving...well, we set the house on fire and killed them as they ran out. If no one answered, we sent the dogs in. Lost all our dogs that way, but by God they moved out. I don't know about your people, but after seeing the insides of a few of those places and what had gone on, burning them down and killing everyone in them was easy enough to do."

Night spoke up right away when she heard that. I knew what she was doing. She wanted to change the subject and fast. It

112

kind of irritated me. I knew why she was doing it. It was out of love and a desire to protect me. Still, it bothered me. Not that I was going to say anything to her. You see, I wasn't sure if I could go back into a basement again.

She asked him, "So what is this place you're taking us to?"

He turned right, still putting on his turn signal I noticed. He didn't have to answer. It was right in front of us.

"My God." She said, "Is this where bicycles go to die?"

"No, just the owners of them," he told her flatly.

I grinned when I heard that. I was the only one who did I noticed. Bike heaven had a lot of bikes. I laid a grid over them all, counted how many were in one square, and then multiplied it out. I came up with five hundred bikes.

"Chief, how many bikes are here?" Night sounded amazed.

He told her, "Ummm...five hundred and twelve at last count, but I think a few have walked off. This is also part of my new job description. I am the keeper of the bikes." He actually sounded a little proud. It dawned on me that he was trying to impress Night. I was mulling that over as they walked over to look at them more closely.

The bikes were stacked in semi-neat rows. You could tell someone, probably the Chief, had tried to maintain some kind of order. You could also tell they had given up on it at some point and just started tossing them in heaps. There were at least seventy-five or more kids' bikes. Freya's little rodents would be pleased.

I saw a pink model with a white basket that I planned on pulling out for the older one. She probably wouldn't like it. Knowing her, she would want a boy's cross-country with flames on it. Maybe if I painted a skull on the white basket...

My musing was interrupted by Night calling excitedly, "G! Come here! Look!" She was pointing at a stack of bikes that had been modified to carry stuff, along with tricycles and a number of trailers for bikes. Half of them looked worse for wear. A few were bent, but it was hard to tell whether it was from the tossing or the trip out here.

I started looking at tires. There were a lot of flats or low tires here. They had also been out in the weather for a couple months at least.

"Hey, Chief. You got any pumps and parts for these bikes?"

He shook his head no. "I know. You got some work cut out for you here. I'll ask Jimmy. He used to ride a lot I think."

I thought, *If you can find him.* Then again where the hell could you really go around here? Hopefully one of the newbies knew bikes.

We looked around a bit more. Well, actually Night did. I began looking for my bike. I didn't want anything fancy. If I could find it a Schwinn five-speed with a comfortable seat, that would be good. If we were going to pedal our way across America, then I sure didn't want my balls getting squashed up into my back pocket every long mile on the way.

While we were looking a crow landed about ten feet from me on one of the bikes. He cawed at me and I cawed back. I saw the Chief look at me a bit strangely but he didn't say anything. Hell, on his strange-o-meter that probably barely budged the needle these days.

We headed back. He told us, "I'm going to ask you two to drop down so you can't be seen in a few minutes. I'm going out past where I picked you up. No need for anyone to see you, or know where I dropped you off. I'll meet you at the same place at 05:00 tomorrow."

Night leaned over the seat and said, "Thanks, Chief."

A few minutes later he told us to duck. We did. I can't say I liked it but I did it. A few minutes later he said, "Clear," and we popped up like groundhogs. A few minutes after that he was easing the truck over to the side of the road. He told us, "Later," and was gone a second after we had shut the doors.

We moved off the side of the road and I led Night to a downed log back in the trees and shrubbery.

114

"Let's sit awhile and talk," I told her. We had a couple of hours before sundown, and I was in no hurry to get back. I waited until she was settled. We sat there for a few minutes, just listening to the trees rustle, until I heard his truck pass by going the other way. We both relaxed a notch.

"You trust him?" I asked her.

She sat there without saying anything for a minute. "Within reason. I can see some possible problems down the line, but I think I know how to handle them."

"You mean his wild and crazy lust for you?"

She snorted. "Don't worry. I'll cool him off if it comes to that." Left unspoken was if she didn't, I would. Permanently.

"Yeah. He is not going to be satisfied being a grunt, is he?"

"No. I think we are going to make him king of the motor pool." I thought about that. It made sense.

"Good plan. I got an idea after looking at all those bikes. What do you think of us becoming cavalry?"

"I like it. I'm thinking we could use the diesel truck, and any more we can find, as slow and heavy movers on the roads. Maybe some bikes with trailers in the mix, too. Then we can use bikes as scouts."

I could see what she meant as clear as day. "Max will have some refinements and ideas. I think he will like it."

"So you want to hear the plan I came up with while you were fondling guns?"

"Sure." As if I had a choice.

"We bring everyone down at 03:30 and set up for a possible ambush. When he shows up we stuff everyone in the truck and drop them at Bike Heaven. I think Ninja should run that part. They get the bikes. They can throw ours on the carriers, and roll back here. Meanwhile, Max and we wait here. The Chief comes back for us and we go load up the truck with the contents of his supply room. Then we all meet back here and roll on out." She leaned back and looked pretty damned satisfied with herself.

I told her, "You're a genius."

115

"Yep."

"You're also sexy."

"Yep."

"You're also about fifteen minutes away from getting laid."

"Twice, I hope."

We walked back holding hands. I was hungry and wanted to move a little more quickly. Instead I did the afterglow thing. It was nice and all. I may even remember that walk for the rest of my life. I was learning. This romance stuff wasn't that hard. If I had known this earlier, I sure wouldn't have burned through a twenty-ounce bottle of moisturizer every month for most of my life.

We came up on the camp and Josh challenged us. I didn't miss the hint of nervousness in his voice when he said, "Who goes there!"

"You been seeing a lot of hand-holding Gnawers come this way, Josh?" Night let go of my hand and kept walking past him. I told him, "Point the gun barrel in a different direction, numb nut."

"Oh. Sorry."

"Thanks. You okay?" He nodded his head. "Good."

I slapped him on the shoulder and headed over to the squad area. I decided to check on them first, make sure there were no problems, and then go see what I could find to eat. It was already getting dark. They should have been getting some sleep because they would be on watch later. They weren't. I didn't kid myself that they were waiting for me. Rather, they were waiting for my news. Each one harbored hope that I would tell them that everything was fine down the road. That I had booked us all rooms at Motel 7, and a cheese pizza was waiting in every room. Afterward, we could all get drunk and talk about how it was all just a bad dream.

"Ya'll waiting for me?" I asked them. A few nodded.

Dalton asked, "Are we going into town, Gardener?" Hope was obvious in voice, so obvious, that if I were someone else I would have been reluctant to crush it.

Too bad. I crushed it. "Nothing good waiting for us down there, people. Well, some supplies. I want everyone up and ready to go at 03:00."

That did not bother them. Getting up early was rapidly becoming part of their lives.

He persisted, "Is there still a town? What's going on?"

Shane asked, "Did you hear any news about what is going on?" And Ben wanted to know if there was any news of Baltimore.

I really would have liked to say something smart-ass and then leave to find some food but that wasn't the way it worked. So I told them what I knew. Then I answered questions. Well, as many as I could deal with. Finally I said, "I have to go get something to eat, and I need to see Max. I'll be back."

I went and found Shelli. She wasn't hard to find as Night was doing the same thing I had just done for Max and everyone else. While she talked, she stuffed her face from an open can of pork and beans.

Shelli handed me a can and told me, "Bon apetit."

One of Freya's little munchkins, Val, said, "We are getting bikes, aren't we?"

"Yep. Did Freya show you the pink one?"

"Yes. I want the black one." I had no idea which one that was, but I was sure I was going to find out.

"You do know how to ride a bike?" I asked her. It never occurred to me until now to think we might have people who did not know how to ride a bike.

She looked at me as if I was an idiot. "Of course I do."

"Oh. Because I can teach you."

She looked at me, her eyes narrowed, and then she said grudgingly, "Well, I might need a little help. Freya says when I get bigger I will have a horse!"

"Cool," I told her. Then I was called away to walk through the plan for tomorrow's adventure.

I guess if most of us had been soldiers in real life instead of online, we would have had a cool name for our meeting. Something like "Command Staff Briefing" or "Tactical Formation Plan." It would probably have to have tactical in it somewhere. I remember looking at military surplus equipment websites online, back in the day, and everything had "tactical" worked into the description. Tactical underwear for that half-naked rappel out the back window. Tactical socks for slipping into the kitchen quietly and eating the last doughnut. Instead we just called it a meeting.

Max was there, along with Ninja, Night, Freya, her munchkins, and Shelli. He ran through the plan, which was almost exactly what Night had told me earlier. The only difference was it was Max, Dalton, and I who were doing the weapons transfer. Everyone else was grabbing bikes. We went through the plan step by step.

Max told us how he planned on organizing us. It wasn't really different than what we had done in town months ago. Well, I had slipped a notch on paper. The reality was it reflected who was good at what. The only difference was we were going to be organized as soldiers instead of cops this time.

He told us we were now proud members of the 1st Freya Division. I was the only one who smiled.

I asked, "Max, don't divisions have thousands of people?"

He stared at me. "G, before the year is over, we will."

I shrugged. "Okay. It's going to be hard to weed out the assholes when you have that many people."

He grinned. "Oh, don't worry about that." I knew that grin. It would not be good to be an asshole in the 1st.

Max told us our ranks. Of course he was the General. Night was his Executive Officer. I had Sword Regiment. Ninja had the Raven Regiment. The two regiments combined were the 1st Division. Shelli would handle logistics. The Chief was going to be 1st Sergeant and in charge of the motor pool. Max continued with a speech about our new responsibilities, and how we needed to work together.

It got tedious quickly so I interrupted him. "What's that leave for Freya? Special Forces?" No one else thought it was funny. Freya rolled her eyes at me. Max and Night shot me their "you're an asshole" looks and Max finished by asking if anyone had any questions. He always did that. I don't know why. We were going to ask our questions regardless if he asked for them or not.

Then we left to go tell our squads the news, and make sure everyone had eaten and was set for the night. Before I settled in I checked all my people who were on watch and made sure everyone else was tucked in.

Morning came quickly. Well, 03:00 did. We still had a while before dawn. I was tired; so was Night. We were both exempt from standing watch, but we made up for it by sitting around with Max and the others, talking about what we were going to do.

I got everyone up and we moved out almost quietly. I made a note to myself to go around later and check their gear. There was way too much rattling and clinking going on. I was going to have to pull Josh aside and tell him to shut the fuck up in the morning. Nobody cared about how badly he had to piss.

We made it down to pickup point and I had to get in Dalton's face.

I hissed at him, "Put that fucking safety back on!" He looked surprised. I bet he thought no one would hear him take it off. I wanted safeties on all the time. I was not thrilled about them even carrying loaded weapons at this point. They were too freaking clueless. If we ever got ahead on food and ammo we were going to need to stop and run them all through a mini boot camp.

We halted far enough from the road that someone would have to stop and stare to see us. We put a watch out in both directions on the road. Then we sat and waited. It was interesting to watch my new people to see who could sit quietly without fidgeting. Dalton was good. So was Josh, to my surprise. Shane sucked at it. I must have sent him the evil glare twice. Yet another one to pull aside later for a chat.

The Chief was on time. Max and Night went down to talk to him. Less than a minute later he was waving the bike snatchers to come down. Five minutes later they were gone. Max came back and sat down about five feet from me. He didn't say a word. The Chief was back about twenty minutes later. He was grinning when we got in the cab.

"Hey! Damn if I didn't feel like Santa Claus letting your people loose amongst the bikes. Those two little girls made a beeline to the kids' bike pile. It was as if they already knew what they wanted."

Max was sitting up front. Dalton and me had the back seats.

Max replied, "Yep. They've got minds of their own."

The Chief did a U-turn and we headed back. He had dressed up in camo fatigues with an "operator" rig for his sidearm. He had a backpack, one of the big ones for expedition use, in the back seat. Dalton and I were jammed together.

Max asked him, "You bringing anyone else?"

The Chief replied, "No. It's best that my son stays here. He didn't want to go anyway. I thought about Jimmy but ...well, I changed my mind. I thought about some of the people I know around here. Of the ones that are still alive, I realized I didn't much care for them anymore." Not much we could say in reply to that.

Chief pulled in around back this time. "Easier to load and harder to see," he explained as he stepped out of the truck. He unlocked the door and we followed him in. "I got some hand trucks for us. Should make loading easier. I want this to go as fast as possible. I'll be glad to get some distance between me

120

and this town." I realized he was talking so much because he was nervous. This had to be a big deal for him.

Max took a look around the room and nodded his head. "Have you got another barrel for that M2HB?"

"No, Max. They probably burned through them all."

He squatted down to look at it. "Chief, this barrel is done for. I would love to have it but it's too heavy for us to carry around. You have any ammo for it?"

"Yeah. Over here."

"Okay. Drag it out, Chief. I'm going to see what we've got in these boxes. G, go ahead and start humping the ammo boxes. When you get out to the truck, pop one open, and see if they came with the stripper clips."

Something was off here but I couldn't figure it out. "Sure, Max." The boxes were heavy. I loaded four of them on a hand truck and wheeled them out the door.

As I did I heard Max tell Dalton, "Go ahead and break that . 50 down. I think we will take it anyway."

"Sorry, Sarge. I don't know how."

"Never mind. Let's move this ammo."

Dalton passed me in the hallway. "We got some good shit, didn't we?"

"Sure did."

The crates had only one surprise. One was halfway full of M-67 hand grenades. I was excited. I always wanted to blow something up, but Max rained on my parade.

"Sorry, G. Those are fragmentation grenades. Not what you were hoping for. Still very good." He was pleased. The other crates had MP-4s with burned-out barrels.

The Chief was surprised. "That's it? That is everything that is good?"

"Yep. It's good, Chief. Real good," Max told him. We were outside and staring at what was stacked inside the truck bed. Max paused for a second. Then he said, "Time to saddle up and move. They are waiting for us."

CHAPTER FOURTEEN

We rolled back down the road. I was surprised. The trailers were easy enough to spot. The bikes, they had laid them down in the trees, and thrown leaves over them. Then they had taken up position farther back in the woods. I was impressed and thought we might actually make it as a bicycle cavalry.

That hope was quickly dashed. I envisioned us pulling away in a tight orderly formation, like jet fighters in formation, or tanks moving on the battlefield. Instead it was a circus. Within the first three minutes we had one collision and a couple of obvious wobblers. The rest, for the most part, looked pretty shaky.

Josh and Ben surprised me. They had obviously spent some time on bikes. I pulled up alongside them and said, "Guess what, guys?" They were laughing their asses off at the collision ahead of us. We had stopped so they could untangle themselves.

Ben answered, "Yeah, what's up, Gardener?"

"You are both now Bike Training and Repair Officers. Split up. Josh, you got Dalton. You know who that leaves you, Ben. Get them up to speed." Then I rode off. Life was good sometimes.

It felt good being on a bike again. It wasn't my old Bat Bike, but Night had picked out one that was pretty close. I rode up front to join Max. I passed Ninja screaming at the two people who had collided.

He was yelling, "God Damnit! You told me you knew how to ride! You better get your asses up in the seats and keep them there!"

Chief was driving the truck. We planned on carrying most of the gear, food and ammo in it. Plus, anyone who was sick or hurt could catch a ride. It was obvious we were going to need at least two more trucks. I pulled up next to Max who was talking to Night. He stopped talking and we turned to watch as some of the gear one of Ninja's people had strapped onto their bike fell off. His squad was having all the luck today.

Max looked at me, grinned, and said, "So much for the movement plan."

"Yep. No doubt about that." Our plan was to have two people riding up front as scouts, about half a mile apart. One squad - I refused to call them a regiment, followed by Max, Freya and her squirrels. They were riding around in circles and giggling at the moment. Next would come the vehicles followed by the other squad. Behind that, about a half mile back, would be a lone rider watching our backs.

After shaking his head Max told me, "Go ahead and scout for us, G. I'll take your squad. Night, take the close point. Shelli, I need you to watch our backs." There was some more talk and then Max bellowed, "Mount up and ride for Freya!"

Almost everyone shouted back "Freya!" This was a new innovation. I decided to pass on it. Freya, who was sitting on her bike next to me, looking almost regal, looked back on them, turned away, and pumped her bike. We were off.

I zoomed ahead of them. There was a bit of a downhill slope so I was able to fly. As I did, I listened to the tires zing against the road and wondered if my brakes worked.

Freya whispered in my head, "Stand by for your feed," and for a second I was riding blind until my brain adjusted to the data flowing in. We were not alone out here. I started braking, and to my relief they actually worked.

I wasn't skilled enough to process data and ride a bike at the same time. Max could. I had watched him do it, hold a conversation, and still watch what was going on around him. I figured I would pick it up in time. In a lot of ways it was not much different than online gaming where you had to watch the main screen, the mini screen, and keep an eye out for management, while shooting alien life forms all at the same time.

I didn't see anyone on the road. We had a car moving toward us that was about twenty minutes out. I would keep an eye on that. Behind us the town was dead. The sun was up and dawn was already behind us. I sat and watched the group come down the hill. It wasn't pretty. It was more like a straggle down the hill. They were strung out and looked more like a bunch of people taking a ride on a pre-Crash Sunday than a formidable fighting force. At this rate we might cover ten miles in a day.

Max saw me sitting there and pulled ahead of the pack. I watched him. He obviously enjoyed getting out and flying, too. He locked them down and overshot me by about ten feet.

"What did you see?"

"There's a car coming. Maybe fifteen minutes out. How do you want to handle it?"

He paused. "Let it go by. Get on out there. Let them see you first. If they want to get frisky then they will probably jump you."

"Okay. Sounds good. It's been kind of boring lately anyway."

I rolled along the highway at a slower clip. Not that I wanted to. I wanted to fly! That wasn't part of my job, though. I was supposed to be looking for possible ambushes and places we might find food. It occurred to me that eventually we would want to push a small team two or three days ahead of the main body. Communications would be a problem. I wondered how

124

Genghis and the boys did it back in the day. Not having the Internet really sucked on a lot of levels.

I was still seeing a lot of dead cars on the sides of the road. I had to slow down even more because more cars were in the road, left there like the ultimate American roadkill. Shattered window glass glittered in the sunlight while broken taillights and turn signal plastic glowed. The highway was marked here and there with bubbled asphalt and burn marks. Off to the side of the road brass casings blinked at me, especially around one knot of cars that led up a driveway to a burned-out farmhouse. Every once in awhile the smell of rotting bodies drifted across the road. Beyond it all were fields, just starting to green.

I was starting to sweat. There were more uphill grades than downhill. *Going to be a lot of sore bodies tonight*, I thought. I might even be one of them. I could feel a twinge in my thigh were the rake had bitten me. That seemed like a million years ago. I figured I was about thirty minutes ahead of the rest of the pack. That is, assuming no-one ran off into a ditch, had an accidental weapons discharge, or had a tire blow-out.

I thought about parking on the side of the road and waving at the car when it went by. That seemed kind of lame. They could do a drive-by on me easily that way. I wasn't going to hide, so I decided to just keep going.

I was starting to feel uneasy. Where the hell was the car? I locked up the bike brakes and swerved to the side. There was no reason for me to do it. It just felt right. I parked, and sat for a minute, listening. Where was my Freya satellite feed when I needed it? Damn. I was going to have to do this the old-fashioned way. I left my bike where the Freya traveling horde could see it. Hopefully they would stop and wonder what the hell had happened to me.

I listened, and did not hear anything alarming or out of place. I was running out of time. The Horde was coming. I dashed along a line of cars that were half on and half off the side of the road. I stopped again and listened.

There they were! Sneaky little bushwhackers. The road was narrowed to a choke point by the cars lining the side; a big part of it was an F-150, which had tangled itself up by sitting on top of a Ford Fusion. Together they narrowed the road to one lane. They weren't Bushwhackers; they were FordWhackers - the worst kind.

I heard someone whisper, "Where the fuck is he?"

"Yeah, he should be here now. Luther, take a look." I froze. Now I knew where Luther was along with the boss man. I took a few more steps. There was a gap between the vehicles on my right. I stepped into it and saw them. Two were behind the Fords. One was back about two cars down on the right. He was off the road. The fourth one was about three feet away from me. I didn't need to see or hear him. I could smell him now.

I whispered, "Hey." He was already turning to look at me. He must have felt my presence. You could not have survived this long without being good at this kind of work otherwise. I shot him at the same time I shot the guy who was back a bit down the road. I didn't want to end up playing hide and seek in the ruins of Detroit steel.

At the same time I started moving at an angle toward the other two. They were good. The one who was taking shelter behind the Fords was pivoting toward me. A split second faster and he would have gotten off his shot. He didn't. I did. The last one did manage to pull the trigger before he died. His short burst traveled through where I had been standing when he began his turn. I had kept moving and I was fast. Very fast and accurate. I would have been dead long before now if I hadn't learned to never stand still.

"Shoot and scoot." Max had pounded that into me. "It will save your life." He was right.

I kept moving. I zigged to my left, zagged to my right, and went through a gap in the cars and then off the road on the right. I stood there and listened.

I got "Standby for data" from Freya. She wasn't seeing anything. I sent "Little late, don't you think?" to her and received no reply. She also cut the feed. *She must be in a snit,* I thought and laughed.

I moved, stopped, and listened again. Once I felt sure I was alone I went to take a look at their vehicle. It was a Honda Odyssey. The outside color was originally silver. They had hit the sides with brown and black spray paint in an attempt to camouflage it. I came up alongside and peered in before I opened it up. It stunk inside.

Nowadays everything that housed humans for any length of time stunk. It was the new normal. These guys were remarkably tidy and organized. That surprised me. I was expecting a lot worse. I started searching the vehicle. I dropped the sun visor on the passenger side and pried the little mirror off and pocketed it. Later I would give it to Night.

As I did I heard, "Put your hands where I can see them and step away from the vehicle."

"Fuck you, Max." I didn't even turn around. Over my shoulder I said, "Come on out, Ninja. I know you're there." I heard Max chuckling as he came up behind me.

He was joined by Ninja who told me, "You did not!"

"Did too."

"No way."

"Dude. I heard you fart. You got to watch that. It ruins the sneaky part." Before he could deny it I tossed him the binoculars that had been sitting on the passenger seat. "Here. A present."

He caught them in mid air and tried them. "Thanks, G. They have a rangefinder!"

"God knows you need it." I laughed, and he flipped me off while he took a look around through them. Max slid the side door back and looked through the odds and ends that he found. He pulled a green ammo box out from behind one of the seats, opened it, closed it, and set it on the road in the "Go" pile.

127

He told Ninja, "Go back and tell them to come on through." I told him, "As you go, take a look at Luther. He's the one over there. He has a nice sidearm. If you want it, take it."

"Thanks, G."

I waited until he cleared the area before I asked Max my questions. "What's up with the Freya chant? You joining the Church of Freya now?"

He stopped what he was doing and looked at me. "G, it's like this. I don't know what she is, and I don't really care as long as she gives us an edge. These people, they need something to believe in and rally around. She was all I had handy."

I considered that briefly and said, "We would have rallied around you, Max." I really couldn't believe I said that, even if it was true.

He nodded. "You have and I appreciate it. But, G, I'm a war leader not a belief system. Way big difference for most people. Think about it." I wanted to ask him about Freya's failure to communicate but I could hear the Horde coming.

They began straggling through the opening in the cars. Max headed over to meet them and Night rode over to where I was standing.

"Hey, Night."

She asked me, "You okay?"

"Yeah, but we are going to have to go off road for a bit, at least until we can get to a road that isn't lined with cars. This is way too dangerous."

"No shit," she said. "We're less than five miles out of town."

"I have to go through some pockets, see what I can find." She and I were doing pretty well. We were still holding a fair amount of the gold and silver I had earned.

She nodded. "Okay. That van run?"

"It should."

"Okay." She yelled to Max, "The van runs. I'll bring it."

He yelled back, "Okay," and went back to keeping the Horde moving. It was just like on the highway back in the day.

Everyone had to slow down and rubberneck at the scene of an accident. As I watched them, they would roll past, look at the bodies, and then look back at me. *Good,* I thought. *Maybe they will listen when I tell them something.* But I doubted it.

I searched the bodies. The total was a couple of gold eagles, some silver, and a hundred-dollar bill. Not bad at all. I took their weapons and boots, put them in the van, and slid the door shut. Night was standing in front of it talking to Max.

"Good. We need the transport." He turned to me. "By the way, G, good job. It's slow going but I can already tell most of them are not going to be able to do a full day. Jail time and lack of food has not helped them either." He slapped me on the shoulder. "I've got to roll. You still have point."

"Yeah, yeah. I know."

I kissed Night and told her, "We need to talk soon."

She nodded her head gravely. "I know."

"Oh, make sure the bolt cutters on the passenger side floorboard stay with us."

"Okay. Be careful." She pulled away in the van. I pulled out behind her and passed by everyone a few minutes later. I got ahead of them and went back to paying attention to the world around me.

The road was starting to creep me out. It was almost claustrophobic in places from all the cars, RVs and trucks jammed along the sides. Every vehicle with its own back story in horror. After an hour and a half, when the occasional break in cars let me see the fields and hills, I decided to pull in and wait for everyone. This was as good as place as any to take a break. We would still have enough light to run through some weapons training, too. God knows getting them up to speed would be helpful.

I set the bike down behind a car and stepped away from the mass of metal on the side the wind was blowing from. It stunk, and I wanted away from the smell as much as possible. It didn't work. If anything it stunk worse.

129

I planned on telling Max the idea that had come to me earlier. We would go off road. I would go ahead of the Horde with the bolt cutters and get rid of obstacles. They could follow me at a distance and we would try to parallel the road as much as possible.

I decided to climb up on the hood of a Land cruiser and see what I could see. I looked back down the way I had come. Nothing.

"Stand by for video feed" bonged in my head. I processed it. We had an occupied farmhouse about five miles down the road and a couple off of it.

"Hey, Freya. Cut the feed and talk to me." The image disappeared and I heard no reply. Oh well, what the hell. I jumped off the roof, hit the ground, rolled and came up with both Rugers out. No reason. I did it because I could, and because it was fun. I holstered them and started scratching my crotch. Might as well get that out of the way before everyone showed up. Damn, I really needed a shower and a shave.

CHAPTER FIFTEEN

"You wanted to talk?"

I spun around, slapped leather, and almost blew Freya's head off. I slid the Rugers back in the holsters and told her, "That was not smart, kiddo."

She laughed. "Look behind you." I didn't turn around; I turned sideways and stepped back. I had a sudden urge to keep her and whoever else was around in my field of vision.

"Well, how nice. You brought the kids." They were both standing there. Both armed and looking far too comfortable with the weapons. "We going to have a picnic?"

"No," she snarled. "We are not going to have a picnic!" Her face, hell, *she* had changed. She had grown again, and her face was cold as death. Gone was the kid I knew. This was something else entirely.

"So was it something you ate that's bothering you?" I asked her.

She screamed, reached forward, placed both of her hands - cold as ice, across my ears, almost interlacing them behind my head, and pulled me to her lips. Lips that were as hot as her hands were cold.

I was paralyzed. I knew her, and thought of her, as a kid. What had me in its grip was not a kid. I was beginning to think it wasn't even human. Instead of a tongue, a steel blade slid out from between her lips and jammed its point in the back of my throat. It didn't stop there. It continued to punch through tissue and bone until it came out the other side. The pain was excruciating.

Then it was gone. My world went black. I heard a voice tell me, "You are dead, Gardener."

"Well, that was not very nice of you, Freya."

An amused voice, similar to Freya's yet much older and colder, said, "I am not nice. I am not even a person, nor has the word *merciful* ever been used to describe my actions. Now open your eyes and walk with me."

I walked alongside the latest version of Freya. I think we must have skipped through some of the earlier versions, because this had to be Freya 15.0 at least. It was definitely a mature product at the end of its cycle.

She was wearing a pearl white dress with a cape of red that must have been awesome before time, dry cleaners, and various fabric-eating bugs had wrought their various forms of destruction on it. Her hair was white and thinning, her skin pale and finely lined. She told me, with a hint of sadness coloring her voice, "You see me as I really am, Gardener."

She stopped walking and faced me. "Not at all awe inspiring am I. None who are alive in your world have seen me this way. They see the old me, the few that still look and dream about the old days." She sighed. "Those few are usually drug-addled idiots who would be hard-pressed to lift the swords they dream about in combat against one of the Old Ones on his worst day."

She shook her head and continued walking. I realized by the sound of her breathing that the stop had been for her as much as it was for me to see her.

We were walking down a path carpeted with pine needles. Tall pines, firs and the occasional aspen lined each side. We stepped on large flat stones that were perfectly placed to allow us to cross a shallow stream without getting our feet wet. Snow was still lying in the shadows, so white as to be almost blue. There was no sun, just an overcast sky late in a winter day.

"Is this Hell?"

"No, you fool. It's Valhalla." She sounded exasperated.

We came around a bend in the path. Not far away was a gray wooden hall. Stag antlers hung on the side and front of the building. It may have been painted once. I wasn't sure, if it had been, it must have been a long, long time ago. In the field next to it four horses, all off-white and in need of grooming, grazed. It looked more like West Virginia then Valhalla to me.

Freya's breath sounded labored. I figured it was a good time to ask her the big question. "So where does Jesus fit in here?"

She stopped dead in her tracks and a long shuddering breath racked her body. She slowly turned to face me. I involuntarily took a step back. Her eyes were huge, blue and fiery. Her face hard planes with spots of red anger highlighting sharp cheekbones accented by fair skin. She slowly let out a deep breath.

"I will answer your question once, and once only. Do not ask this of me again!" She took another deep breath, held it, and slowly let it escape. Her eyes dimmed, as did the spots.

"It is a question I should have anticipated given the time and cycle of the world you live in. He won. We lost. Rather, we faded away as you will see. Even Odin is no match for an Archangel." She was nearly spitting as she said, "We exist because he is merciful. We only want to live again, at least for a time, however short it will be before we once again lose the hearts and minds of the minority that believe in us."

I looked at her, and said, "I think I'm getting it. You're like Nordic vampires sucking on your believers' energy."

"No!" She screamed, "We not only take but we give! Who gave you your hearing? Is your sight so much sharper? I gave it to you! At great cost! I reward those who believe in many ways, both now and afterward. You are a warrior. One of us. You must see this and believe."

133

She had swung from extreme anger to where she was now ready to cry. Women were weird that way I had found, especially during certain times of the month. I wished I could see the moon. It had to be full.

We approached the hall and its double doors. Every inch of the doors was carved with scenes of warriors, horses with Valkyrie, and of course, Freya. The doors swung open by themselves. They had to; I would have been severely disappointed if they had not. One got stuck about halfway, but we ignored it.

I let Freya enter first. I might be dead but I wasn't stupid. It was reassuring to know that I still had my guns and bayonet. What was not so reassuring was that I had no way of knowing whether they worked here.

So this was the great hall of warriors. It looked more like a senior citizens' home for short, old, Harley types, with sharp pig stickers. My Norse history occupied, at best, a short paragraph of memory in my brain. It amounted to hot ladies on horses that rode down from Valhalla and did something? Smite? Give warriors rides to Norway? Then there was Odin and Thor who didn't do much that I could remember. There was the warrior hall. I think that was where you went if you died in battle. A Viking VFW hall in the hereafter. Oh, there had to be some big-breasted maidens in there somewhere with low-cut bodices and pitchers of ale? Or was it mead? Yep. That was it.

Freya stopped short and I almost ran into her. With a grand sweep of her arm she said, "Welcome to Folkvangr, Gardener."

"I thought you said it was Valhalla."

"No. Valhalla is elsewhere. I told you that earlier because I didn't want to confuse you. Valhalla is a name everyone knows. It put this into context for you. This is Folkvangr." She was sounding exasperated again.

The men, and occasional woman, were not paying us much attention; probably because they were asleep.

She added, "I also take women who die nobly in battle. Odin gets the other half, and he does not take women."

"Is he gay?" She didn't answer that. I looked out over the warriors of the hall. They were either asleep or muttering to themselves. Their weapons were casually stacked next to them or slung on the chairs they sat in. Some had them hung off of their belts. I noticed no one had horns on their helmets. I guess Odin got the horny ones. Over there in his boys club wherever it was. The few women I saw, well, they were old and needed to lace up those bodices. I shuddered and looked away.

"Have you seen enough, Gardener?"

"Yeah." I remembered what she had told me in the cave about cycles and power. It made sense now. "So what do you need me to do?"

"It will be easy for you. Just kill in my name. From the others who witness it, and believe, will come the revival. In turn you will have my aid when possible."

"That's it? I don't have to polish your boots or attend Freya church?"

She replied, "Men do not attend my church, and no warrior worth his steel would bow to me."

"Okay."

She looked at me. I think she was surprised. Then she smiled. "Thank you, Gardener. Wait." She walked through the mass of sleeping warriors to the front where a large chair sat at the end of the biggest trestle table. From the warrior on the right, a big guy, she took a sword. He twitched a bit as she did. Then he went back to sleep. She carried it back, holding it in front of her.

She stopped in front of me. "Here is my first personal gift to you. It has a name that no longer means anything. Take it, and give it a new one." She handed it to me.

It was a beautiful sword. Somewhat crude, but I liked the pommel - it was a head buster. It was also shorter than I expected, more of a Roman short sword than a long movie style blade. It felt good in my hand. Perfectly balanced and alive.

135

"Nice, I'll take it. Thanks." I looked around. "You think any of these guys have a sheath for it?"

She laughed. "I'll take care of that. You need to go."

I opened my mouth to say something and found myself alone. Back in the same place on the road. The only difference was a sore throat and a crick in my neck. In my hand was the short sword. *That was different*, I thought.

I started looking for the Horde. They arrived about fifteen minutes later. Freya and her Freylings were with her. Nobody seemed to be acting strange the way I would have expected if Freya and her little rugrats had levitated out of the Horde to come see me. It must have been that space-time continuum thing that I used to read about in sci-fi books. I shrugged it off. It wasn't really all that big of a deal.

CHAPTER SIXTEEN

Max and Night rode over to where I was standing.

"What's up, G?"

"I figure we could go off road here, Max." I pointed west. "Maybe head for that hill and spend the night."

He looked at it. "Yeah, I saw that earlier. We can get some weapons time, too. Let's do it."

Night was grinning at me. She reached into her basket and pulled out an emergency crank radio. "Look! We can get the news and music!" Whatever had been bothering her had left, at least for the moment. "Where did you get the sword?"

"Tell you later. Where did you find the radio?"

She grinned. "In a suitcase off to the side when we stopped to untangle Ben's pant leg from his bike." Night still loved looking in the suitcases, boxes, and bins that we came across. They were a source of mystery, and often delight, for her. I had given up on it because too often they were a source of sadness for me. I simply saw them as the debris of dead people who did nothing to deserve their fate except to be born in the wrong time or place.

Ninja was shepherding his squad through. Night had the bolt cutters in her basket. I was beginning to think her bike basket might be like her purse used to be: an endless black hole of storage. Ninja stopped long enough to admire my sword, grab the bolt cutters, and move on. I winked at Freya when she rolled by, followed by my squad.

Max told Night to roll with them. "Gardener and I are going to run point for the vehicles until we get to the turn off that leads to the hill." The Chief was idling behind us, with the minivan behind him.

"Let's go, G." We started threading our way through the maze.

After about five minutes he slowed down enough that I could come up alongside him. Long ago we had perfected the ability to converse without looking at each other. Without talking about it we split the road in half. He had the right side. I had the left. He looked straight ahead while I kept checking behind us. We had done it this way since we first started walking street patrol back in Fairfax.

Max asked, "Night talk to you yet?"

"Nope."

"Dalton is working for somebody."

"And being an asshole?"

"So, she told you what she's been hearing him say?"

"About her?"

"Yeah."

I didn't say anything.

"I'm surprised you're taking it so calmly. You are changing. Wait a minute. She didn't tell you anything, did she?"

"Nope. You just did. Don't worry. I'm not going to go off the deep end."

Max sighed, and said, "Shit. Well, for God's sake, make him talk before you kill his sorry ass."

I wasn't planning to kill him right away. This was the new, improved me. My new mantra, freshly thought up, went through my head: *Maximum information, maximum pain.* I smiled. Got to change with the times.

I waited until we had gotten to the turn off and made it up the hill where we were making camp. Then I went in search of

Dalton. On the way, I passed Max and Ninja talking and gave them the hand sign "on me." I didn't look back to see if they were coming. I didn't need to.

We were making camp at the top of the hill. A burned-out farmhouse had once occupied it. A couple of bullet-ridden vehicles were off to one side. Daffodils bloomed near where the front door had been. The usual litter of brass cartridges and personal effects were scattered across the dead front lawn. Someone could start a small business collecting all the spent cartridges. Too bad I had no clue what was involved in reloading. My entire education had turned out to be worthless.

I found the squad. Night was nowhere to be seen. Dalton was whistling "Inagodavida" from *The Simpsons*.

"Hey, guys! How was the ride?" This was greeted by moans and laughter.

Dalton was sitting next to his buddy, Shane. Both were sitting on the bench backseat of a full-sized American car that someone had ripped out and placed there years ago. The 100 percent natural plastic had held up well. Where it had cracked, someone had mended it with duct tape. It faced a concrete statue of Mary, which also had daffodils blooming around it. *Someone's idea of a meditation space?* I wondered.

Ben was sitting on a stump looking at a scrape he had picked up, probably when his pant leg got tangled up. Josh was standing there talking to him.

I looked at it and told Ben, "Go find Shelli and get some hydrogen peroxide on that. You don't need an infection. Then let it dry out."

While I talked to him I watched Max come up quickly and quietly behind the other two. Ninja circled a bit more around so we all had clear fields of fire. I turned around to face Dalton. He registered that something wasn't right, but he wasn't sure where or what. Shane was oblivious.

Max set the barrel of his Colt .45 behind Dalton's head and said, "Kerclick."

Dalton froze. He looked at me, and I shook my head. Shane was still going on about how funny it had been seeing Ben fall on his ass. I told him to shut up.

Dalton smiled at me. "Let me guess. That's Max standing behind me making the sound of a .45 being cocked."

Shane looked over his shoulder at Max and asked, "Why did you make that sound, Max?"

Dalton answered for him. "Because he carries it cocked." Then he sighed.

"Shane," I told him, "you're a dumbass, but right now you are not in trouble. You will be if you don't get off your ass and go stand by Ninja."

"Oh. Okay. Well, see you guys." He got up, left, and didn't look back. I watched as Ninja moved to meet him. He would take his weapons for now.

"So, gentlemen. Care to tell me what's up?" Dalton had nerve. Too bad. We could have used him.

"You are charged with being an agent of the Feds, trying to convince your squad mates to rebel against their leaders, and talking shit about Night." I hoped I had hit the right degree of formality with that. Out of the corner of my eye I also noticed Ben and Josh startled a bit. I was on the right track.

"What tipped you off, Max?" I had spoken the charges but Dalton chose to address Max instead. I laughed. He could ignore me now but we would see about that later.

"Back in the armory, you called me Sarge. That is what set me to thinking. How did you know I was one once? Also, the way you said it. It rolled too easily out of your mouth, as easy as if you were still active."

"Okay, Dalton. I want you to ease that Glock out. Pinch it; don't grab it. That's it. Now toss it." This was going more smoothly than I expected. I wasn't sure if I liked that or not.

Max told Josh, "Go get everyone who's not on watch. Ben, I want you to come around behind me and pull his bag away from him. Go through the contents."

Both of them did as Max directed.

Dalton said, "You know, Max. I was in your unit a couple years after you left. They still talked about some of the shit you did."

"That's nice. What are you doing now?" he replied.

"Well, Max, maybe we can make a deal. I know Gardener would kill me in heartbeat. Isn't that so, Gardener?" I just smiled. "Yep. Max and I, we know your type. Max here is the same but he has management skills. Ain't that right, Max?"

Max just tapped the end of the .45 against his head. People were coming in and making a semi-circle around us. I repeated the formal charges so everyone would be up to speed.

"Shit. This is why I am willing to dicker with you, Max. I feel like I can. Ya'll got this formal hearing going on instead of just shooting me in the back of the head and leaving me for the dogs."

"Found it!" Ben yelled. He held it up. It was almost identical to the radio/cell phone I had pulled off the body of the hunter team awhile back.

"Put it down, then put the bag and his clothes over it, Ben," Max told him. "They could be monitoring us and it wouldn't do to get them riled up yet."

"So I'm a Fed. When did that equal a death penalty in America? Yeah, we fucked up some," Dalton paused, "maybe a lot. Still, it's your government and it is trying to help you." He was going to go on but Max tapped him on the head hard enough for it to hurt.

"Shut up. You want to live? We can work something out...maybe." He walked around so he could face him. "Tell us why you are here, Dalton. Tell us everything."

He laughed. "You sure your gunslinger there is going to go along?" Max looked at me and I nodded my head. I wasn't sure where Max was going with this but I would go along with it for now.

Dalton nodded his head. "You know, Max, you could be running this region's teams in no time. Maybe the East Coast. You've got the creds and you sure haven't let yourself get sloppy."

Max shook his head no. "Talk." The way he said it told everyone, including Dalton, he was giving him his last chance.

"Okay, Max. Your word?"

"My word I will let you live."

Dalton began talking. I doubt if he told us everything, and what he did tell us had his slant on it, I am sure of that. It was interesting though.

"My brief was to go in country and evaluate the damage caused by 'PowerDown' in this area. We had reports, and we had drones, but it was spotty. Plus, no one wanted to believe how bad it was." He actually looked sad. "It is that bad. Worse actually. We were a six-man team two months ago. I am all that's left. We thought the worst was over. It wasn't." The last was delivered flatly.

"My mission stayed the same, with the addition of spotting bandit gangs and calling them in." He looked puzzled. "I expected rounds on target after calling in but nothing happened most of the time. I found you all but you were going the wrong way. I thought I might be able to convince Shane, and a few others, to put a round in your head, and then I would lead them back to an installation." He looked up at us, held up his palms, and said, "That's it."

"No," I said. "What was it you said about Night? Something like: 'We will save her. She might be a good fuck.' Maybe you described to Shane and some of the others what you would like to do? Maybe more than once." My voice was very quiet. I felt no anger. I just felt flat.

He replied, "Hey, Gardener. Sorry. I've been in the bush awhile and I do like Asian woman." He grinned at me as if we were best buddies and I would understand. Oh, I did. I really wanted to wipe that smile off his face by exploding his head but I didn't do it. I stood there.

I heard some of the others in the background shouting, "Kill him!" and another say, "We should. We can't trust him."

Max silenced them. "Get me some rope. I want everyone moving. We are not staying here tonight." He took the rope Ninja handed him and said, "Move them, Ninja. Now!"

Then he walked over to Dalton, grabbed him by the hair, jammed the .45 in his ear, and walked him over to a tree. "Put your arms back." He began tying him up.

"You know, Max, I don't consider this letting me go free. I am confined here and helpless."

Max laughed. "You said you were in my old unit. Anyone from that unit would be able to get themselves free in thirty minutes or less." As he said this he jerked the rope hard enough that Dalton gasped. "Okay, your arms are done." He cut the rope and handed me the rest.

"G, you can tie his legs for me." Then he smashed the radio/cell phone underfoot and walked off. "Follow us and catch up when you can, G."

Dalton yelled after him, "Hey! Wait, Max! Don't leave me with this sociopath! C'mon!"

After I tied his legs, I sat down cross-legged in front of him. I took out the Ruger, sat there and spun the cylinder around and around. It was starting to wear. The bluing was coming off, leaving the silver underneath to show through.

Dalton gave up talking to me about five minutes after he apologized for calling me a sociopath. He gave up because I didn't look up at him or answer. I waited about thirty minutes after everyone had left. Then I stood up, holstered the Ruger, and drew the bayonet.

He looked at me and said, "Max promised."

"I know." I slashed his legs lightly. Then his stomach. Just enough to bleed. I stepped back, slid the bayonet back in its sheath, and told him, "Good luck."

I turned, and began a loping run to catch up with the others. I thought "Freya?" Instantly I heard "Yes?"

"Call Woof and his friends to where we were." Then I cut the connection. Somewhere a few miles away Woof and the pack turned around, and began running back.

I caught up with everyone about thirty minutes later. They had not gone far and were just setting up camp again. I went over to where my squad was setting up so I could assign watches. While I was talking to Shane, telling him he was on my shit list, the screams started. We were close enough together that a comment spoken casually could be heard by almost everyone.

Max, who was standing not far from me, asked, "Did you leave him alive, G?"

I replied, perhaps a little louder than normal, "Yeah. I think he is spilling his guts now," and grinned at Max. He approved. That was obvious. A few faces, especially Shane's, went pale listening to the screams. I caught him looking at me. I winked. He swallowed, and looked away. He didn't know it, but I was going to use him as fodder until he proved to me he was worth keeping alive.

We had enough time left in the day to run through the basics of firing the weapons they were carrying. They got a chance to feel the recoil and swap out a magazine. I had them use an SUV as a very large target and they actually hit it. They had fun blowing out the windows, too. Then we walked over and looked at the bullet penetration inside. After that, we cleaned weapons, did bike maintenance, and ate.

Food was always fetched informally. It was assigned the way getting haircuts in a barbershop were once. Everyone knew who was up next without making a big deal of it. We ate as a squad, including Night.

I took the last watch as we were short a body now. Plus, people were very tired.

CHAPTER SEVENTEEN

We were headed toward Ohio. We looked for side roads whenever possible. Railroad tracks and power lines also usually had trails or rough roads we could follow.

We took fire from one sniper who didn't hit anyone. As soon as the first round went whizzing overhead, Max dropped off and moved into the brush. We passed a crossroads and kept going straight. It must have been the right choice as nothing more happened. Max joined us a few minutes later shaking his head. He said that it was probably more of a warning since they had only fired a couple shots.

We did have one stroke of luck. Freya found us a cow. It was a lonesome cow and happy to see us. When it saw us, it probably had visions of a barn and food delivered every day. It wasn't a milk cow either. I heard one of Ninja's people call it a "Hereford." It tasted great. We took two days off and stuffed ourselves and then dried the rest.

We also looked for greens. The problem was none of us, other than me surprisingly, knew what to look for. The time I had spent learning about edible plants with Donna while I was healing from the rake wound came in handy. We also started checking abandoned farmhouses for gardens, looking for spring lettuce and spinach.

Every once in awhile we would head down to a main road to scavenge gas for the van. We were running the truck on heating oil. There was no lack of heating oil around here. In the rural areas almost every house used it. One intact tank would fill up the truck and every container we could find. The other thing that drove us down to the main road was the need for tires. We were going through tires quickly. We carried tires, extra bikes, and bike tires strapped to the top of the van. More tires were strapped to the top of the truck cab.

It didn't take me long to realize that Max was running us in an oval. I didn't have to ask him to know why. We were not ready to run into any real trouble. We had barely gotten to the point where Josh was teaching everyone how to ride in echelon and how to draft. We practiced how to give and respond to hand signals. We went through ambush drills, approaching drills, and fade to defend. We still sucked, but we were getting there.

The night before, Max told us it was time to push on. No more going in circles. Our next big problem was crossing the Ohio River to get to Ohio. The Interstate bridges were watched and guarded. Ohio already had a history of charging people to use their Interstates before the crash.

Their state police had tried to close every bridge in southern Ohio at one point. They couldn't keep them closed from what we could tell, but now they were coming back and trying to lock them down again. In some places they were being backed by what was left of the National Guard. I took a look at the bridge near Marietta; I think that's where it was.

It looked like something out of a WWII movie. They had sandbagged machine gun emplacements on the Ohio side including a Humvee with a chain gun. They had guards underneath the bridge. They had an actual trench line behind all that. They were determined to hold that bridge.

What we wanted was a railroad bridge crossing the Ohio River. We needed it to be next to or close to a road so we could bring the vehicles up as close as possible. We had spotted a couple of likely choices, and now it was time to start heading for them. We eventually decided to try and cross south of Pomeroy and then head toward Chillicothe.

We chose a condemned bridge called the Pomeroy-Mason. It was on the schedule to be dropped into the river in 2009 but that had not happened. We approached it early in the morning. We came out on Route 7 about twenty miles below the bridge. It was too damn hilly around here to do it any other way.

Having the truck and the van was a nice benefit but also a pain in the ass. Gas for the van was getting tougher to find. We weren't the only ones running around out here, and the population density was starting to pick up. These hills and the people living here had done a fairly good job of repelling the invaders.

I was running point with Ben right behind me. He had been an architect in his previous life so we figured he could do the best job of evaluating the bridge for us. We chose it because, as far as we could tell, it was still closed for traffic. That morning we left the group early - just after dawn but before sunrise - and rolled down the road toward the bridge at medium speed.

I could smell the river. It smelled good. I wondered if it was getting closer to how it had once been since industrial production was long gone around here. The fertilizers and other chemicals that used to wash into the river should have dropped considerably by now. Then again, PCBs, from what I remembered, hung in there like radiation. It was still pleasant to ride alongside it. It reminded me of the Potomac River, and a life that was ancient history.

We were coasting down toward where the bridge met the river on the West Virginia side when I saw him. It looked like he was fishing, but I took nothing for granted. I signaled Ben to drop off and cover me while I headed toward him.

The man heard my tires crunching on the dirt and loose stone and slowly turned to face me. I could see his hand resting on the

147

butt of a revolver thrust into his pants. He was wearing suspenders, a ball cap, brown canvas pants, work boots, and a t-shirt with an open long sleeve shirt over it. He had a five-gallon bucket for a chair, and a beer cooler next to it.

"Who's that?" His voice was no longer young but not quite old. By his posture and voice I placed him in his early fifties.

I stopped the bike about thirty feet short of him. "Just a traveler. We want to cross the river on that bridge."

He laughed. "Ohio is a shit hole. You ought to stay on this side of the river." Suspiciously, he asked. "Where's the 'we' you mentioned?"

"Well, one of them is watching my back. The rest are not too far away. I'm here to find out if the government is going to be waiting for us if we go over that bridge."

He spat off to one side. "Ain't no fucking government around here. We ran them off." He paused. "Except for the ones that were related to someone's family around here. Not that they are worth a good goddamn anyway. I got me someone watching my back, too."

"You mean the woman over to my right about thirty yards away with the shotgun?"

There was a moment of silence, then he admitted grudgingly, "You got pretty good eyes, son."

"Yep. So how about she points that barrel in another direction and we talk?"

"Well, shit. Might as well. Fish ain't biting."

The sun was starting to come up. The birds had already been up for awhile. I noticed the woman hadn't really moved the barrel much. I understood.

He had enough light to size me up now and he didn't seem surprised at how I looked. Then again, I suppose the dress code for possible bandits and road warriors was no longer as strict anymore. Once we'd hit the real *Mad Max* stage, the Hollywood stuff got left behind.

148

I was wearing my hair cut as short as possible because of ticks. Night cut it for me with a knife. She called it the "razor cut special." Since I usually forgot to brush it, sometimes over a period of days, it had a tendency to stick up in patches. My current hat was a straw one I'd found in a farmhouse awhile back. It wasn't a cowboy hat. It was more of a Florida grandpa's Panama. I had punched holes in it so I could cinch it up under my chin with a leather thong, or just push it back. Otherwise I would have spent all day stopping my bike to go chase it.

I wore high-end body armor with plates that I never seemed to get a chance to take off. I wasn't even aware of the weight anymore. The vest the plates fit into was rotting in places from sweat, had a lot of snagged spots, and a couple bullet holes which marked it as having a previous owner. It also smelled a bit. I really needed to wash everything I owned. Twice.

My pants were surplus military in the woodland pattern. I think every pocket had stuff in it. My boots were getting a bit beat up and I needed to find new laces soon. My gun belt, between sweat, spills, me laying flat out in various types of dirt and grass, and getting scratched by thorns looked as if it was a hundred years old. I liked the look. The cleanest things on me were my weapons. Max had insisted on that since Day One. Clean weapons. Clean feet.

Not long after my trip to wherever the hell Freya had taken me, I had come back from taking a leak and found a sheath for my short sword waiting. Even nicer, the leather rig was cut so I could wear it on my back at an angle or around my waist. I put it on, reached back, and the grip was there, right in the palm of my hand. I think I was carrying close to twenty-five pounds just in iron and steel strapped to my body alone. Was I in shape? Outside of being hungry most of the time I felt better than I ever had in my entire life.

I gave him a short minute to finish digesting what he saw and gave him my best warm and winning smile. He stepped back. I guess I would have to pack away my warm smile. It wasn't working.

"We can trade for information and goods." That helped. He seemed a little less alarmed hearing that.

He must have come to the conclusion that I was reasonably safe. He pushed the cooler toward me with the tip of his worn sneaker and said, "Have a seat. I am. My legs ain't as right as they were awhile back."

"We okay sitting out here in the open?" I asked him.

"Yeah. This is Big Tom's area now. He and his family thinned out them freaks and such enough that we don't lose but a person every other week or so. Not like a few months ago." His eyes narrowed and he literally shuddered. I don't think he was even aware that he did.

I waved Ben in but I told Bucket Man what I was doing first. No need for misunderstandings. I told Ben to start surveying the bridge while I talked.

As he walked off the man yelled at him, "Don't be trusting that wood too much!" Looking at me he said, "That bridge is a piece of shit, and has been since I was a kid. Never stopped them from running freight across it though. Talk to me. What you want?"

I told him, "We want to push a couple vehicles and some people on bikes across it." I wanted to know what he thought of that. I also asked if he knew anything about the other side and anything about further into Ohio. "What have you heard lately in general?"

He looked at me and nodded his head. "Okay. I will swap news for news. We trade what we know. I'll guide you across the bridge. That won't be free. We also got some stuff for barter. I'll have Bettina put it out. You say you got more people?"

I nodded.

"Might as well have them come on down shortly and move into them woods over there soon." He indicated the woods behind us. "Best bet is I take you, and whoever else, up on the bridge myself and we work out how we are going to do it. Then we do it as soon as the sun comes up tomorrow. What do you think?"

"Sounds good." I called Ben back. I would send him with the news to the Horde while I stayed here with Bucket Man and the woman.

"So what's new in the world? By the way, you got a name?" I asked Bucket Man.

"Call me Phil."

I stuck my hand out. We shook. A handshake was more meaningful these days; probably a lot closer to what it meant when it first started. You had to trust the person to let them get that close to you. Then, for a brief second, you were connected and vulnerable. That meant something now.

"Call me Gardener." He froze for a second. I let go of his hand.

"I should have known. Not a lot of six gunners with cowboy rigs in the world." He looked at me, and only half skeptically asked, "You really jump off a rock, and while you were in the air doing somersaults kill five deputies who had gone bad?"

I pretended to think for a minute. "Naw, I think I only got three while I was in the air, and two when I came up."

"Damn. That's when you took down the other twelve with your guns a blazing?"

"Yeah, well, it was less than that and I had help." I was getting a little uncomfortable with this and decided to change the subject. "So what's up around here? You got any Feds, Burners, or Baptists running wild?"

He looked at me shrewdly. "You been away for awhile, haven't you?"

"Why?" I asked him, flatly and bluntly.

He held up his hand hastily "No offense! Just claiming to be one of those in front of the wrong people can get you killed these days." He shook his head. "Recruiting and converting is the story I hear. Both here, and over there." He jerked his head to indicate across the river. "Makes sense. I think, and this is just me thinking, mind you, but I'm thinking we're heading to a bunch of kingdoms around here until the government steps in and slaps them down."

"You really think that's going to happen?" I asked him, curious at what he would say.

"Oh yeah. I heard they ain't being too gentle about it either." I looked at him, waiting for more but he changed the subject.

"You get across the river and you're going to be in refried hillbilly land for awhile." He laughed. "Pretty much the same as you got here. That should start petering out in about fifty miles or so. I don't know much more beyond that, except stay away from Chicago. Word is they still got Eaters out there."

"That what you call them here? Cannibals?"

"Yep. Why? What you call them?"

"Dead."

He stared at me, laughed, and then said, "You know, I could get to like you." He pulled his bucket over so we were sitting next to the bridge abutment. Despite his earlier comment, he was not taking chances about us being easily seen. We talked about fishing for a bit. I told him about the monster carp in the Potomac, and we both talked about catfish. He was telling me how to run a trotline with a lot of hooks dangling from it when the advance crew from the Horde rolled in.

They were learning. I watched Phil as he watched Ninja and two of his squad come in. Ninja saw me and kept coming toward me while the other two split and stopped before he got up to me. They had their weapons out and were scanning in different directions before they came to a stop. Ninja was flying his Raven flag. I was going to have to look at how he managed to do it. It looked like some kind of flexible plastic stick was duct-taped to the front fork on his bike. He had promised me a Sword flag. I was going to have to bug him about it or end up making it myself.

The rest of the Horde rolled in a few minutes later. They looked good. Shelli was sitting up on top of the tires on top of the cab of the truck watching everything, her M-16 ready. Max and Freya were in front on their bikes.

The two Freylings were doing their usual, which was whatever the hell they felt like doing. In this case Val came speeding toward me, hit her brakes, and skidded sideways, stopping about three feet in front of me. She looked at me and grinned.

I laughed, and said, "Awesome." She checked out Phil for a couple seconds, and then went off toward the water, the other girl following behind her.

Behind the truck came the van. My squad was flanking them. I looked over at Phil again.

He was shaking his head. "Going to be interesting getting them across the bridge. Not that it matters; if this is all you got then you won't be making it out of Ohio anyway."

"What the hell is that supposed to mean?" This was from Ninja who had stopped in front of us without all the braking drama. Max was thirty feet away waving the trucks to the right where a dirt road led into some trees that would help screen them from view.

Instead of answering, Phil looked at me. "Who's this?"

"My brother." They didn't shake hands.

"Because you don't have the hardware to go up against what I hear is running around out there. You ever watch *Blackhawk Down*?"

Ninja shook his head no. I said, "Yeah, I did."

As I finished, Max, who had turned away as the vehicles rolled past him and was walking toward us, said, "Shit. I was there. What about Somalia?"

Phil wasn't looking as nervous as I expected he would. Of us all, Max was the most impressive, both physically and for the aura he generated.

153

I knew I gave off a "Don't fuck with me" aura. Actually, I had been told I radiated actual coldness. "It's as if the temperature drops around you sometimes" is what people said. The only one who had never told me that was Night. She was also the only one, other than Max, who I had never made back away from me.

Max had that aura also. What he also had, that I didn't, was something that made you realize that not only did you not want to go one on one with him, but that you wanted to follow him. He asked Phil, "What? You talking technicals? Or military hardware and vehicles run by ex-military types?"

"Look. I'm sorry I brought it up. It's all of the above. Plus, some weird combos of nut jobs with a mission. From what I can tell, once you cross the Ohio, you leave the Feds and God behind."

I told him, "We'll worry about that later. Show us the bridge." I told Max how Phil wanted to do some trading.

Max told Ninja to go find Shelli and the Chief while we went to look at the bridge. Ben was watching from a distance. I waved him over. He was going with us.

CHAPTER EIGHTEEN

We followed Phil up the same dirt road where the trucks had gone. It ended next to the railroad tracks. The rails were rusty. In between the ties a few scraggly weeds were starting to come up. Behind us a brunch of crap was piled on the tracks as a warning to any lost locomotive that it was too late to turn back now. I looked at the plaque set into the stone support of the bridge.

"Hey, Max, this bridge is eighty-four years old." He didn't say anything. Instead he looked at the decking on the bridge.

Phil laughed. "Yeah. It's down right historical. Now listen up. Stay on the rails in the center if you can, or on the far edges." He pointed out one of the many gaps I could see. "The wood is bad, and so is the iron that supports them in places."

We made it out about halfway across when Phil said, "Okay. This is as far as I go. I'll see you back there." The Ohio was running high and fast below us. Spring run off was my guess. Phil paused as we watched what looked like a body and four cars go by. One of the cars, an SUV by the looks of it, hit the center support column hard - hard enough that a chunk of brick fell off as the bridge shuddered under the impact. A few seconds after that Phil took his leave of us.

I looked at Ben. "What do you think?"

"You mean other than I'm scared shitless being up here?"

"Yeah, other than that," Max said.

155

"I'm not really qualified to rate a bridge's safety. If we are going to do it, I suggest that they drive as fast as they can and never stop," was his reply.

Max and I looked at each other. "No shit," we said in unison.

I asked, "You want to go to the end, Max?"

"No. You and I will do that tonight. I think you might as well plan on spending the night over there. Ben, you too. Just in case." He didn't have to spell it out. We understood. "Let's head back and see what the man has got to trade."

Bettina was back. She had spread a stained blue sheet on the ground and was kneeling behind it handing people the items they wanted to look at more closely. Every male that wasn't on watch was there.

It wasn't hard to figure out why. She had taken the time to change into a low-cut blouse, and she wasn't wearing anything under it. Every time she leaned over, anyone who was standing at the right angle got to see an eyeful. She had some decent-sized melons hanging out there. My view from the side told me that.

Freya and Night were standing off to one side watching, talking, and laughing.

I walked over and told Night, "I guess Ben and I are going to be spending the night on the other side of the bridge."

"Okay. You're not going over there to take a closer look at the merchandise?"

I knew the correct answer to that one. "No. I don't see any weapons or ammo."

Freya, ignoring me completely, told Night, "Well, I hope she at least does Ninja. It better be soon, too, before that boy explodes." They both thought that was funny. I left to try and get some sleep.

Max and I moved out that night around 10:00. At the last minute he decided to leave Ben behind. It was dark with just a sliver of a moon visible through fast-moving clouds. Max pantomimed in two gestures why Ben was staying home. He didn't have the eyesight we did, and Max didn't want to lose him to the river.

We got up to the bridge and Max stood there for a minute looking around. Then he looked back at me, grinned, and started running. I watched him go. He was leaping like a mountain goat. *Fine. Let's play,* I thought, and took off after him.

Even with our night vision it was tricky. I started gaining on him. He didn't look back, but somehow he knew and picked up his pace. I swear that asshole was running on air some of the time. He beat me to the other side by ten feet and I heard him laughing as he did. Not at me; I think it was from pure joy and the adrenalin rush.

He went to the left and I went to the right, as usual. We moved into the bushes on the other side, stopped, and listened. I heard the river, the wind, and nothing else. Max intentionally made a noise, most likely inaudible to most humans over thirty, and we started sweeping the area. It was clean. We met back in the middle. Max saluted me, and he was gone. I found a good position and settled in. It was going to be a long night.

My watch had died awhile back. I hoped Night noticed the old windup models I'd seen on the sheet with the items Bettina had for trade. She had an interesting pile of trade goods from what I saw. Pocketknives, some glasses including sunglasses, silverware, jewelry, and a bottle of aspirin that looked half full. I was going to talk to Night. We should start picking stuff up like that to trade along the way. I was daydreaming of that and had progressed to where we had a national chain of stores when the Horde started coming over.

Max had everything loaded in the truck and the van. It was a gamble if we lost them, but it made it easier for our people. They came across first, and I noticed a few were white in the face when they made it to my side. Next came the vehicles. Chief wasn't messing around. He got that truck over in a hurry, and the van hugged his tailgate the entire way. I heard constant splashes in the river that tracked them as they rolled.

157

Max, being Max, sat on the hood of the truck the entire way across. I suppose he told them he was spotting. I knew better. I didn't relax until I saw Night on my side of the world.

They pulled the bikes off, and we were moving within five minutes of crossing. I came out of overwatch about two thirds of the way through the remount and noticed Bettina was riding in the van. I had to laugh.

I looked over at Ninja who grinned. "I hope she came with a dowry, Bro."

"She did. Oh yeah, she did." He grinned again, and before I could up with something else to say he was on his bike and moving. *Damn nice melons,* I thought to myself. Then I mounted up and put my legs into it.

We rolled through a handful of red brick buildings and a scattered grouping of houses that were burned-out shells. Some of the buildings were fairly big, left from when America used to make things. One was in use. I spotted a few people watching us from windows and one of them, rifle in hand, from the roof. Nowadays, if you had anything worth stealing you always had someone watching.

Between the ruins of the factory buildings I saw a freshly cultivated field. God only knows what kind of chemicals had leeched into the soil from whatever industry had once been here. They probably knew that. It was a trade-off: be able to defend the crops from the walls of the old factory buildings and maybe get cancer, or plant them further out and probably lose them to someone else.

There were not quite as many cars on the side of the road here. We had a Finder now working between the point person and the main body when we rolled. For now at least, the person on point carried a spray paint can to mark possible Finder lodes. The Finder's job was just that - to find stuff we could use. They carried two five-gallon gas cans, hoses, bags, a small maul, and tin shears.

It worked out pretty well. If they found gas, they would punch a hole in the tank and drain it into the can, or cans, and leave it on the side of the road. The assigned Hopper for the day would see it, and the truck or van would slow down enough for the Hopper to get out, grab it, stow it, and hop back in. Hopper was a light-duty job. Everyone was rotated through it except squad leaders and Night. It helped balance out that we were exempt from standing watch. Not that we weren't pulling watch on occasion anyway.

I asked Max about it, and he said, "G, it's all about getting it in everyone's heads. Set the rules now, not when there are thousands of us."

Freya was doing the same thing. The getting in people's heads part. She was doing blessings on the food before we pulled it out to the squads. She was making a point of standing someplace where she was visible to everyone and calling the crows to her. Once she had a pair of hawks drop bunnies at her feet. That was good for a few gasps.

I started practicing with Sword one afternoon when we went down into camp early in the day. Freya watched, as did everyone else. The difference was she came and stood about ten feet from me, while everyone else pretended to be doing whatever they were supposed to be doing.

I had no clue what I was supposed to do which I was sure was obvious. She, along with the Freylings, watched for about ten minutes, and then she said something to Val, Val ran off, and when she returned, she was bearing a long object wrapped in white cloth. She actually went down on one knee when she presented it to Freya. I stopped attacking the oak tree that was standing in as my enemy to see what Val had brought.

Freya unwrapped a sword. Not just any sword. This sword looked like what I imagined Excalibur might look like. It also looked very sharp. She walked toward me with it held straight up in front of her.

She said, not just to me, her voice carried to everyone, "This is how to use a sword." Then she screamed, leaped, and proceeded to become a fast moving demon. She cut my oak tree down in three strokes. It fell as she stepped away from it and turned to me.

I told her, "Nice. I was going to get to that."

She didn't smile. Instead she drawled a slow "Riiight."

That is when I became a student in the Freya School of Swordsmanship. We practiced whenever we could and, much to my surprise, she was an excellent teacher. She was patient and didn't expect much at first. That was good because it turned out there was a lot more to it than I expected. Everything we did, we repeated over and over and over.

I even dreamed about the exercises and sword fighting when I slept. The dreams were intense and realistic. Too realistic sometimes. I woke Night up at least twice by screaming in rage because my assailants had lopped off my arm or head in the dream. Failure with a sword was the same as with a gun. It was fatal.

Southern Ohio had slim pickings. The area we were moving through looked as if its best days were long since past. It had been that way in Virginia; towns that looked as if their best days were several generations ago. We made a point of looking for maps, tourist brochures, and local newspapers when we could. As far as I could tell this area had made a living off tourists, and it had not been a good living for a long time. I mean when one of your attractions was an old maple tree... Well, you were scratching for reasons to make people look twice.

We didn't move very fast. We couldn't. We added another two diesel-powered trucks. They were in perfect shape, which was not surprising considering we took them off a dealer's lot. While running two more trucks meant we could spread the loads out more, and, in theory, have more range, it actually slowed us down.

This was also when we decided we needed to start recruiting. We had to put drivers in the cabs, and we had to feed those engines. More trucks also meant we needed more bodies to guard them.

The other problem in running this many trucks was that we were now advertising that we had goods that might be worth taking. Before, we could have been a well-organized family grouping that, while worthwhile to take, was offset by the fact that we were well-armed. It was a simple cost benefit analysis that any bandit group could do. It also helped that we could move away, or around them, since we could see them.

Most of the bandit groups we saw were static. They staked out watering holes. Avoid those, and you avoided the bandits. Getting bigger meant word got out, calculations were run, and the potential upside started making sense to them. That we might even be worth pursuing was becoming a possibility.

Logistics is everything. That idea struck me like a hammer blow. Sure, kicking ass was good. Having people that could kick ass was better. Yet for it all to work was a job in itself. If the main rule was "getting there first with the most," then it was all about logistics. Twenty well-fed, well-armed, and trained soldiers were worth three times that number of hungry, poorly-equipped and motivated troops. I vaguely remembered that was one of primary tenets of the old US Army back before all their thoughtless wars and budget cuts.

CHAPTER NINETEEN

We pulled into a town that we'd been told had a Saturday Market. On occasion we would meet other travelers and exchange gossip and trade. There was a rapidly evolving protocol on how this was done.

If a group was a lot smaller than us, it would usually shy away until there was a decent distance between us. We would stare at each other and wait to see what the situation was. Then usually, since we had more people, one of us would meet them halfway. Sometimes that was it. Sometimes whoever went out to the middle would hold up two fingers. If the other person agreed they would do the same. That meant two more people could approach with trade goods.

If the group was our size or a little bigger, both groups would pull off, get in a defensive circle, and we would end up talking. Having the Freylings buzzing around on their bikes helped. It gave us a kinder, softer image. That's how we had heard about the market.

The word was ammo was available there for the right price. A lot of stuff was available, supposedly, including clothing.

Night got a wistful look on her face, sighed, and said to Shelli, "You think they will have toilet paper?"

Shelli's reply was, "Oh sweet Jesus, I hope so." They were serious. I made a mental note to see if I could find some. It

162

sounded like it would go over better than a new magazine for her pistol or a pocketknife.

The town was doing what we had tried to do: provide a secure environment for people to do business and then take a percentage for doing it. Our plan was to come into town on a Friday night, make camp, and find out what the deal was. Then go to the market Saturday, trade a bit, and buy a lot more. We would hopefully come across some locals who felt like going west, and maybe make some money on the side. All the new people were told they would get paid before we went into town. That came as a bit of a surprise to them and went over very well.

There wasn't much to the town. At most, it had a couple thousand people before PowerDown. Now, Freya's guess was three hundred or so. We came in while there was still daylight, and we were met right away by a couple of well-armed men who directed us to the "Parking Lot." There, a middle-aged woman met us and explained the rules.

They were pretty simple. No weapons unholstered inside the marketplace. No rifles or shotguns of any sort. If you had a dispute, you waited and settled it outside of town the next day. If you were caught thieving or passing off bad goods on purpose, you died.

I liked it. I could have written them.

It was an interesting night spent there in the Parking Lot. Since we were paying for security the other traders let a little of their reserve slip. Plus, I think most of the people wanted to relax and have a good time. They just needed the opportunity. There was a band of sorts playing, alcohol was flowing, and by the time it got dark people were trying their Karaoke skills.

I noticed Max wasn't drinking. Instead he was going from group to group, talking to whoever would listen. Shelli, on the other hand, was getting hammered. I found Night, we danced a bit, drank a little, and then we slipped off. Afterward she wanted to sleep, so I left her, walked out of the lot, and sat on somebody's car hood to look at the stars.

I was sitting there thinking of other times and places where I had done the same thing. Most of those times involved getting high and drunk. That, and hoping to get lucky, which was something that had happened far too rarely but when it did it was memorable. Then my walk down memory lane, one that was admittedly becoming somewhat maudlin, hit a pothole.

An incoming feed and the ice of Freya's voice overrode it. "I am sending this to Max. I cannot judge speeds accurately yet, but I don't think we have a lot of time."

"Well, Freya, if I had a clue where this was, I might be able to make a guess." She shifted views and my stomach lurched. I muttered, "Nice smooth transition there, Freya."

She told me, "This is the town they just went through." Her bird stared at a road sign for only three seconds before it decided its right wing armpit was itchy. I saw enough to know the name of the town, and to get familiar with this particular crow's armpit. He or she had mites.

"Okay. I need to find a map and Max." I jumped off the car, thinking this was going to be interesting. We had company coming. Heavily-armed company. Max would be able to do a better analysis of the hardware than me. I saw fifteen vehicles and one of them looked like a Humvee with a .50 mounted. They also had motorcycle outriders and a couple of dump trucks. We should have thought of that for ourselves. It wasn't as if we had never used them.

I walked past security into the Parking Lot. The guy working security had decent equipment. He called out to me, half mocking, "See anything interesting, cowboy?"

"Just death riding in a dump truck."

He laughed, "Scared you back inside, did it?"

I stopped dead, and looked at him square on. "No. Dancing with death is why I was made."

Damn. I felt good. I suppose a few years ago someone might have said I had issues. Actually, when I thought about it, people had. Well, I never felt as comfortable with the world I lived in as I did now. You might say I had found my calling.

I walked past the fire pit where people were still carrying on. It occurred to me that there had to be a strong Burner influence among these traders. They may have kept it concealed, but the fire, alcohol, and, by the smell in the air, their favorite substance, was kicking that influence loose. I would have liked to stay. A thin blond was dancing with a coffee-colored woman and they both were well dressed in nothing.

Everyone was up when I got to our vehicles. I said "Hey, sleepyhead" to Night, and went over to where Max was talking to a stocky black male who had two guys standing slightly behind him. All three were geared up.

I heard the black guy say as I walked up, "All right. I don't know why, but I believe you. He had his people here two weeks ago looking for a cut of our market profits. I should have sent them back without their hands."

"What do you know about him and his people?" Max asked.

"He runs a mix. Mostly Army, but also a few bad-ass locals. He was born around here, so the locals are probably related. He was Army, but I hear he got a Bad Conduct Discharge. You really had to fuck up to go out that way." They were all nodding their heads.

Max saw me walk up and told him, "This is Gardener - my brother and my go-to guy. Gardener, this is Jose."

Night joined us, and Max introduced her as his XO - his Executive Officer. I saw the looks. I heard the *WTF?* pass through their heads. I saw one guy smile. That bothered me, so I asked him, "Hey. You have a problem with the lady?"

He looked at me, cocked his head, hesitated, and then said, "No. Actually she reminds me of my ex. She was fucking evil." He grinned at Night who just stared back at him.

Max cut in brusquely, "We don't have time to fuck around. What are you going to do, Jose?"

"Fight. What else?" He shrugged. "What do you want to join us, Max?"

"We want ammo. A lot of ammo. We keep whatever is left over, and we get half of everything they leave behind when it's done. That includes the Humvee with the .50 caliber."

Jose thought for a few seconds, and then said, "You drive a hard bargain. Fine. I agree. Now let's see if any of these maricons will fight. See me in fifteen minutes with your people at the post office. It's the next block over." He strode off toward the fire pit.

"Where's Ninja?" I asked.

"Getting the squads geared up," Night told me. "Have fun with yours." She laughed. I did not like the sound of it.

I went to find my people. Ninja had everyone getting their gear together. It was obvious why Shane and Josh were having problems. They were both drunk.

Shane was happy to see me. "Hey, Gardener! You see that blond? Damn, I would poke her in a heartbeat."

Josh swayed a bit and laughed. "Sheeeit. She wanted me. Didn't you see the way she looked at me? Those hungry eyes." He made his hands into claws and snarled. They both thought that was pretty damn funny.

I took their rifles, stripped the magazines, and then made sure they had nothing chambered.

"Why you unloading our guns, Gardener, sir?" Shane asked.

"Because you are both drunk, and if you don't sober up fast, you're going to be dead before sunrise." They both stared at me and blinked like owls.

"Dead?" Shane asked.

"Dead," I replied. "Guys, we got maybe seventy five people headed this way who plan on killing us and taking what we have." I didn't know if this was true but I figured it would help

166

motivate them. "When they get done with that, my guess is they will be getting out the BBQ sauce."

That got their attention. I watched their eyes get round. Shane, under his breath, said a long, drawn out "shiiitt." I wasn't angry with them. They had thought they were safe, and I knew they'd needed to unwind.

I told them, "Just get it together. C'mon, started putting your gear on. We are moving in ten." I started helping them.

Ben showed up. His eyes were red, and I smelled the smoke on him. Well, to each his own. He was able to get himself dressed. He just lost focus a few times.

"Quit staring at the buckle, Ben, and move."

Ninja called over to me, "Time, G!" We joined him and headed over to the post office. Behind us was controlled bedlam. I heard Jose yelling at someone and calling him a pussy. All the traders were bailing. My guess is they figured they could get enough distance between them and the threat if they moved fast, especially if we were going to delay them. I say "delay" because they would not be leaving if they thought we were going to come out on the winning side.

Jose started running through his plan. "We hide in the houses along Main Street. They will come racing in. We hit them with Molotovs and seal the end of the street with a truck. That will create a kill zone, and that's exactly what we will do." He looked around to approving nods and a couple of "OORAHS!" from his men. I noticed Max check those two out. If they lived through what was coming, then I bet that they would be coming with us.

Max shook his head. "No go." Night was shaking her head, too.

"Why? What's the problem?" Jose was genuinely puzzled.

"The problem is we will all die," Max told him. "And I don't die. I kill."

"Yeah. So what you got that's better?" I, along with everyone else, heard the sneer implied in Jose's response.

Max's face didn't change. "Why are they coming? They want the market goods. They will wait somewhere until a little before dawn. They will send in some scouts to confirm that everyone is here and asleep. This party...it's done every time?"

Jose nodded his head.

"So then they will race in, but not on Main Street. They will want to come as fast as possible to the market off a side road They probably have already scouted that. They will come in loud, horns honking, guns firing to panic everyone. They will park that .50 right over there." He pointed to a side street. "And they will hose everyone down. Then they will snatch and go."

"Yeah. Nice, but the traders are all gone." Jose swept his hand in the direction of the market.

"Then what will they do, Jose? When the scouts report there is nothing here. Will they turn around? Or will they come for you?"

We all saw the light go on above his head. He tried to dim it with bravado but it didn't work.

"No, Jose. We won't kick their asses. We will kill a lot of them, but in the end we will be dead."

I saw Jose scan his people's eyes. His mistake, if it was one, was doing this in front of everyone. They heard it, thought about it, and it was obvious they followed Max's logic to the same conclusion.

Jose laughed. "Let me guess. You got a better plan?"

Max, still not smiling, answered him. "Yep."

Max's plan was based on deception. "I want trucks in the Parking Lot. I want it to look like there are people there, and everything is the way it is supposed to be. I want a couple people; Shelli, it's going to be you and the kids. I want you to get up, mess with setting up a table. Then just before dawn I want the kids to lead you off to the bathroom. I want a volunteer other than Gardener to wander around doing background shit until the last possible second."

How did he know? I wondered.

168

"We are going to set up in the buildings around the lot. Molotovs ready. I want that parking lot to melt down into the oil it was made from and then burn some more. I want a strike team to come up behind them, and take the .50 and everything around it. Jose, you have the buildings. I know you know the drill."

Jose nodded. Most of his men also knew it. Urban warfare was something they knew all too well. "Where are you going to be?" he asked.

I thought, *Give up, dude. You lost. They are his now.*

"With Gardener, Ninja, and Freya. Plus, I will take two of your people, and give you the rest of mine." He pointed out the two who had given themselves away earlier as Marines. "Those two right there. We are the strike team. Night, pick some people and set the stage. Jose, I need you to handle disbursing the ammo and setting up the houses. The rest of you, on me. Let's go, people!"

I stepped on his exit line. "Hey, Max. Shane volunteered for the Parking Lot job."

He didn't blink an eye. "Great! Shane, I knew you would. You're a good man." Shane was having a problem processing what just happened. He knew I had just fucked him, but he wasn't really sure how, and the public praise was sugar on the shit sandwich he'd just been handed.

Jose barked, "All right! You heard the man. Let's do this."

As I walked over to say goodbye to Night I thought, *So Max just got himself a Top Sergeant if he lives through this.* I hugged Night. We didn't make a big deal about it. I just liked holding her before we split up. I wasn't a romantic; I was selfish. I wanted that last grope in case she died. At least that's what I told myself.

Chief stopped me as I walked away and handed me his magazines. Then he punched me on the shoulder and said, "Don't lose them," and walked away. The rest of the team, except for Freya, was collecting also. Eventually Max wanted everyone with automatic weapons to carry twenty magazines. We had never come close to that yet.

Freya just stood there and watched. I noticed Jose's men had a problem keeping their eyes off of her. She had grown some more and was now probably eighteen physically. I watched their eyes. They weren't looking at her thinking, "I am going to do that. Yes indeed." It was more like they were puzzled and attracted. It wasn't lust I was seeing. I had no clue what it was. I was going to have to ask Night. She would know. She always knew this stuff. I put it out of my mind. It was time for me to do what I did and for others to die as a result.

We moved to the edge of town. It didn't take long since it was only two blocks away. I watched Max talk to the two new guys. They went from somber to grinning and back to somber in a few minutes. Two of Jose's guys came running toward us. One was carrying two cans of ammo and a daypack on his back. He was making tracks for it being so heavy. The other guy was carrying an ice cooler. Our Molotovs I was sure. They set them down. I heard the one with the cans point at the daypack and say, "Full magazines," and then say they'd be right back with more of the same.

Max passed out the magazines and sent one of the new guys with Ninja; he took the other, and pointed to where he wanted me to be. I had the first house the vehicles would pass. Max placed himself where he thought the .50 would be. Ninja and his guy filled the gap between us.

We were standing behind the corner of a building. The ammo had disappeared. One can to Ninja, the other to Max. He also had the Molotovs. We were watching Jose's men run toward us with the second and final load.

"G, I am keeping all the ammo and Molotovs for Ninja and I. You understand why?"

"For the same reason you are putting me behind them when they come is my guess."

170

Max nodded. "Yeah. Wait until they get past you and the shit hits the fan. Flush whatever you don't kill toward us."

I grinned at him. "Okay. I'll let a few live. Can't let you get too bored."

He laughed. "If it all goes right I am going to be running that . 50 and I want you at my back." He reached out and put his hand on my shoulder "G, you are not going to have any fancy titles for awhile probably, but I want you to know; I wouldn't have anyone else next to me when it gets crazy."

"I know." I wanted add something sarcastic but I couldn't think of anything. "See you on the other side of whatever, Max." Then I walked away. It was time to find some place to wait.

CHAPTER TWENTY

I was never good at waiting. It helped that I got to watch Freya TV in my head.

They were still coming. They were pushing a little harder now to make up for lost time. One vehicle had a blow out, and instead of leaving them behind, they all waited. That told me a couple things. They didn't think it was safe to leave a vehicle alone. It also told me whoever was in charge, despite what Jose said, looked out for his people. I hoped I'd get to cut off his head.

Freya turned on the audio. Just like the video, it drained her. Perhaps more so. We just checked in, and then it was gone.

She dropped the others and whispered to me, "For Freya. Remember, for Freya." It didn't occur to me until later to wonder if she had pushed the same message to all of us. Not that I really cared.

About twenty minutes later, way off in the distance, I heard two motorcycles and then lost them. The scouts were on their way and it was about damn time. I had smeared my face and hands with charcoal, as had everyone else. There was always plenty of charred wood around to use for it. I was going to look like I had blackheads for the next couple days. The stuff was a bitch to get out of my pores.

I was set up on the second floor. Max told me back when we were first starting out that only good troops consistently checked the second floor. Most would check the first floor, and if it looked right, they would move on. I was sitting back from the window. I could still see, not as well perhaps, but I was harder to see from the ground.

They were good. They were also where they were supposed to be, which was even better. I caught a very quick glimpse of one of them moving quickly and quietly on the other side of the street. I waited. Five minutes later they were headed back. *Better hurry, people,* I thought. *Sun will be up soon.*

Ten minutes later I heard them coming. Some of those trucks really needed new mufflers. I reached into my top pocket and put in my earplugs. It was going to get real noisy soon. The first motorcycles went by out front. I could hear one on the next street over, too. Then came the vehicles.

Max was right. They came in noisy, fast, and shooting rounds off into the air. I even heard a few lame-ass rebel yells. I wanted their heads. My heartbeat was picking up. I said to myself, *I want their heads!* I liked the sound of it. Shivers started running up and down my back. I stood up, grinned, and breathed deep.

I didn't move. I just stood there in the middle of the room and listened to the show start outside my window. They had hit the parking lot just like Max said they would. They were getting return fire from Jose. I heard the .50 starting to chug. I heard Ninja and Max's weapons returning fire.

Not yet. I was starting to tremble. *Not yet,* I told myself again. *Patience.* It was such a weak and pathetic word, that I decided, *Fuck patience.* My teeth were starting to grind. I threw back my head, stretched out my arms and screamed, "Hit me, Freya!" Bam! Video on. I saw the street. A technical was parked right outside my window. *My, my,* I thought. *Command vehicle.*

I gathered the air around me deep into my lungs, screamed, "Freya!" and went out the window in a headfirst dive.

Goddamn! Sometimes it felt good to scream and this was one of those times. As I went out, I did a somersault, pulled Sword out with my right hand, and the Ruger with my left. I landed right in the middle of the hood of an F-250 with a very satisfying crunch. I screamed again.

There was a driver in the cab. A passenger sat next to him. I shot the passenger in the face. Part of me registered the shattering of the front windshield and loved it. I loved breaking stuff. I leaped as high as I could and came down on top of the cab. I landed in a crouch, letting the momentum drive me down. At the same time I punched the sword through the roof of the cab and into the driver's head.

I looked at the General and his aide. They had watched too many movies. Black leather, peroxide, and metal inserts in the face. So very *Mad Max*. I know the real Max and he dresses as a professional. Nice armor though.

I shot the aide in the face. I swung Sword backwards in arc overhand, back and then down. One-handed wood chopping. It ended somewhere around the General's chin, which was now cleft. Fucking helmets. My sword was stuck. I straightened up, and as I did, I kicked him in what remained of his face and jerked the sword up. It came loose.

I screamed, "Asshole!" Then I jumped to the ground, rolled and came up. Two men were standing in front of me. One had just shot at where I had been a second before. The other shot a quick but high three round burst. I punched the sword through the chest of the one on the right. It went through his armor as if it was made of Chinese cotton. At the same time I shot the other in the face. I screamed, "Freya!" Goddamn, I felt good.

Freya tried to keep feeding me video. I blocked it. I didn't want it. I was too busy. It also required thinking, and I was not in the mood to think. Hell, I didn't want to think.

Ahead of me were three vehicles. Two were on fire. Bodies littered the street around them. The .50 gunner was slumped sideways at his mount. Beyond them I could see black oily smoke rising in the air. The smell of burning petroleum products filled the air.

I watched as one of the dump trucks came out of the smoke. The driver had it in reverse and was determined to come through the same street I was on. He glanced off the Humvee hard and hit one of the vehicles behind it and stalled out. That's when a Molotov arced through the air and landed in the bed. *Must be Ninja,* I thought when I saw it. He always threw with an arc like that. Before it even hit, the soldiers in the back were leaping out like popcorn. The bed was the pan, and they were not going to wait for the fire.

At the same time I saw Max run out of the office building he' been in and head for the .50 caliber. The new guy followed him, limping, while I started running toward the popcorn hitting the street. Ninja and his new guy were engaging the ones that bailed on his side of the street, but they could not see the other side of the truck. Max made it to the .50 and it was chugging rounds off to the far right. He wasn't even looking back, and I knew why. He thought I had it. I know I wouldn't have watched mine if he told me he had my back.

The thought that they might get to him enraged me. I sprinted forward, and then went to an all-out run. The four who landed had picked themselves up. One had sprained an ankle or worse, and was grimacing in pain while leaning on a buddy who was looking down at it. Probably to see if any bones were sticking out. The other one was looking at Max. He was probably trying to figure out whose side he was on. The fourth was looking toward the smoke, wondering which way to go. I made all of their minds up for them.

The one with the bad ankle saw me coming and looking at me drew the other's attention. I had my sword held straight out in front of me. The buddy saw me, and stepped in front of his hurt friend. I skewered them both. I was moving too fast to stop, let alone hold onto the sword. I heard him grunt. I saw his eyes widen, and then we were going down. I saw over his shoulder

175

as his buddy winced when the blade ran through her armor. When we hit I saw wisps of blond hair that had not stayed tucked up under her helmet. Then I was rolling off of them.

I kept rolling and took the legs out from under the one who had been looking up at Max. He went down hard as I got up. I didn't even think about drawing a weapon. Instead I kicked him in the face and watched his head snap back. Even with all the noise and my earplugs I could hear cartilage crunch. I snarled and kicked him again. I was drawing my foot back to kick him again when I remembered the fourth guy. I dropped my foot and looked around for him. He was standing there, staring at me, completely horrified. I grinned at him and then his face dissolved when I shot him.

Ninja went past me, slapping me on the shoulder as he did. His Marine was following him. We locked eyes for a second. His registered nothing. No surprise, fear, or horror. It was all part of the job. It did one thing - his look and Ninja's contact; it took me down a notch. Enough to start thinking again. I went back for my sword. The woman wasn't dead yet but the sound she made when I pulled it out told me she wasn't going to be around much longer. I didn't really care or register anything. Like the Marine, I was now on the job.

I was also hungry. I put that thought aside, sheathed my sword after wiping it off as best as I could, and followed Ninja. His Marine had grabbed the man who had fallen by Max and dragged him into the building. I tossed him my wound kit and looked over at Max. The Humvee was moving, just skirting the edge of dying flames and bubbling tarmac. I thought "Video Freya" and saw that we had won. "Kill video." It went dead.

"Thank you, Gardener. That was lovely." This came from Freya. She sounded as if she just had a really good orgasm. I was surprised that I found that somewhat disconcerting.

Freya opened audio long enough for Max to tell us, "Cease fire. Round them up. We move immediately. Gardener, bring

176

the General's head to the Humvee." I looked at Ninja, who looked back and shrugged.

Okay. Not a problem, but I might have to duct tape him around the nose to hold both sides together. I jogged off. It was a moment's work. I sat Mr. Head gently on the ground while I cleaned my blade. It took longer to clean the blade than it did to take off his head. Then I picked it up using both hands and jogged back to Max.

As I jogged, I looked down at Mr. Head and said soothingly, "I know, I know, you have a splitting headache." I thought it was funny. I was still laughing when I passed Ninja and the Marine who looked at me strangely. Max was back at the .50 and watched with interest as I came up to him.

"Jesus, G." He laughed. "Hold him up so they can see it in that building across the way. " I did, and I made sure to hold him away from me. He was still dripping.

Max's voice boomed, "Give up and join us! Live as warriors! Or die here and now." Then he sent a burst that ripped across the top of the windows on the second floor. I saw a couple of people look out at us, and then disappear back inside. A few minutes later they filed out. There were seven of them.

Max told them, "Stack your weapons and stand over there." He indicated with the barrel of the .50 where he wanted them. I noticed he kept it pointed at them. Ninja came out of building and stood off to one side of the new recruits while he checked them out warily.

"Ninja," Max told him, "go get the rest of the new recruits. Tell Jose I want him and Chief to organize all the vehicles. Tell Shelli to give priority to the wounded."

He looked out at the seven. "Any of you a medic?"

One of them stepped up and said, "I am, but I don't have a lot of supplies."

"Fine. Help the man in the building behind you." He turned back to Ninja. "I want all wounded who can be moved brought up here. Have you got any wounded inside?" he asked the remaining six men.

"Yeah," one of them replied.

Max told him, "Get them out here." He looked down at me. "G, you can get rid of the head now." I flipped it away. It hit the asphalt like a ripe cantaloupe and splattered open. Some of the six looked a little taken aback by it. People are never as hard core as they like to think they are.

We started getting it together. We did not leave immediately. Stripping the bodies, getting the vehicles in order, and treating the wounded took until noon. We had gotten off amazingly light. One dead, two wounded, and they were minor wounds at that.

Shane did not make it out of the parking lot alive. There was no body to recover. The bad guys who were caught in the parking lot inferno were left there. It was still too hot to look for toasties, and no one really cared anyway. The other side was not so lucky. The badly burned and severely wounded were put down quietly.

Night, Shelli, and the Chief were running around like maniacs. I went to check on my squad. None of them seemed too shaken up by the loss of Shane. They did seem a little more distant and polite to me, which was different. I shrugged it off. We all sat down and cleaned weapons. They warmed up a bit as they described what they did during the "Big Toast" as we were all calling it.

They didn't ask what I had done, and I didn't tell them. It was already fading in my mind anyway. Usually I only remembered brief seconds of action. They would remain in my head as frozen frames of events. If I stitched them all together I doubt if I could get even a ten second video out of it. I told them to go find Night or Shelli if they were hungry, and I went to find Max.

He was talking to Freya and it was obvious that it was important. Everyone was giving them their space by walking wide around them. "Hey, Max. Hey, Freya."

Max grinned. "Hey, G." Freya looked at me and smiled. Her color was high I noticed. *It takes all types*, I thought.

"You were magnificent today, Gardener," she told me. She looked a little older. *At this rate, I thought, she'll be ancient by the time we make Indiana.*

"Why thank you," I told her. I looked at Max who was trying really hard to suppress a smile. "So what's next?"

"We get the survivors together. I want to ask them a few questions. We do an oath ceremony. We find out where their base is, and then we go take it."

I nodded. "Okay. We find anything good to eat?"

"Go find Night. I think she found something for you." He grinned, and continued, "I think it has chocolate as one of the ingredients." I was happy. This was turning out to be really good day. As I walked away Max called out to me, "Freya's right. You were good today."

I waved without turning around. I had chocolate to find.

CHAPTER TWENTY-ONE

The oath ceremony was a new one on me. One of Ninja's squad came looking for me. I was standing with Night talking about nothing when he found me. I couldn't remember his name if I ever knew it but Night did. He stood there, maybe ten paces from us, and didn't say a word. I was going to let him keep standing there but Night had pity on him.

"Yes, Keith?"

"Sorry to disturb you, Ma'am, but you two are requested to join Max and The Freya by the post office for the ceremony."

"Thank you, Keith."

Then much to my amazement he did a quick nod that was suspiciously close to a bow. I almost stifled my laugh. "What the hell was all that about?"

Night giggled. "You mean the bow?"

"Yeah."

Primly she replied, "It's a sign of respect."

"Right," I said skeptically. "I don't see them doing that to anyone else."

"Of course."

I was getting a pretty good grip on this relationship stuff so instead of saying that was ridiculous I replied, "Of course."

She smiled, took my arm, and said, "Come on. Let's go see the Witch Queen get crowned."

We found Jose, who had lived, and Ninja getting everyone who could stand in ranks. There was not that much of a difference between the two groups except we still had our rifles and they didn't. Together we would still not qualify for Horde status, but we had more than doubled in size. Even better, they were all warriors.

Max stood alone at a distance from it all. I had seen enough movies to know the stage was being set for the "General talks to the troops" scene. I wasn't sure where we were supposed to stand. Night didn't hesitate. I felt her hand tighten a bit on my arm and I went with it. She guided me to the front center of the drawn up ranks, swept them with her eyes, and turned to face Max. I mimicked her and as her arm fell away I did my best imitation of a soldier standing at attention.

Out of the corner of her mouth Night whispered to me, "Now march up to Max, salute, and then stand on his right."

I sauntered over; I didn't even attempt marching, and stood on Max's right and waited for the show to begin. It didn't take long. Max looked over at me, nodded, and then stepped out a few paces to address the ranks. I didn't even think about it. I did the same but moved away from him so we would have some room to work if we needed it. A couple of them stared at me as I did. I just looked at them and grinned. They looked away.

Max had his hands on his hips and was surveying them. He didn't say anything. He just looked them over, and as long as it seemed to take, I think he eyeballed every single one of them.

He began. "Welcome to the Freya Legion." I wondered what happened to "Division." I guess Legion was better sounding at this point.

"Who is your leader?" They looked around.

I didn't see them focusing on one particular person but from the middle I heard, "I am!"

Interesting, I thought. The one who claimed leadership was a black male. Maybe in his early thirties. My guess would be six foot and one hundred ninety pounds. It looked as if he was in

181

good shape. From the way the others were looking at the ground I also think he was a self-appointed leader. He strode out of the group and stood about six feet from Max.

Max looked at him, nodded, and then shot him in the head. He re-holstered his Colt .45 and flatly told everyone, "No. There is only one leader here and that is me. Anyone here have a problem with that?" he asked. The stillness was only broken by my laughter.

After waiting for a handful of seconds, he continued. "You will be fed, paid, and armed. In exchange I will ask of you a few simple things, and offer you the chance to do great things. We are warriors of Freya, and you will respect the goddess of war as personified by her priestess."

This was her cue. Freya walked out and stood besides Max. "You will show your respect by calling her name out in battle. Those that prove themselves will be rewarded in time with her gifts, and the chance to stand among the Chosen. Do any of you have a problem with that?"

A few looked at each other. I saw one shrug, and heard a lot of quick nos.

"These are our rules. No officer will eat or sleep before his people are taken care of. Pay will be disbursed according to the share rule. We will not leave anyone behind. We do not steal from one another. We do not rape. We are professionals." He came down hard on the word *professionals*. He paused. I watched as heads nodded during his recital. The first and last rule had gone over well.

"The penalty for failure is death." That did not go over as well. Too bad. No one decided to object. No surprise there. Wannabe Leader was still stretched out on the asphalt, still bleeding and still very dead. I noticed that it looked like there were ceramic plates in his armor. I was going to have to remember to ask Max if I could trade him something for those. Mine were taking a beating lately. My chest was starting to talk to me about what had to have been a handgun round. I knew from experience that it would feel even worse tomorrow.

"Before I ask you to give me your oath, I am going to ask you a question. You have my word that if you find what I have asked, or what I am going to ask, too difficult, you will be able to go free. Free meaning armed, with one magazine, and the rifle you came in with." He paused. "When we leave here we will head off to take your base. I expect you to give me any details I want to make this happen with a minimum loss of life. We will restock, and proceed to Montana where we intend to settle. Any questions or objections?" He waited.

Much to my surprise I saw a hand rise. It was a short, wiry Latino. "Maybe you let us talk to our friends at the base. We tell them what you offer, and we can do this maybe without killing any more." He grinned. "At least today."

"Fine," Max told him. "It has possibilities. Any takers on my offer?" There were none, but they were going to need watching until after the taking of the base. I wondered why we were even bringing them. We should leave them here without weapons, and pick up the survivors on the way back.

"We will begin then." Max looked at Freya and stepped back. She had to have been coached by Max or Night for this. I expected swooping birds, a bolt of lightening, and drums. Instead it was a ceremony that might have been held in a post office lobby by a bureaucrat who was in a hurry to eat lunch.

She told them, "Raise your right hand and repeat after me. I solemnly swear to render total obedience to the Legion and accept the rules as were explained to me. So help me Freya."

They did. I noticed a few stumbled on the "So help me Freya" part. She stepped back and Max again took center stage. "All right. I want you," he pointed to the Latino soldier who had spoken up earlier, "to come talk to me." He then looked over at Ninja, who in turn nodded to Jose.

Jose bellowed, "Dismissed! But don't go any fucking where!" Next stop was the base. I hoped they had more chocolate.

Freya surprised us all. When we rolled out to hit the base she had come roaring out on a Harley. She took lead for the vehicles and she was a hell of a sight to see. She wasn't wearing a helmet and her golden hair streamed behind her in the wind. With her sword out of its wrapping and strapped to her back she was a head turner. I half expected to see the Freylings following her on their own motorcycles. Since they were shorties, I figured maybe Hondas or Vespas. Nope, they were riding in the van. No motorcycles for them, at least not yet.

Everyone rode inside a vehicle with the bikes stacked on top. Max wanted to make time. His idea was to make us look like we were the bad guys returning from another successful raid. He put Jose up front, and a couple other familiar faces in the first two vehicles, and we were waved right in. Ninja and his squad were in the third vehicle. They jumped out and secured the gate without killing anyone. The Humvee with the .50 was right behind them and it was all over.

Capturing the base was easy. They might have been able to put a hurt on us, but they didn't bother because once we were inside the gates, it was all over. Most, probably ninety percent, of their fighters had rolled out on the raid. Less than twelve percent had come home. It broke a lot of hearts. I understood now why they waited when the vehicle broke down. Four people in a vehicle meant eight back at base counting on them. This was based on my rough estimate of at least two dependents for every soldier.

The toughest part was the weeping and wailing by all the dependents once they saw how many of their people had been lost. They were not pissed at us. They knew how it worked. Your average American at this point was familiar with how quickly life could change. They especially knew how thin the

184

line was between living and dying. Many in the camp were still processing a lot of recent bad memories. Crying jags during the day, and people screaming from what they were seeing in their nightmares, were as common now as breaking wind and cursing the government had been once.

Taking the camp was both a good and bad thing. It was a rich prize by our standards. The drawback was keeping it up and running. Keeping everyone fed was a full-time job. I thought our plan was to travel continuously until we reached our destination as a Warrior Horde. We were not a Warrior Horde. Not when half the people were either children or support staff.

That's why they had used static bases. Even then it was only a matter of time before you stripped the countryside and had to move on. We had vehicles now, but they needed fuel and maintenance, and skilled people to do it. Everything, to me at least, had just tripled in complexity without any real gain in our ability to fight.

We stayed at our new base. I expected us to keep moving, but that was unrealistic on my part. We couldn't. We had personnel issues amongst other things, such as figuring out who was going to be assigned where and whose ego needed to be accounted for as part of moving people around.

We had gone from a semi-tight group of fifteen to one hundred thirty-two people in a matter of a week. It would have been higher, but a small group from the base slipped away the first night. Max was asked if a team should be sent out to hunt them down and bring them back. If not the people, then at least what they had taken with them.

He replied, "I have no claim on them. They swore no oath to me. We don't want people who do not want to be a part of what we are going to build together. Let them go. Anyone else who wishes to leave can go." After he said this he walked away. I paced him and he told me, "Get word to Night. I don't want anyone leaving with more than a couple of magazines, clothes, a weapon, and some food."

I talked to Ninja, and we made sure one of our people was on the gate all the time. I also had one of ours sitting behind the .50, just in case. I made sure they understood that I didn't want the barrel of the .50 pointed inward. That way we could maintain the fiction of "guard duty."

The personnel problem was just a reflection on a lot smaller scale of what was helping pull the country apart. We all spoke English, but there were groups that did not list English as their first language. This was not counting Night and Ninja who knew but rarely spoke Chinese. We had the "Americans" who were Anglo and black. Despite the color difference this group had more in common than they had differences. The next largest group was a mixed bag of Spanish speakers, representing three different countries south of the border. They were also a little hesitant about going to Montana. They wanted to head south.

The other group was the minority and represented the United Nations. We had an Indian family, a Korean family, and a Vietnamese family. Shelli told me that the only food item everyone could agree on as a staple was rice. I thought that was funny, as we didn't have more than two days' worth. No one asked me but I like potatoes.

The other problem was we had no common vision of the meaning of success. People disagreed on what we were working toward as a group. If the United States fully recovered, or at least began recovering substantially, who wanted to be a member of a heavily-armed gang then?

I listened in on one conversation. People always underestimated how good our hearing was. There were still some who thought the worst part was over. They believed that America would return to its former high standard of living and everything would go back to the way it was. The person saying this mentioned that it might be tough for a while, but there was no way things were going to get worse. The clincher, at least for them, was seeing the power back on in places.

Then we had the religion issue. Surprisingly the Latino contingent did not have a problem with Freya. If we had the paint and airbrushes Freya would have had a spot across from Our Lady of Guadalupe on the trucks. As long as she didn't claim to be "The One" they had room for her. The Asian and Indian contingents were the same except they cared even less. It was just another weird white people thing they had to pay lip service to.

It was among some of the white and blacks that the Freya concept hit the most resistance. We had some hard-core Jesus believers there. I didn't have a problem with them as long as they left me alone. Without their kind, I would have gone hungry more than a few times in the past but I didn't like them. Too many times in my childhood and later, someone had told me about the love of Jesus right after they had hurt me badly.

CHAPTER TWENTY-TWO

I wandered around the base. I didn't have much else to do. I could have sat in on the non-stop meetings that were going on. I didn't bother. Partly because I saw them as a waste time and because all the talking irritated the hell out of me, but mostly it was because meetings bored me. I wanted to scream, "It's not that fucking complicated, people!" I was smart enough to know that the people I cared about would not appreciate my doing that so I stayed away.

The base was interesting for about an hour. They had grown by providing protection for families during PowerDown. In exchange they got motivated troopers. Was Metal Face, their commander, a bad guy? I don't know. He had held them together during a bad time in American history. He had kept everyone fed without resorting to gnawing on each other. He did it by robbing and killing other people, which was frowned on, especially by the people he robbed and killed. But was this right or wrong? I didn't know.

I stopped and looked at their defenses. Someone had gotten hold of razor wire and knew how to set it up. They had used that as a first line of defense in some places and I could see bits of cloth, and the occasional nasty-looking bone, or bones, hanging from it or scattered on the ground underneath. It hadn't held in places, but it had made a difference.

I was standing there looking at one of the places where the wire had been breached. The burned-out hulks of cars gave me a pretty good idea of how they had done it. I heard his footsteps and looked around.

He flashed a yellowed smile and said, "Hey." I returned his greeting and looked back at the wire. "Figure out how they did it?" he asked me.

"Yeah, I think so. They ran the cars into the wire and went over the tops?"

"Yeah. We had to light up the cars." He came up and stood next to me. "They were persistent. They made it all the way into the laager twice. Both times were touch and go." He paused again. "I didn't think we were going to make it." He shook his head. "Lost my stepson the second time around. Boy had to be a hero. Dumbass." The last was spoken softly and proudly. He spit in the direction of the wire.

"So, you're Gardener." He didn't say it as a question. Rather it was a statement.

I turned to face him. "Yep."

He looked me up and down. He told me, "Watch your back. Some people loved our leader." He stared at me until I nodded. Then he added, "And don't be a fucking hero."

I watched him walk away until he disappeared into one of the living quarters building. *Interesting,* I thought. *I never get the love.* Then I laughed and thought, *Fuck 'em. Fuck them all.*

I decided to go see what was happening in the kitchen. Night might be there. If not, well, I could always sit and listen to the radio. They had an FM radio and it was kept on 24/7. It was a tradition from the prior management, and no one saw any reason to change it. I found it somewhat soothing, plus, while I didn't sit around it like the regulars, I sat close enough to hear it and their chatter. Funny, I sat there in plain view, and at first they were guarded about what they said until after awhile I became invisible. I liked being invisible. They seemed to like ignoring me. It was all good.

189

I had timed it well. I sat on the five-gallon bucket that I used for a seat and leaned back against a brick wall under the shade of a sycamore. It reminded me of the Tree back in Fairfax. I never would have thought I would end up nostalgic for a day laborer gathering spot but life is what it is.

It was the top of the hour and they were running down the schedule of broadcasts for the next four hour programming block on the radio. The announcer had a sweet voice with a bit of an English accent. I thought that was strange but it didn't seem to bother anyone else. She announced:

12:00 to 12:15 The Missing Persons Report and Local News
12:15 to 12:30 Personal Hygiene with Nurse Kim
12:30 to 12:45 News from Home and Abroad
12:45 to 2:00 Music that Made America Great!
 2:00 to 3:00 The Food Hour!
 3:00 to 4:00 Classical Music

I settled down just in time to catch the Missing Persons Report. "Bob Johnson. Your wife is alive and waiting for you in the Cincinnati Hope and Pride Camp Number 3. Tonya Jackson. If you hear this please contact your local Missing Persons office." This went on for almost ten minutes. Then came the Help Wanted ads. "Machinists are wanted at all Camps. Don't hesitate! You will qualify for automatic Level 1 benefits! Toledo Camp Victory needs Pharmacists and Nurses. Don't hesitate! You will qualify for automatic Level 2 benefits!" I was going to have to find out where these camps were. We would want to stay at least thirty miles from them.

Leaving here, we would be threading the needle through some urban areas that had been heavily populated at one time. We would be going north for a while was my guess. It was too tight of a squeeze to try to go through the Cincinnati, Dayton, and Columbus area, especially with two interstates running through the area. No wonder the radio was talking about multiple camps in Cincinnati.

If I were doing the road planning I would head north toward Zanesville and make a left somewhere around Mansfield and head west. Stay between the interstates and use the farm and secondary roads. At the rate we were moving we would be in Indiana by late summer.

I was trying to recall what I knew about the area ahead. Ohio was totally foreign to me. I didn't think Ohio was ever used as a background for a movie or TV show that I had seen. It was one of those "old" states. Like a movie star from the seventies, you knew they had been big once; it was just before your time. The only thing I knew about Indiana was it grew corn, and I had known a girl named Rae Ann who told me she was born in Terre Haute. Well, I liked corn and she was a nice enough girl so who knows. It might be a good place.

I might have been daydreaming thinking about this, but I was still watching my perimeter, especially since I didn't consider this place home or even safe. And even more so after the old gaffer warned me about watching my back.

In the past few years I had learned a lot about body language. Sometimes I watched that more than I listened to the words coming out of the mouth of whoever was talking to me. I watched a woman cross about thirty yards in front of me. She had a leather-bound book under one arm and a scowl on her face. A half step behind her was a tall, spindly white man who did not look too happy.

I checked her course, saw that it was going to intercede with Freya, who standing by her motorcycle talking to a couple of the new people. The Freylings were behind her playing with some of the other kids. It looked like hopscotch. *Playing* is not the right word. Even from here I could tell they were being their usual little bossy selves.

I also saw a handful of other new people come out of the living quarters where the woman had come from. They were headed in the same direction. Damn. I recognized trouble when I saw it. The people following were armed. So was the Bible couple. We all were. I stood up, looked around to see if I had any backup. Of course not. I started walking toward Freya and the belief collision I was sure was about to happen.

I changed my mind when I saw three males heading my way. Within the blink of an eye people started disappearing and the entire vibe changed. "Freya! Reach out to Max and Ninja." Then I broke off the connection. I was going to need to concentrate. Out of the corner of my eye I saw her stiffen. She looked at me and at the people headed toward her, and smiled. I grinned back. She knew, and I knew. It was that time again.

I focused on the three headed my way. All were armed, with one casually carrying a shotgun. The other two were wearing sidearms. I stopped, and looked beyond them. No one was down range, and a wall was behind me. It didn't get much better. They were about twenty feet from me. I knew when they hit the twelve to fifteen foot line they would stop, say something, and then try to kill me.

I was not big on getting shot, let alone dying. I shot the guy with the shotgun, and then the one on my right. The one in the middle looked at me as if he wanted to say something. I holstered both guns and drew my sword. His eyes opened wide.

I screamed, "Freya!" and started walking toward him. I never took my eyes off of his, even when I gutted him. He folded over my blade groaning out a plea for help to his mother. She didn't come. I grabbed him by the hair to hold him up while I pulled out the sword. Then I let him drop while I checked out what was happening with Freya.

The discussion she had been having with her new friends came to an abrupt end when my guns went off. The little cluster of people looked somewhat disconcerted to see me approaching them at a rapid clip with a grin and a bloody sword.

192

I called out to them as I approached. "Hi, Peeps. How's the coup attempt coming along?" I wasn't surprised when they didn't answer.

The woman with the leather-bound Bible looked at me. She was not afraid. She was pissed. She also did not look as if she had slept in a week. Either that, or she was kin to a raccoon. Regardless, she did not have the "how to interact with people" thing down very well.

She started screaming, "Dark Sider! Dark Sider! She's a Dark Sider!" at Freya. She turned to her little group. "She's a Dark Sider witch! Kill the bitch!"

Nice rhyme, I thought as I closed the distance. I made a note of whose eyes bounced back and forth between the Bible lady and my bloody sword, and whose were locked in on Freya. The latter would have to go first. The others would be a step behind in reacting.

That's when Freya screamed, *"Tystnad!"* Saying she screamed it is an injustice to both her and the word. Her scream made my ears ache and the hairs on the back of my neck stand up. It made me feel simultaneously cold and hot. Or perhaps so cold inside that it was hot.

I picked up my pace. I quit smiling. I wasn't going to pick and choose. I was just going to get in the middle of them and start swinging. I could hear boots pounding the pavement. I recognized the sounds those boots made. Max was coming with the cavalry at a dead run. As far as I was concerned, he could count body parts.

Then Freya changed the equation. She looked at the Bible lady and said, "You want to kill me. You have no heart." Then she drove her hand into the woman's chest. When it came back out it was clenching her heart. Her shirtsleeve was red to the elbow, and I knew from personal experience that it was going to be a real pain to get that stain out.

Freya raised her arm so everyone could see it, and then squeezed the heart until it turned to a bloody pulp in her hand.

The woman, much to my amazement, was still standing, at least until the pulp-squeezing part. She screamed, but hers was pathetic compared to what Freya had launched. Then she fell over.

Freya looked at the remaining witch-burning party and asked, "Anyone else want to kill me?" They were not an easily cowed bunch. They had seen and survived some shit to still be alive at this point. A year ago they would have puked all over their boots. Now they just looked pale and uneasy. The moment had passed.

Max, Ninja, and Night were there. Right behind them was Jose with half a squad. It wasn't over for the haters. It was for me. I felt tired but I knew I wasn't going to be able to go anywhere. Max looked seriously pissed.

I was impressed by how Jose's people deployed around us. They made an arc with us on the inside, their eyes and barrels pointed out. Two of them went pounding past me. I watched as they headed toward the .50 to secure it. Someone was ahead of me in the thinking department. I had not even thought about it.

"G, talk to me," were the first words out of Max's mouth.

"Well, Max. Looks as if she had a heart attack to me." He didn't appreciate the humor. I started again. "I think we just had a coup attempt."

He nodded. "Yep. I think you are right." He turned to Ninja. "Get Sword squad. I want the armory secured. Then roust everyone out of the living and work areas. I want them disarmed. We are going with Jose and our people only for now."

He turned to me. "Get these people disarmed. I want them over by the wall and sitting for now. If they give you any shit..." he paused, and turned to make eye contact with them, "kill them all."

That's when "the one" spoke up. You always have "the one." He is the one, way back when, who never stopped asking stupid questions in class. He was the one who made the meeting go on forever. He was the loudest mouth at the bar during "Happy

Hour." This time, he approached Max. He probably thought that Max was safer than me.

"Look, buddy." He had his finger out, and was jabbing it in the air to emphasize his point. "Your bitch killed our Pastor in cold blood. What the hell are you going to do about it!"

Max moved fast. I forgot sometimes how quick he was when he decided to move. Somehow, a quarter second later the man was up in the air. A quarter second after that Max was down on one knee and slamming the man across it. There was a "Snap!" like a stick breaking, and he was dead. Max stood up, the man rolling off his leg like a log, and said, "Move them, G."

I moved them. Night came by about a half hour later. She told me why everyone seemed to be in the wrong place when the coup went down.

"It was a plan, G. Max and Ninja were told they had to see something outside the walls. Shelli and I were being shown an old water pipe in the basement of the storage building. Supposedly, we might be able to get water from it. Max and Ninja killed the people that had led them outside the wall. Freya sent an alarm. Shelli and I disarmed ours."

She was outside with me because by now everyone was. Ninja had replaced all the guards on the roofs and on the .50 with our people. The .50 now had its barrel pointed inward. It seemed to have a calming effect on everyone who was sitting.

Max walked over to where he could be heard by everyone. "Listen up. What happened today could have been avoided. I know there are a lot of rumors going around, so I am going to explain some things to you people, and then I am going to let you make a choice." He continued, telling them:

"Congress shall make no law respecting an establishment of religion, or prohibiting the free exercise thereof; or abridging the freedom of speech, or of the press; or the right of the people peaceably to assemble, and to petition the government for a redress of grievances."

195

He paused. "I hope you all recognize that. It is the First Amendment to the Constitution of the United States." He came down heavy on the United States part. "For those of you that join us, that means exactly what it says. I don't care who you worship. All we ask is that you use our battle cry. If that is a problem, so be it. We will not tolerate discrimination in any form. If you are good enough to kill, and perhaps die, to protect your brothers and sisters, then you are good enough to stand with them and me anytime, anywhere. We leave in the morning. Those of you coming with us, I expect you to be ready to swear an oath to affirm it. Those of you who wish to stay…" He paused. "Stay. Due to the unpleasant incident earlier you will not be issued arms until we leave. That is all."

He walked over to me and said, "Cut them loose, G."

I cut them loose. "You heard the man. Go do what you got to do." They were a quiet bunch as they got up to leave. Only a couple of them met my eyes as they went past me. I watched them go. They all left except for one older lady who was sitting on my bucket. I walked over to her. She had a cell phone out and was staring at it.

"That thing work?" I asked her, somewhat surprised. I heard that some still did, but I hadn't seen one. What did surprise me was the stab of nostalgia I felt.

I had startled her. She looked up at me, while at the same time she quickly snapped it shut, and dropped it into the front pocket of her BDUs. "Oh no," she answered quickly.

"Then why were you looking at it?" I was not trying to be threatening. I was just curious.

"It's silly, I know. I just like to hope my son will call me." The way she said it told me she regarded it as far from silly. She actually believed he might, but she also knew he may never. It wasn't just a phone. It was her lottery, airline, her escape ticket, her lucky charm. It was a connection to her past, and a fragile bridge to a future that was probably never going to happen.

196

A couple of different replies went through my head. I discarded them all. "Sure. Amazing things happen all the time. You better go get ready." I extended a hand to help her up. It was fragile and bony. I let go of it quickly. She thanked me and walked off. I noticed she touched her front pocket to reassure herself her phone was still there at least twice before she disappeared inside.

I watched her and wondered if she knew the screen was cracked. She probably did. I shook my head and wondered if they still made iPhones. I had wanted one really badly once upon a time. I wasn't sure why now.

CHAPTER TWENTY-THREE

I saw that the Chief had pulled some of the vehicles into the main area to make it easier to do our load out. I walked up on him as he was talking to Shelli.

He was telling her, "We are going to have to pack heavy. You can find room for those potatoes in the four trucks I gave you."

"You want to eat?" was her waspish reply.

"Damn, Shelli. I saw them potatoes. They are half rotten at best. You already have one too many vehicles. Where the hell do you think fuel comes from? The fuel tree?"

They were both getting red in the face. I decided to walk the other way. I figured I would go find my squad and see what they were doing or not doing. I didn't make it. I was sidetracked by Max.

"G, walk with me." I knew what that meant. Super Duper Secret Plan time. We walked out the gate, past the wreckage of cars, debris of burned-out buildings, and suitcases that had not been opened by the owners. I looked down and stepped over a pair of women's underwear. They were pink and made of rayon, which was worthless for bandages, and huge.

Max caught me looking at them, laughed and said, "Someone fed a squad for a week on rump roast."

"Either that, or she is a size ten for the first time since junior high," I replied.

Most people considered talking about cannibalism tasteless. The idea that it had been a rare occurrence, only done by crazies, was becoming the popular cover story for what had really happened. Max and I, since we didn't live through it, did not have any inhibitions about mentioning it. It was probably that way after World War II in Germany, especially with those who had helped feed the camps with the innocent. Now when I heard someone vehemently denying munching on long pig I knew that they had.

Max stopped walking. "G, I've got a choice for you."

"Yeah?"

"You can run all the troops for me or do recon."

I didn't even hesitate. "Recon."

"I figured as much. You can have two others to take with you. Your choice with a couple of exceptions."

"Okay. I will take Night and Ninja."

He laughed. "Those are your two exceptions."

"Shit." I thought for a moment. "I'll take the Marine who was with me a few days ago. Hmmm...how about Jose?"

"Another exception."

I saw where he was going with this. "So, I guess I should call our team 'The Expendibles'?"

"It's not like that, G. I need someone with a Freya link. I need someone who can scout, map a route, and deal with any locals. If the locals don't want to deal, then I need someone who can deal with them. That's you."

Yeah, that was me. Negotiator and ambassador of good will to the world at large. I had to laugh at what I was thinking. Max looked at me quizzically.

"Nothing," I told him. "You ever realize how weird all this is, Max?"

He looked at me, then off into space, and back at me. "G, my life has been weird ever since I got on that plane at Camp Lejeune a million years ago for my first deployment. At least what I am doing today makes more sense."

He looked at me, and I realized that he enjoyed this. So did I. We weren't going to admit it, but we did.

He clapped me on shoulder. "I need the name of the third man for your team."

"Go ahead and pick him, Max. How much time do I have before we hit the road?"

"You have two hours. I want you to keep about fifty miles ahead of us at a minimum. That's why you get such short notice. You are going to need to move through the night to get a decent lead on us."

"Okay. I'll go find Night. Then I'll gear up. Where should I pick up my people?"

"I'll have them ready at the gate. See Shelli for rations. I'll tell her to take care of you."

There wasn't much for me to say after that. As we walked back, Max explained more of what he wanted me to look for, but I was only half listening. Instead I was trying to think of a place Night and I could go where we would have some privacy.

As we went through the gate Max stopped, looked at me, and said, "I know you haven't listened to a word I've said. Try the basement. The room in the back is clean. Take a blanket." Then he grinned at me and walked off.

I went to find Night. I found her standing by Shelli and Chief talking about food and fuel. We did the greeting thing and they started talking where they had left off.

"Hey, Night." She looked at me somewhat annoyed. She was a stickler about good manners sometimes.

"Yes?" she replied. Yep, there was a faint edge to that yes.

"I'm out of here in one hour forty-seven minutes. Max has me running long distance recon." Then I just looked at her. She looked at me.

She looked at them, and said, "Shelli, Chief is right. Dump some of that shit." Then she took me by the hand and headed toward the living area.

I said, "Ah, Night. We need to go the other way."

200

"What other way?"

"Toward the basement building."

She grinned. "First we get a blanket. Then we go there."

Later I asked, "How did you know about the blanket and the room?"

She smiled down at me and brushed her hair back. "Shelli can't keep her mouth shut about her sex life." I wasn't a big fan of Shelli's, but by the time we left the basement I harbored warm feelings toward her. Actually, I had warm feelings for the entire world.

Night sat with me while I packed. It didn't take long, which was a good thing, as I didn't have much time left. We went by the kitchen so I could find Shelli and draw my rations or "rats" as Ninja liked to call them. He would grin manically whenever he said that, which was far too often.

I was getting tense, and Shelli was taking forever to pull it together. She and Night were chattering away and grinning at each other as if we had all day. We didn't. One of the things Max taught me, and it had taken awhile to sink in, was that punctuality was everything.

Getting casual about time and getting places could get people killed. There was no such thing as being somewhere at 14:00. If that was when you were supposed to be there then you better have your ass there, and ready to go, fifteen minutes ahead of time.

I wanted to check my bike, check the vehicle we were using, check out the two guys going with me, and look at a map and go over routes with them. Instead I was listening to Shelli and Night discuss how many cans of peaches I could carry.

I was about ready to get testy with them when Night looked at me and said, "It's okay, honey. Just relax." It didn't make me less tense, but she was the logistical brains of our bunch so I backed down a bit.

I finally stuffed the "rats" into my pack. I was going to have to repack later. I told Shelli thanks and headed for the door with

Night and Shelli following me. I was surprised at what was going on outside as we exited. Most of the troops were lined up in formation. They were even organized, well, somewhat, like real soldiers. I looked at them and thought there must be another oath ceremony planned. The dependents stood in their own group away from the troops.

We never had done much in the way of formal presentations and parades. We never had the time, Max and I thought it was bullshit, and two thirds of the people were new anyway. I think the only thing we could do as a group was "Dress right. Dress." Anyway the second thought through my head was, *Shit. Who fucked up now?*

I was also surprised to see Max, Ninja, and Freya standing in a group in front of the troops with Jose off to one side. As I walked up to Max I heard Jose bellow "Present Arms!" I looked at Max for a clue, and all I got was "C'mon. Stand over here, G." He beckoned to his right.

Then Jose bellowed, "Order Arms!" They all went back to standing there with varying degrees of precision. I noticed my old squad was grinning at me. Max made a short speech where he told them what we were going to be doing. Then he talked about my role in suppressing the coup, which I didn't think was all that big of a deal. Hell, I thought that was my job.

He continued. "Many of you are veterans who served honorably in the United States military. We will run this Legion the same way those units you served in were: with pride, professionalism, and dedication. In keeping with those traditions we will recognize acts by individuals who uphold these traditions." He turned to me. "Major Gardener. It is fitting that you receive this unit's first award. The Bronze Star."

He turned to Ninja who handed him a small box. Out of it came a genuine Bronze Star, which he held up for everyone to see, and then he handed it to me.

"Thanks, Max," I told him. I was a little confused. When did I become a Major? I guess I should have gone to a few of the meetings.

Things happened fairly quickly after that. Ninja had my bike loaded in the back of the "walkaway." A walkaway was a vehicle that we could drive long enough to get some distance between the Horde and us and then walk away from.

The Chief pulled me aside. "Hey, buddy. Good luck and all that shit. Stay safe. You got two gallons of gas and this vehicle should be good for it. Heck, you find some more gas, and some decent tires, you could probably push this Tundra to the Rockies." Then he laughed. "Well, maybe not, but you know what I mean."

"Yeah. Thanks, Chief." I went over and checked on my guys. I had the Marine from the Strike Force team. I always wondered how Max could say "Strike Force" and keep a straight face. It always sounded to me like some kind of Asian-animated cartoon. As in "Woo Hoo! Let's put on our funny spandex costumes and space ray something." Then you had to watch five cereal commercials.

The Marine's name was Ricky. He was from Iowa, and he looked like it. By that I mean he was tall, lean, and very white. Not his skin color, but his persona. The other guy was a squat Mexican who called himself "Loco." He was covered in tattoos and was from East LA. He had been in the Army and had been discharged back in the big wave of cutbacks. He said he was running a florist shop in Cincinnati when things got weird. I let that pass without comment. I think I surprised him by doing so.

I said good-bye to Night, told Loco he was driving, and climbed into the passenger seat. We pulled out, and I stuck my arm out the window and waved. That was easy to do as we had no windows. There were also a couple of bullet holes in my door.

"Where to, Major?" Loco asked.

"Straight ahead. Keep it around twenty-five miles an hour, and if you call me Major again I will kill you." He turned his head to look at me, expecting me to grin. I didn't. I heard Ricky chuckle, and watched Loco shoot him an evil eye in the rearview mirror. I sighed, tilted my hat down over my eyes, and said, "Let's make this as easy as possible." I was going to go on, but Ricky interrupted me.

"Hey, Loco."

"What?"

"You did a couple tours, right? You were in Columbia?"

"Yeah. So?"

"So, I laughed because you don't realize who you are fucking with." He looked at me. "You and me will do fine. You see, Loco, I saw Gardener here in action. I know his type. I don't mean any disrespect, Gardener, but you are a fucking stone killer from another dimension. That's what we are going to need, Loco, my man. Because we are going to be out there with our asses hanging out and no backup, no air, no nothing on call. So, yeah, I want to live, and I don't what end up hanging in no fucking basement providing mutants with entertainment or body parts. You don't want to be catching an attitude, know what I mean?"

I didn't even look to see what Loco's response was. I just said, "You done?"

"Yep."

"Fine. We got about two hours. Supposedly, we are clear for the next forty-five minutes. After that, I am going to assume trouble."

Loco cut in with a comment. "We're being watched now."

I tilted my hat back up. "Tell me more."

"Don't have more but I can feel it." I sat quietly and went into neutral. Yeah, there was someone out there. Not close by, but out there.

"Park it in the next place that looks good. We're moving on foot from here." I knew what Max had said but I thought, *Screw it.* Ricky wasn't the only one who liked living.

CHAPTER TWENTY-FOUR

Walking across America is not a good idea in the best of times. These weren't the best of times. Some might have said the worst was past us. I didn't think so. I thought I had some idea about how big this country was. I was wrong. America is fucking huge and right now it was also hot in Ohio.

We had been away from the main group for two days now. They were behind us maybe forty miles or so, and they would begin to move tomorrow. The schedule had been reset due to logistics problems. That meant they would be narrowing the distance between us pretty damn fast. We needed to roll out on the bikes but I wasn't in a hurry.

The breeze felt good on my face. I took another sip of water that I didn't need or really want but Max had taught us to drink or "hydrate" as he called it. I already knew to do it but not to the extreme he wanted us to practice it. The two guys with me must have gone to the same school Max had because they drank a fair amount of water, too.

I remember asking him what he remembered about the roads in Iraq and Afghanistan. I expected something like crazed Muslim fanatics in cars or IEDs. He looked away for a second and said, "Water bottles."

"What?"

"Yeah, they were everywhere in some places."

"Oh." For once he had me at loss for words.

Well, we didn't leave our water bottles behind. Loco and Ricky had CamelBaks. As soon as I could find one I was going to carry one. My idea of just carrying a couple containers and a filter was turning out to be pretty stupid. What worked for me back in Fairfax and at the farm did not work as well on the road. If I spent any time on foot, carrying water got to be a major pain in the ass. We were spending far too much time dismounted and walking; far more than I had planned.

We were sitting off Route 124 east of Wilkesville and not too far from a strip mine on one of the many hills around here. I had a look at it from above and it was ugly; a scar gouged into the earth filled with water. It looked like a pond, a big one too but nothing grew around it. I bet some local asshole would have told me it looked like money. If it had smelled bad he would tell me that was the smell of money. I shook my head, stood up, and stretched.

We had been watched on and off since we left the main group. I hadn't felt it since this morning but now it was back.

We were sitting under the shade of an oak tree about a hundred yards off the main road and about a quarter of the way up a small hill. Our bikes were laid down in the grass and dirt next to us. The terrain was starting to flatten out which was not really a good thing. I already felt more exposed than I cared for. I could only imagine what the Great Plains would be like. At least the bike units behind us would be able to pick up the pace.

"Hey, Gardener."

"Yeah, Loco?"

"You feel it?"

"Yeah. They're out there again." Loco was sharp. He might be as good as I was at feeling when someone's eyes were on us.

"Shit. This is getting irritating."

"Yeah, Loco. The problem is I can't find the fucker." It was true. Even looking through the eyes of one of Freya's birds hadn't helped.

207

"The birds not picking it up?" Ricky asked. He usually felt it but it took him longer, and he usually lost it quicker. Everyone knew about Freya and her special power with birds. None, except us lucky ones, knew how it all exactly worked. Those who didn't know had theories. All the theories basically agreed it was magic powers. They were right. It was magic as far as I was concerned.

"No. Nothing. Whoever or whatever it is, is pretty fucking slick."

"I think it's one of those fucking drones from the gov. Them birds don't get up high enough to see that shit," Loco said.

"Probably. So far they have been quiet. Mount up. We need to find a vehicle and gas," I told them. I loved saying "Mount up." It was really cool to have a reason to say it without sounding like a total ass. I had to bite my tongue and only say it occasionally. I didn't want to ruin the coolness of saying it.

I picked up my bike, straddled it and coasted down to the road. Behind me I didn't hear anyone bother to groan or complain. It wouldn't have done them any good and it would have just pissed me off. They were good though. As good as we had available. I would rather have been out here with Max and Ninja but life never did pay a whole hell of a lot of attention to what I wanted or didn't want.

We had begun to figure out how we were going to do this. We had to. If we didn't, we would probably die. I wasn't big on dying and I sure didn't want to get stuck or bitten by anything sharp again. My leg never did come back completely after that damn dog bit down on it. I didn't tell anyone, including Night, that I sometimes lost feeling in places. That wasn't all bad I figured. It beat the alternative. Plus, if I did get hit there again, I wouldn't notice it until I had time to deal with it.

You would think that three guys, all of them experienced in dealing with the different faces that violence wore, would be a team right off the line. It didn't work that way. It helped, of course. It also helped that we all knew the difference without talking about it.

There is a team and then there is a pack. A team works up to a certain point. That point is when you run into situations that practice hadn't covered. A pack could care less what the situation is. It is just more of the same. No discussion is needed. Looking over your shoulder never crosses your mind. You know your brothers and sisters will be where they need to be when they need to be there. If they aren't, it is because they are dead or dying.

I didn't have to practice with Max and Ninja. I knew. That was where our group had to get to and the sooner the better. I also missed Woof. I had seen him a few times but he was keeping his distance. I think all the new people bothered him. I understood. They bothered me, too.

We may have been out in the middle of nowhere, at least as I defined it, but PowerDown had left its skid mark across the face of the landscape here. At one time this highway had probably handled thirty cars an hour during its busiest times. We had not seen any today. None. Zero. It was rather freaky. None of us liked it, but that was why we were out here. To find problems and solve them before the rest of the Horde encountered them.

This highway had its share of abandoned vehicles, although far less than what we had seen before. Yet enough that someone would eventually make some money working salvage here. Hell, at the rate America had gone through its vehicles during PowerDown, Detroit might actually make a comeback building replacements. That thought was quickly followed by the realization that it was unlikely. They had already proven they could fuck up a wet dream.

Instead of dwelling on our not being a pack yet, I told Loco and Ricky, "Ya'll know the drill. Loco take the road. I'll take the left side of the road." I didn't bother saying who had the right side. Ricky knew. We didn't push someone out at point. Instead we rode in a wedge-shaped formation. Loco was our car guy.

209

That was why he had the center of the road. His job today was to find us something that would run.

We had left the Tundra not far from here. I had just made the decision to dump it and move forward on our bikes when the truck decided it wasn't going any further anyway. Ricky took a pothole that turned out to be deeper than it looked, busted a tie rod and drove the truck at an angle into a telephone pole. We hadn't been moving that fast which was a good thing. Since the airbags no longer worked it was even better that we had belted in.

It was a walkaway truck anyway so the crash was no big deal. At least that was what I had thought at the time. How hard could it be to find a vehicle? I mean it rained vehicles along this road for awhile.

We should have made it further ahead. The problem was we had to stop and clear the road far more often than I wanted to. When we couldn't do that we had to find away around the obstacle and then mark that we had been there. A couple times we were visited by crows that sat on the telephone wires and watched us. Loco had asked, "Those Freya's birds?"

I replied, "You know anyone else who does that shit?"

He didn't answer. I didn't care. I suppose I should have made it into a teachable moment, and maybe even answered civilly. I didn't because it was a stupid fucking question.

Working the cars we passed wasn't our job. The Horde had people whose job was to check vehicles for goodies. If they found anything they would leave it in piles on the road and when the trucks rolled past it would be picked up and picked over. At least that was the plan.

Who the hell knew what reality was going to be. The problem we continually bumped into was how labor intensive and time consuming everything was. I had learned that as soon as I had become homeless. The farm had reinforced it. Everything that had happened since was just added reinforcement. Well, if it was true everywhere then unemployment was going to be a thing of the past.

I personally thought car stripping was a shit job but some people loved it. They actually thought it was fun. My guess was that it attracted the same kind of people who thought going to the mall was fun back in the day. You want to smell something foul? Bust into a Lexus that has been sealed up tight for months with dead people in it. No thanks, not for me.

The car strippers usually just busted the trunk open and left the passengers to grin at whoever passed by next. Popping the trunk still created quite a stink. No clothes were salvageable, that was for sure. We passed on the deadmobiles like that. I was sure others wouldn't and hadn't. There were gold wedding rings and diamonds to be found.

We were having problems finding a vehicle. Not because there weren't enough of them. The problem was finding one with a stick that we could roll and jump-start. Nobody bought vehicles with stick shifts anymore. It helped narrow the search down. The batteries were also either dead or gone in a lot of the vehicles. Fuel injection might have been great back in the day but it wasn't helping us now. If we saw an older truck we stopped and looked. Otherwise we kept pedaling.

Loco and I had just stopped to look at a Ford F-150 when Ricky said, "Got company ahead." We stopped looking and rolled up near Ricky to take a look. Yep. We had company.

CHAPTER TWENTY-FIVE

They were on foot, and far enough away that the heat from the asphalt made them look as if they were emerging from the ocean. They did not look like a crack unit of road warriors from here, but they had survived this long so they had to have something going for them.

"Okay. I'm going to stand in the middle of the road. If they keep coming then we'll see if they want to talk. If they scatter then we hunt them down." I looked at Ricky and Loco. They were okay with that.

I strolled out into the middle of the road and watched them approach. In the background I heard Ricky and Loco take up positions on either side of me. Ricky had a car to take cover behind. Loco had to make do with flopping down in the grass on the side of the road.

I was carrying a Marlin 30-30 on a leather sling over my shoulder. It was also known as the Appalachian AK. I liked it, but figured I would be swapping it out for a real wood stock AK or M-14 as soon as I found one. I wasn't a big fan of rifles but they were useful when you had to really reach out for someone.

I reached in my shirt pocket, pulled out the two cigarette butts I kept there, and stuck one in each ear. My hearing was good, really good, thanks to Freya. That had turned out to be a mixed blessing. My vision, which had always been good, was also better. Putting cigarette butts in the ears was my idea. My head really rang the last few times I had to slap leather without some kind of hearing protection and the headaches were a bitch afterward.

It was easier to find gold nowadays than a couple of aspirin. Shelli wanted me to look for willow trees while we were out here because they grew aspirin or something. I had just pretended I hadn't heard her. If you started going down that road with people, then you ended up taking requests for all kinds of shit. I don't do personal shopper very well.

While my mind was running random crap like that through it, the rest of my brain was watching the people approaching. One was an old man with gray hair and a really good Old Testament prophet beard. He was walking in front and had spotted me about a minute ago. A young guy with long hair and a decent beard was pulling a garden cart with a tarp-covered load. Off to one side was an even younger kid with no beard, probably because he didn't have the juice to grow one yet.

They were all armed. Cart Puller had something slung over his shoulder - I couldn't tell what it was - and a handgun on his hip. Grandpa had a handgun and a genuine black plastic assault rifle of some sort. Youngster had a shotgun and no handgun that I could see. They were all wearing knives as well. No body armor that I could tell. Decent boots and each one had a daypack. This might be interesting.

He looked at me for a couple of seconds. Then over his shoulder he said, "Boys, pull the cart off to the side and take a break while I talk to this gentleman." He scratched himself and said, "All right if we sit down somewhere? My legs have been talking to me all day."

"Yeah. Sounds good." I indicated the car that Ricky was behind. I gave the hand sign for him and Loco to "form on me." I watched the old man's eyes. He was good but I knew that he had not seen either one of them. They were good but I found it curious that he was that bad. Damn. Here I was hoping the dumb asses in the gene pool had been thinned out but it was looking as if some of them had survived.

Yet, there was something wrong here. The feeling of being watched was back stronger than ever. Plus, the boys, they weren't relaxing right. I did a quick "caution" hand sign as Ricky and Loco came up. They didn't say anything. They just continued on and walked over to the boys.

The old man started talking. "Where you coming from? How's the road?" While he was asking me questions I noticed Loco had split from Ricky and was at an angle from him but in one of the boys' blind side. I liked that and relaxed a hair. We were taking a lean against the side of the car and the old man was looking at me, waiting for my response.

"Funny. I was going to ask you the same things."

He laughed. "Well, we could take turns."

"That we could." I looked around. "You feel like you been watched along the way?" He looked startled for a second. Then he looked away and spat. He almost made the grass.

"Yep. I figure every step of the way we are going to be watched by somebody. If it ain't the gov up in the sky, it is going to be some assholes in the woods. Supposedly this area was swept by one of those police battalions they got." That got my attention.

"Regular Army or the Guard?"

"Shit. What I hear is there is a mix of all kinds. The one that went through here was mostly Guard. They're supposed to be heading for the National Forest down the road. Got some real assholes living in the woods." He shuddered but I don't think he even noticed he did. "Got some fucking, pardon my language, Eaters running around still."

"Yeah. We called them Gnawers where we come from. Same thing I suppose," I told him.

He spat again. "Yeah. So I've been running my mouth. What you got?"

214

I thought, *Nobody wants to stay on the subject of who ate what for very long.* So I decided to give him some information. "We're headed for Iowa out of DC."

"Iowa?" He laughed. "Damn. You got a hell of a long walk ahead of you. We're headed for West Virginia. Got family there. I suppose the gov will be showing up there eventually but they will pay a hell of a price rooting us out."

"What makes you think they'll bother?"

He looked at me as if I was an idiot. "Son, they want us all where they can see us."

Now it was my turn to laugh and say, "Like that has worked out so well for everyone."

"Yeah. No shit," he replied glumly. We talked a bit more. I told him a bit about the road ahead of him. He told me a bit about the road waiting for us.

"Whatever you do, stay out of them camps. Hell, don't even go within forty miles of them. I don't know why you be going this way. Going to be tough to squeeze in between all the roadblocks and patrols. You should go south then head back up. A lot of gangs are working that area, too. Some serious looting going on from what I hear." He chuckled. "Some of them chuckleheads are stealing TVs and such."

He shook his head, and then added, "Plus, watch out for them Prius cars and such."

Huh?" That one caught me by surprise.

"Them electric cars. The gov loves them. You see an electric car and you are looking at a gov person or someone in tight with them."

"Damn." He was right. I hadn't seen but a couple of hybrids along the way and they were totaled. He was talking about West Virginia and his people when it clicked in my head. I casually asked, "So you and the boys been together for awhile?"

He replied, "Oh no. We hooked up about two weeks ago. They came into town." He laughed bitterly. "Town. Shit. Nothing but a handful of people nowadays. Lot of people drifting here and there and a lot of them you never hear from again. So yeah, safety in numbers and all that. Why?"

"Don't know. Let's go see." I started walking over to them. Ricky and Loco were grinning at something the bearded one had said. They looked over and I hit them with the "danger" sign. Ricky, the dumb ass, dropped his grin and went stone-faced but Loco said something back in reply and laughed.

Old Man wasn't following me. I stopped and said, "You coming?" He shrugged, and I waited until he was next to me before continuing toward the happy little group.

I stopped about five feet from them. Old Man stopped with me. As soon as he did I moved again so I was about three feet from him and had a better angle. I called it anchoring a person.

You get someone walking with you, approach a group, and just stop. The person with you usually stops without thinking. Then you move again. They never follow because they know it makes them look like a little puppy. A lot of what I did was just playing off cultural wiring and conditioning. "Staying out of the pattern" was what Max called it.

The boys looked a little unsure now, especially Bearded Boy.

I told them, "Well, we're out of here," and grinned. "We got one more thing to do. Ya'll don't mind if we poke around in that cart? Of course not. Why don't you two boys stand back a bit?" I waited for a couple of seconds.

Sure enough, Bearded Boy objected. "You're not the law. Why don't you fuck off." He was going to keep going but I drew the Ruger.

In the silence that followed I told him, "Shut up or die." He shut up.

"Loco. Take a look." I drew the Colt. "Old man, settle down. We're just looking." He had opened his mouth and changed his stance.

Loco began trying to untie the cords that they had used to tie down the tarp. It was blue, of course. I sometimes thought if I

216

ever started my own country the national flag would be a blue tarp. He was having problems with the knots they had used.

I said, "Just cut them, Loco." The old man's lips compressed into a tight line when I said that. He started to put his sunglasses back on. I told him, "Don't."

I watched his face ripple with his thoughts. *Fuck him. Do it. No. He'll do something. Probably painful. I'm a man, damn it!* I saw him decide to put them on. I pulled the hammer back on the Colt. He changed his mind.

Loco cut through the cords, sheathed his blade and began pulling back the tarp. I didn't know what to expect. Hell, it could have been filled with dried people jerky headed for some Gnawer market. It wasn't.

We saw the same stuff we saw in the backs and trunks of cars. A suitcase. Some trash bags - the official suitcase of the homeless, a couple of cardboard boxes with pots and pans, and what looked to be dried spices. Also three sleeping bags, each tightly rolled, and some plastic water jugs, one of which I noticed was leaking. Seeing that it was another cart full of the same old shit let everybody relax a notch.

I smiled at the boys and said, "See. No big deal." Bearded Boy smiled weakly. The other two were still pissed. I understood that. Too bad.

I was going to tell Loco to just grope the Heftys. I changed my mind. He obviously knew what he was doing. The tension went back up a notch when he stepped away from the cart, looked at it, then walked around one side, knelt down, and then stood back up.

He looked at me, and said, "We got something here." I knew it as soon as he had taken a knee by the change on the boys' faces. Of course then they had to go for it. Ricky was for shit as an actor but he was fast on the trigger. I already had a round in Bearded Boy, maybe a split second before Ricky. Loco was on them, too. We were fast, but it was sloppy and overkill. Overkill because none of us knew the others well enough to bet our life

217

on them doing what needed to be done. I sighed mentally and thought, *No wonder Max walked us through the whys and whats afterward.*

I looked at the old man who was frozen in place and white in the face. "So...what are we going to find, old man?"

"I don't know. Really!"

Neither did I actually. I didn't even know what had alerted Loco, but I would keep that to myself. Instead I said, "Show him, Loco."

Ricky looked at Loco and said, "False Bottom?"

"Yep. Same old shit. Different country." Loco started tossing luggage out of the back of the cart when a voice I recognized blasted the word "Run!" into my head and followed it with an image of a smoking crater. I went from zero to sixty in nothing flat yelling "Bomb!" as I passed Loco and Ricky.

They understood that word. I had a five-stride lead on them but they were moving at full throttle right behind me. I felt like I had been running, and not fast enough, for an eternity, or maybe just three or four seconds, when the same voice screamed "Down!" and down I went.

I hit the ground hard, ate grass, and skidded to a stop. Almost on top of me was Loco. From the "Oof" I heard, he hit as hard as I did. Ricky was about two strides behind us. I covered my ears, and buried my head in the grass I had just mowed with my face and waited. The ground shook, the boom not even muffled by my hands and Marlboro butts in my ears, and dirt and other crap rained down on us. I knew my head was going to be hurting for certain soon. Damn, that was loud.

I waited a few seconds, got up on my knees, and while I finger-combed crap out of my hair and clothes, looked back at where we had been. There was a small crater where we had been standing. The old man was nowhere to be seen. Well, he did say his legs were hurting. They were probably not bothering him now.

I stood up and gave Loco a hand up. He and Ricky started doing what I was doing. The only difference was they were saying "Holy shit" while I was thinking it. I rearranged all the gear I had hanging on me.

"Take a look, guys," I told them, "while I check in with headquarters." Mentally I sent Freya the word that meant I wanted to talk to her: "*Svärd.*" I didn't get why I had to say that. I wanted to say "Earth to Freya" but no, we had to had to have a nifty cool Norse word. She was there instantly as I had expected. I didn't bother with verbal foreplay.

"What the fuck was that about?"

"I don't know." She sounded genuinely puzzled.

"Damn. I bet you can hear my ears ringing from there."

She laughed. "No, all I hear in your head is the usual." I didn't bother to ask what that was. I knew her answer would be insulting.

"Can you patch Max and Night in?" I was surprised by how much I wanted to hear Night's voice. Everything we verbalized in our heads went out to whoever was tied into the Freya party line so she heard and felt it as well. I felt her smile.

"No Max. He is disciplining people." I felt her fierce joy about that. "Here is Night."

As soon as she came on I sent images of how much I missed her as she did to me. I thought, "Wow! This is intense. Maybe we could..."

Night cut me off, laughing, "No."

We went back and forth, then settled down and actually talked for about five minutes about nothing really. It was a delight just to talk to her. Well, actually I listened. She did most of the talking. Then we got down to what had just happened, prompted by Freya who said, "You two want to hurry up? I have birds to talk to."

"So what do you think?" I asked Night.

219

She was silent for a few seconds, and then said, "Who were they going to be running into next?" Then she sent me an image of the Horde.

"Oh. Yeah."

Freya joined in. "Me?"

We both answered, "Yep."

I signed off to find Loco and Ricky staring at me with more than a little bit of awe. Loco said, "Were you talking to Freya?"

"Yeah."

They both shouted, "Freya!" and slammed their chests with their right hands clenched into a fist.

Okay, I thought, *I missed when that became popular.* They were looking at me as if I was supposed to do something. Probably bang back. The weird thing was I did feel something stir inside of me when they did that. Something I was familiar with. I wanted to roll. I wanted to pull the sword I had strapped across my back and cut someone's limbs off. I wanted to yell, to let free, to give voice to that which lived within me.

Instead I said, "Cool. Let's move."

CHAPTER TWENTY-SIX

We moved. We were able to put some miles under our wheels for a change. The road was clear in places. More so than we had seen so far. We passed houses, some occupied. Once we passed a man and a boy walking the road, rifles slung over their shoulders. I waved, and the boy waved back.

The sky was blue, a deeper blue than I had ever seen. Every year it seemed like the sky became bluer. I forget who had explained why that was to me. The sky really was getting bluer because each year there were less planes up there painting it gray with their exhaust. I still saw contrails, but they were rare enough that they were pointed out when someone spotted one.

We had one nice surprise. Nice surprises were rare. Nasty ones were far more likely. Loco found a portable radio that worked. He and Ricky were excited. I could not care less. If they played music it was from a world that was gone. I didn't really mourn its passing either; it was never my world anyway. The news was full of lies from liars. The weather forecast was generally useless. It was never for the area we were in and if it was, it was usually wrong. I was a better weatherman. More and more I was finding that I cared less for the artifacts and news from a civilization I thought of as "Machine World."

They were excited, though, and I think they were surprised that I wasn't. I noticed Loco look at Ricky and get a tiny shrug.

Loco and Ricky started talking about baseball and whether the Yankees were still playing. The Yankees? Well, if money could save you from PowerDown then they might still have a roster. Otherwise there probably were some bulked-up Gnawers running around New York. A-Rod had to have enough steroids in him to pump a Jewish Granny up to minor league Gnawer status.

I wasn't surprised at what was playing, or interested but I sat with them anyway. Who knew, maybe we would hear something useful. The FM stations were what I expected. Government-approved broadcasting. Pure propaganda. A couple of robot stations playing music. Loco and Ricky started arguing about which station to listen to. I was surprised that their musical tastes were different. I told them to switch to AM and it got more interesting. We had the usual Christian preachers telling us that what happened was God's vengeance on a nation that had lost its way. Someone was selling charms that prevented nightmares, and then we hit gold. We heard:

"Standby for a broadcast from the Revolution Network. We are also available on the 'Net at revolution.org.is or revolution.org.no." They went to the panpipe music that the Burners always used and a woman's voice, with a bit of a Brit accent, said, "This broadcast will be brief, as usual." She chuckled, and added, "No surprise there." She continued. "We will prevail. Despite the brutal tactics of the warlord puppets and mass murder of citizens by the government police battalions, we will prevail. Know this! Freya is upon you government dogs. You think by killing us you have stopped us?" She laughed scornfully. "No. Oh no. You have only guaranteed your death. She comes! She comes! Fire and sword! Fire and sw...."

The transmission went dead. Loco and Ricky looked at each other gape-mouthed. I just grinned. Shorty was stirring people up. How, I wasn't sure.

A few seconds later, another voice came on. This one was male, and, by the accent, southern. "The broadcast you just heard was from a robotic transmitter placed in your area by terrorists. Please contact federal law enforcement should you know anything about this. A reward will be paid for successful prosecution of these individuals. Thank you and God Bless America."

"All right. Leave the radio somewhere so the follow-up people will see it. Maybe it will be here. Maybe it won't."

Loco asked me, "Gardener, any chance..."

"No," I said flatly. I relented and told him why. "We don't listen to the news, Loco; we make it." It was bullshit of course but it sounded macho so it was okay. They liked it. We rolled on.

We pulled up outside of some little crossroads that once existed because it was at the intersection of two minor state roads. That had worked in their favor until PowerDown. Then they had been overrun. Loco and Ricky glassed the town while I studied it. I really wished I had Woof and his friends with me. I had asked for them but Max said he wanted them to work the gaps between the scouts. I was going to ask again. I liked talking to Woof, perhaps more than to most people. We saw eye to eye except when I stood up.

"We got people," I told them.

"Yeah, I see them," Loco replied.

He passed the binoculars to Ricky who took a look. He handed them back to Loco and said, "Looks like a checkpoint of some sort."

Loco replied, "Yeah. You see the flag?"

"Flag? Hand me them binoculars again." Loco passed them back to Ricky. "Yeah. Okay. I got it." He held the binoculars to me. I took them and scanned back and forth. Luckily the wind was blowing lightly. The flag unfurled enough in the breeze for me to get a glimpse of the device sewn to the white cloth.

223

"Ya'll see what's on that flag?" I was looking at Loco when I asked.

"Not really. It ain't the star-spangled banner, that's for sure."

Ricky added, "That's got to be something else." He laughed and said, "Maybe it's the local warlord."

I didn't laugh. "Probably. I don't like the watchtower." There was a platform built on top of a two-story building that had a lookout with a rifle on it.

"That could be trouble," Ricky noted.

I agreed with him. "He does have a couple blind spots once you are inside of town." I pointed them out. It looked as if they were trying to wall the main area in with dead cars. So far they had only managed a hundred foot section. Half of that had been covered in dirt. Somewhat. It did not look too impressive.

I told them, "Let's sit tight here. See what happens for a bit. Spend the night. Look at them again tomorrow. I want silence now until tomorrow. No cooking either." I told them the watch schedule and sat down and began cleaning and sharpening my weapons. I had to figure out how we were going to do this.

The flag had a cross and something else emblazoned on the white field. It probably meant they were Christian militia types. I wanted to figure out some cool strategy to do this instead of just showing up. Something more military; something Max would come up with. I couldn't think of anything other than showing up and if it got weird, well, then kill them all. I shrugged, and thought, *I am what I am.*

I watched the village as darkness came upon us. I saw the light of a couple lanterns glowing for a while through windows. Lantern light was different than light from a light bulb. It glowed more than it illuminated. Tomorrow we would go down and say hello. After that we'd see what happened. I got up, stretched, and went to relieve Ricky of the watch.

We woke up before dawn, sat for a while, and listened to the daytime world wake up around us. We watched as the village came to life. Nothing new there. I watched a guy come out of a

224

house and enter the woods to take a piss. Sanitation was going to be a problem if they didn't get power restored everywhere. Either that, or people needed to start digging holes for outhouses. The women would probably make sure something happened either way.

I counted twenty-two people. Enough people to make a village but I wasn't sure it was enough to make a village work None of the fields looked cultivated although there were a couple of gardens. I didn't see any sign of animals like cows and goats. Those had been devoured. No chickens either. Someone was going to make some serious money breeding livestock and selling them from what I had seen so far.

This told me they were being supplied. The question was by whom and from where. Were they a threat? What did they have? Was it worth letting the Horde know? Could it be taken? Damn, thinking about it made my head ache.

Too bad. This isn't about you, came from the inner voice I called "Mr. Responsible Pain In The Ass." Fortunately I didn't hear from him very often and almost never listened to him.

"Okay, guys. You ready to go meet the neighbors?"

Ricky said, "Yep," and Loco said, "Sure." They both looked at me, waiting, I guess, for me to tell them my plan. I didn't want to say, "Yeah. That's all I came up with." So I added, "Maybe they'll invite us for breakfast."

The two of them looked at each other, back at me, and grinned. Loco said, "Right."

We cut around the back side of the hill we were on so we could approach them from the road. No use advertising that we had been sitting up there spying on them. Some people might take that the wrong way.

We walked toward the town with me out front and Ricky and Loco back about six feet. Ricky and Loco liked wearing their rifles so they hung in front of their chests instead of slung over their shoulder the way I did. I understood why but I didn't care for it. They were totally focused on the rifle as their weapon of choice, something I considered a disadvantage.

Me, I figured if I was engaging people at rifle range then I had fucked up. I preferred getting up close. My range was fifteen feet or less. At that distance it was personal, which worked in my favor. I wasn't just a target then. I was a flesh-and-blood man who was armed and in range of more than just their eyeballs. I was there on all levels. They could smell me, see me, and read me on levels they probably were not even aware of. The reality that death was just a split second away and looking straight at them was unnerving to most people. Not all, but most. The ones that weren't unnerved were the ones I shot first.

I was thinking about this because we had been spotted and the lookout was beating on a trash can lid with a piece of wood. I noticed they had left their flag up all night. One less chore to do in the morning, I figured. Men came busting out the doors from a couple of houses, trying to dress while holding onto their rifles at the same time. Impressive it wasn't. I heard Loco snicker. Not a lot of body armor in this bunch.

While they rushed around, I realized we were going to have to tone down the military look some. Out here it made us stand out too much. Camouflage was the wrong camouflage. Looking around at the villagers approaching I realized modified L.L.Bean was what we wanted.

I slowed our pace down so I could watch as they got their shit together. It was sad. Max, or anyone else who led people with training and the weapons to use, would have gutted them. Either they didn't have anything worth taking, or they were backed by someone who had the muscle to make sure that whatever was taken was quickly recovered. Then again they could just be survivors trying to get by. I discounted that. Just getting by didn't cut it anymore. You didn't get participation awards anymore. Hell, second place was a hole in the ground if you were lucky.

A crow cawed somewhere off to my right. I cawed back, for no reason other than I felt like it. Not every bird belonged to Freya but increasingly I felt as if all crows belonged to me and my people. In front of us the village welcoming committee was forming. I noticed they were looking around as if they expected someone else to arrive any minute. That someone stumbled out of a house, noticed we were watching, slowed down, adjusted his robe and began walking toward us. He was armed with a black leather-bound Bible. *Truly a weapon of mass destruction,* I thought, *when deployed by the wrong people.*

We came to a stop. In the old days, and even older movies, a dog or two would be in the street barking and watching. Maybe a couple chickens working the dirt for bugs. Not in this world. They had all been eaten. The policy of neutering everything with four legs hadn't helped matters. Hell, if Woof was still intact he had a good chance of becoming immortal.

The others also slowed down their pace. They were trying to time their arrival to end up in front of us with Bible Man in the lead. Since he was going for dignified that meant they had no choice but to wait for him while we stood off from each other. Maybe twenty feet separated us. While we awaited his arrival we both studied each other.

It was, in many ways, a dance with each movement falling into an expected pattern. There were different movements depending on what music was selected but they almost always started off the same way. The greeting. This would determine the tempo of the second movement and whether or not there would be a third movement. Me, I listened to the music in my head, which seemed to be beamed in from another planet entirely. I was okay with that. I had to be. It was the only station I had.

Bible Man was interesting. The gray-streaked beard, the glittering eyes, the sense of purpose that you only get when you are truly freaking insane. He was a keeper. The other two flanking him had drunk from the same Kool-aide. Hell, Bible Man probably brewed and dispensed it for the community.

I grinned at him. Much to my delight he grinned back. I call it a grin. The reality was we had just shown each other our teeth in a socially acceptable kind of way. The two guys with him, and every man I had seen so far, had a beard if they could grow one. There were a lot of beards nowadays. Ricky had one. Loco tried but he was not from the first class beard-growing limb of the old genetic tree.

Me, I shaved. I wasn't good at it but I would rather scrape and cut myself than have a beard. Plus, Night didn't like them. I told her I shaved for her and reaped the benefits whenever I could which sure as hell wasn't much lately.

Bible Man focused my attention by starting the conversational ball rolling. "What do you want?" It was spoken in a half confrontational, half curious tone. I could understand that.

I replied, "So, you guys Amish?"

"No." He seemed insulted that I asked him that. "The Amish don't carry guns."

I thought about it for a few seconds and said, "Oh, I guess that is why we haven't seen any." He didn't like how the conversation was proceeding. I saw that plain as day on his face, probably because it wasn't going the way he had planned.

He tried again. "Why are you here?"

"Because it is on the road we are following." I kept a stone face when I answered him. I was starting to enjoy this and I decided to see how long I could continue. Plus, it sounded mystical. A guy like Bible Man should be able to appreciate that.

The guy on his right decided to jump in. He said, "Brother Thomas means, what do you want from us?"

Brother Thomas looked at him and snarled, "I will ask the questions here, Elder Bob."

228

As he did I learned a bit more about Brother Tom and decided I didn't like him. Not that I wasn't already prejudiced against the entire "Crackin Christy" subset of American Christianity.

Brother Tom decided to try another tack. "So, join us inside. We can provide clean cold water for you to drink, and we can talk." He went for a warm smile.

I smiled back and said, "Why, thank you, Brother"

CHAPTER TWENTY-SEVEN

We headed for the two-story building underneath the watchman's post. Brother Tom and I fell in step together and everyone trailed along after us. Behind me I could hear Elder Bob trying to chat up Loco and failing miserably, especially after Elder Bob told him, "We have beans we can trade. I know you people love them."

Brother Tom heard that and said, "You don't look like traders. Other than beans we don't have much to trade." I could tell by the way he emphasized that they didn't have much that he was talking to his people as well as to us.

"No, we are not traders. Rather we are an advance party for people who might be interested in trading with you," I told him as we came to the double doors that led inside the building. The wall was cracked in places from the impact of multiple rounds and the glass in the doors had been replaced by plywood with strips of metal to reinforce it.

Brother Tom saw me taking it in and said, "Yes. We had our share of troubles. Tell me more about this group that you say is following you."

"Well, not much to tell you really." I looked around. We were in a fairly large room that was empty except for a couple of picnic tables that had been pushed together to form one long table. About halfway down the table were a pair of nice silver salt-and-pepper shakers. There was a china cabinet, which held dishes, and a side table that was empty. At the head of the table was a rough-hewn wooden chair that looked a lot like a throne. I was sure the resemblance was on purpose. On the wall behind it was another version of the same flag that was flying outside. This one was actually a satin bed sheet that had been spray-painted. Whoever did it had held the nozzle too close and the paint had run.

Brother Tom sat in the throne-like chair at the head of the table, of course. Elder Bob sat on his right, and Brother Tom gestured for me to sit on his left. His four men, who had followed us in, took their seats beyond the salt-and-pepper shakers. The empty space in between was supposed to be filled by Ricky and Loco.

Ricky was starting to sit down when Loco growled at him. Loco walked away from the table and took up position against the wall by an open door that probably led to a kitchen. Ricky started to take the same wall but Loco looked at the far wall and back at him. Damn, he was slow about some shit but he got the message and moved over to the far wall by the china cabinet. Brother Tom did not like this at all. He opened his mouth, thought about the loss of face involved, and shut it. Inwardly I grinned.

"So where are you coming from? You know how it is. We don't get the news the way we used to." He smiled. I am sure he thought it was his best "talk to me" smile. Before I could say anything he banged on the table with his fist and yelled, "Woman! Where the hell are you? You've got thirsty men in here. Bring us some water!"

He continued. "I am sorry that all we have to offer is water but this is a poor village. Perhaps we could convince you to tithe a small amount to the church. You are good Christians, are you not?" Oh yeah. His boys hadn't missed a word of what was being said and surely popped a woody of nonverbal delight over the implication apparent in his comment.

"Well, Brother Tom, you know there are many roads that lead to the Father's house." I remembered hearing someone say that once and liked it. It had lots of weasel in it without being nasty.

He thought about it for a second, or pretended to, then he said, "Yes, but there is only one God and one true path." He smiled at me. Then he again yelled, "Water! Woman, get your ass in here now!"

I heard her voice say, "Coming!" before I saw her. That was a good thing. I needed the extra moment it gave me. A cold wave splashed over me and a jolt of pure energy lit up my nervous system.

Carol came through the door struggling with a five-gallon plastic container two-thirds full of water. Another woman, right behind her carrying coffee mugs on a silver serving tray, said, "Sorry, Brother Thomas. This stupid bitch, I mean woman, had problems with the pump."

She curtsied, set the cups on the table and told Carol, "Don't splash the water all over the place when you pour."

Carol looked like shit. She probably hadn't been that skinny since she was twelve. Her hair was dull but when she looked at me, for a second before dropping them, her eyes told me she was still alive.

I slid my legs up over the seat and dropped them on the floor. Then I bent down and began retying my boots. I had to. I knew if anyone saw my face then it would begin. It would begin soon, just not until she was out of the room.

I heard her bare feet move across the floor as she left the room and Brother Tom ask, "Do you have a problem with women knowing their place amongst your people?" I didn't look at him first. Instead I looked at his men and then at Loco.

I heard Loco say softly, "Holy shit." Then I turned to Brother Tom and said, "No. Not at all."

Brother Tom did not like the look on my face. I'm not sure why not. I was smiling my happy smile.

Much later and a thousand miles west of here I overheard a new member ask one of the vets, "Does Gardener ever smile?" His question was greeted by silence, and then one of the old timers replied, "Kid, you don't ever want to be around when he smiles." Another voice added, "When he starts smiling, people die." Then they began arguing about whether or not my eyes changed color, too. I quietly turned, walked away, and when I was sure no one was looking at me, I laughed. They thought I smiled because I enjoyed killing.

The killing isn't what made me smile. In fact that part rarely registered with me. I smiled because of how good it felt to walk the edge. I didn't feel more "alive" so much as I felt completely focused. Everything that made me who I was - all the software, all the hardware - began running at peak capacity. All the internal bullshit, all the nagging pains in my body, and all the doubts disappeared, and I knew. I mean I *knew* what had to be done. Usually that meant killing pieces of shit masquerading as human beings. I was okay with that.

I was especially okay with it right now. I reached back, gripped the hilt, and slid Sword from its sheath. I had learned through practicing this move that if I did it exactly right it sang a very nice metallic zing song as I did. I loved that. I smiled a little more and Brother Tom's eyes widened a whole lot. Not for very long. My right hand gripped the hilt next to my left; I pivoted and swung into him. His head separated cleanly but the wood used in building his throne was made of better stuff. I left the blade buried in the wood and drew both the Ruger and the Colt, firing as I did. Elder Bob's soul was only a step or two behind his leader's, as were the souls of the rest of his loyal brethren sitting with us.

I looked around the room and inhaled the smell of blood and gunpowder. Perhaps two seconds had passed. It was time to move. Loco and Ricky were staring at me. Well, they could still earn their keep.

"Ricky! Block the door." I wanted one of the picnic tables in front of the door we had come in. "Loco! On me." I retrieved my sword and headed for the door Carol had gone through.

Loco understood what I wanted. I hoped Ricky did. Loco went through the door and cut right. As soon as he did, the doorjamb and part of the wall exploded. Someone had a shotgun. That meant I had next to no time to clear it before they cycled another round. I dove through the doorway, somersaulted, and slammed into the woman who had just fired the shotgun. She went down in a heap and I got a good look at unshaven legs and stained underwear before I shot her.

We were in the kitchen. Someone was screaming over by the stainless steel table to my left. Loco was up and I watched as he sent a three round burst toward the back door. I holstered the handguns and struggled to unsling the Marlin. Somehow in my semi-somersault move the sling had tangled up in all the crap I carried on my belt now. I yanked hard and snapped the swivel.

Shit. I could worry about that later. Whoever was screaming by the stainless steel table finally shut up which was very nice of them. I looked over at Loco and he signed to me that he was headed out the back door.

I signed back "wait" and yelled, "Carol!"

From behind the stainless steel table two heads popped up. One was Carol's. The other was a scared and pissed-off girl of maybe sixteen who was trying to pry Carol's hand away from covering her mouth. I pulled the Colt and tossed it underhand to Carol. She caught it nicely but she had to let go of the girl who began screaming "Help!" Carol clubbed her with the Colt. The screamer disappeared and Carol grinned. Her teeth had turned yellow but the smile was still great.

My lost focus was restored by the sound of several bursts of gunfire coming from Ricky's side. *Shit.* I would have liked to get a look from above to see what was happening outside but my Freya connection was on the blink. I had noticed that once we put more than forty miles between us, the connection was

234

sporadic. Our goddess, at least at this point, was about as reliable as most cell phone phones were back when the Burners were taking down cell phone towers every day.

Well, shit. I was paid the big bucks to make these kinds of decisions. Behind the table was a stainless steel sink and counter. Above them was a window. Going out the door was stupid at a time such as this. I pointed at the window and gave Loco the "two" sign. Two minutes, two seconds, two whatevers. Then I pointed at the door. Hopefully he understood. I wanted him to go out the door after I went out the window and distracted whoever was out there.

He nodded, and I started running. I leaped, launched off the table, and went through the window with the Marlin reversed and the wooden butt making contact with the glass first. It was not pretty. It was real glass not spun sugar like Hollywood uses. A jagged piece of glass raked across my arm and I knew it was going to be added to my collection of scars.

I remember watching a football player being interviewed about how he felt on Monday after a game. His reply was that he woke up every Monday feeling as if he had been a car wreck the previous day. That pretty much summed up how I usually felt after a day like this.

I might hurt tomorrow but right now I was juiced and flying. I hit the grass and weeds outside the building and came up looking for targets. It was not a problem finding them as I almost landed on a guy who thought looking through the window was a good idea. It wasn't for him.

I jacked the lever action on the Marlin and looped wide around the corner. There were three more of them forming up in a stack to go through the door. I shot the guy who was watching the others' backs. He was quick. I was lucky that he shot high. I dropped the Marlin and drew both of the Rugers. That was good for both of them and Loco sealed the deal by shooting through the wall. Kind of sloppy but effective.

235

I yelled, "Clear!" and then spun around to make sure it really was. Loco came out the door fast, saw me, cut to the left, and fell awkwardly to the ground. I had forgotten about the guy on the roof. I looked up, saw him backlit from the sun - a black silhouette, and shot him. *That was too fucking close, you idiot,* I thought as I ran toward Loco who was struggling to get back on his feet while holding his arm. "Inside!" I yelled, my voice croaking from dryness as we headed back in.

I dropped him with Carol who looked pretty calm considering everything that was going on around her. Then I want to see what was up with Ricky.

Nothing was. He was dead. I counted two bodies in the door and one outside. He had died with his weapon in his hands so he was guaranteed a seat in Freya Heaven. At least that was what she said. Me, I wasn't in any hurry to find out. I took a second to put a compress on my arm where I had cut myself and started checking the perimeter.

The first thing I did was find the ladder the lookout used to get up to the roof and climbed up to take a look around. Off to the east, about two blocks away, I saw two pickup trucks pull out onto the county road and haul ass away from town. Good fucking riddance. It also meant that we needed to get moving. Like soon.

I went back down the ladder and realized I was hearing noise. People noise. I walked around the building puzzled and a bit pissed at myself thinking, *I forgot the rooftop guy. What else did I miss?*

The sounds were coming from a storm cellar with big weathered wooden doors almost flat to the surface of the ground. They were secured by a long bolt with a nut at the end that kept it from slipping through the twin handles. I looked at the door handles and listened to the voices crying. All I heard were female ones.

Visions of basements past went through my head and took with it any sense of invincibility I still harbored. Instead cold dread and immense sadness washed over and through me. A little voice said, *You don't have to do this. You know that, don't you?*

I thought, *Fuck you, little voice,* unscrewed the nut, and flung open one of the doors as I stepped to the side.

Their heads appeared like gophers blinking in the light. All three were female and the oldest looked to be twenty-six years old but having seen a hundred too many ugly things. Their clothes were dirty, and, like Carol, they had done made it to skinny and were gaining on emaciated. I stood there looking down on them, my guns drawn, and I almost felt foolish.

The oldest one said, "Hey."

I replied, "Hey. That all of you?"

"Yep."

"Thank you, Jesus!" shot through my head. I was going to have to check, but I wasn't going to do it right away.

The little blond, a real one at that, asked me in a whisper, "Are you one of the Blessed?"

I kind of laughed and replied, "Probably not the way you mean it. If you mean a local peckerhead, then nope, I'm not."

She replied, "Good." They started climbing out and I backed up to give them some room. I didn't holster the Rugers yet.

The oldest one smiled when she saw that and said, "Not the trusting sort, are you?"

I replied, "You know anyone who is alive that is?" She didn't have an answer, which was answer enough.

I herded them into the building and when they saw Carol they squealed, yelled her name, and ran stiff-legged to her. I followed along behind them and saw she had patched up Loco. The girl she had knocked upside the head was still out. Not a good sign. Carol looked up and smiled. When she looked past me, I saw the smile fade.

237

I squatted down next to her and asked Loco, "How you doing?"

He grinned. "Not bad. It missed the bone." He looked around. "Ricky?" I shook my head and his grin disappeared. "Aw shit."

I told him, "Yeah well, he took three with him."

Loco nodded and said, "Yeah. That was some crazy shit, G." I shrugged. There wasn't much to say about it. It was what it was.

Carol said, "Let me look at your arm, Gardener." While she did she casually asked, "So, where is Max?" She kept her head down when she asked so I couldn't see her eyes. It was just as well. She couldn't see mine either because in asking that enough had already been said between us.

Later I stripped Ricky of his CamelBak. He wouldn't need it anymore. I had Loco search the bodies while Carol and her friends searched the houses for anything of value. I didn't let them go too far because we hadn't checked every house. I was gambling on my sense that everything, at least for now, was good. What was making me antsy was the feeling that it wasn't going to last.

While they did that, I dug a shallow grave for Ricky. It wasn't much and he deserved better. When I got done I found everyone and we held a brief service. I said, "In Freya's name we bury this warrior. May he meet us at the gates when we arrive. Amen."

Then I got everyone moving. As I did I heard one of Carol's girls ask, "Who the hell is Freya?"

She replied, "Why do you care? If Gardener is okay with it, then you should be."

CHAPTER TWENTY-EIGHT

I wanted to hear Carol's story, and the other girls'. I also wanted to know more about the cult or whatever the hell it was here. That was going to have to wait.

I pulled Loco aside and asked, "What do you think?" I didn't have to qualify my question or go into detail. He knew what I was asking.

He looked up at the sky, pursed his lips, did a quick scan of the horizon and where the sun was, and said, "Get out of town, off the roads, and up on a hill for now. After that it's your call."

"Yeah. I don't think we are going to be able to push them hard." He nodded. I added, "We're also going to need to feed them sometime."

"Yep."

I looked around. The closest good hill was about three miles away. Once we made that I would think about our next move. I indicated the hill and told him, "That's it. You got point."

I found Carol, told them the plan, and told her crew to drop about half the crap they were carrying. When the women grumbled, I looked at them and said, "Keep up. Shut up. We can do this." They all nodded tight-lipped. I still didn't know what happened here but they seemed very okay with leaving it behind. "You okay, Carol?"

She replied, "Yeah. Let's get the hell out of here."

"Okay. Follow Loco."

I took a knee and watched them go. I was going to give them a long lead. If anyone came hunting us I wanted the women away from the first contact. I noticed nobody looked back.

I looked at the town. I should do something special to let the people coming know we were not people to trifle with. I laughed out loud and said it again. I loved the phrase, "not people to trifle with." I was bad. Yes I was.

I was also alone. I ended up using the spray paint we carried to leave markers for the Horde scouts who screened the main body advance. I spray-painted "Freya Cometh!" on a wall. The hell with it. I was going to have to work on the scary calling card part.

I started pushing my bike toward the hill. I was almost to the hill when I got a bad feeling and froze in place. I waited a bit and then slowly eased down into the grass and waited. When it felt right I crawled to a small rise and looked around it back at the town. They had come in on foot from somewhere outside of town, probably from the north. No blowing into town yelling and hooting from the packed bed of a pickup truck. Someone had their shit together. That was not good.

It took me another forty-five minutes to make the last half-mile to the hill. I wanted to avoid any chance of being spotted. I also had to leave my bike. I figured I could go back for it later. That was going to be another problem along with what do with Carol and her friends. *Hell,* I thought, *we'll have to take them back.* That made me smile because it meant I would get to see Night. I was okay with that.

I ran across Loco before I found the rest of them. I gave him the hand sign for "multiple enemy", and he nodded and pointed at his binoculars. I followed him in. He had armed all the women with the weapons we'd had them carry off from the town. Hopefully they knew what they were doing. The odds were pretty good that they did. My guess was that for the first time in over a hundred years, what remained of the American

240

population was proficient with firearms. It was somewhat jarring to see Carol armed. She seemed pretty comfortable with a weapon, too.

I settled down and drank some water. Loco took the first watch. I would take the second, which would last until just before dawn. I was going to be dragging tomorrow and probably hurting

After Loco disappeared into the bush Carol and I sat there studying each other. I don't know what she saw but I saw the same woman I had known for years but the etching around the eyes and the eyes themselves belonged to a different person. She was the same but not the same.

I was thinking about that when she told me, "Show me that arm. I want to clean that gash again." She pulled off the wrapping and we both looked at it. Stitches would be better but I told her to butterfly it for now. She started cleaning it out. I looked at the top of her head as she bent over my arm and wondered how soft her hair would feel under my hand.

I pushed that thought aside and asked, "So how was it, Carol? How did you end up here?"

She stopped for a minute. I was getting ready to say, "Don't worry about it. Some other time," when she sighed.

She said, "I really hoped I would run into you or Max. It was...ugly, Gardener. No. Not ugly. Beyond ugly." Then she began telling me her story. The three women behind her lay silently in the grass and watched us both as she began to talk.

She went off on a tangent that surprised me. Well, no, actually it didn't. I figured she would wait a little while before bringing him up again. I should have known better. Carol was always direct and to the point.

"Loco says Max is a big warlord now. He is leading over a hundred people." She asked me, "Is this true?"

"Yep," I replied.

A little softer she asked, "And he has a woman?"

241

"Yep."

Something was up. I could see her mind whirling away. She may be Carol but I wasn't the same Gardener she once knew. At least that was what I wanted to believe.

"Okay. You want to hear how I got here. I owe you that. Then I want to ask a favor of you. Will you listen all the way to the end of my story before you ask me any questions?"

I shrugged. "Sure, Carol."

She looked at me. I mean really looked at me. I don't know if she felt it. Probably not, but I did. The connection was still there and it powered up as if it had never been shut down. Life truly is a complicated bitch sometimes.

She took a deep breath. I watched her breasts rise and fall. *Need to focus* went through my head. Even underweight she was still beautiful.

"You guys left and I went home. I talked to Bobby and we decided to start getting it together. You know, just in case." I nodded my head and so did the women seated behind her. "Anyway, we didn't have a lot of money. Bobby had been out of work for a while. We had been making ends meet with venison he was killing and selling. Plus, the kids...ah shit..." One of the women reached out and patted her back. "I think I am going to skip some parts here and there, Gardener." She looked up at me and I saw her eyes were shining.

"You don't have to say anything more, Carol," I told her. I was curious but not curious enough to have her open up the doors to rooms best sealed off. I had seen and heard enough to know how bad this story could be.

"No. I am going to tell you this story and you are going to listen!"

I held up my hands, smiled, and said, "Okay, tell me."

The flare-up passed as quickly as it had come. She said, "When the power went down I didn't think it was a big deal. Nobody did. It happened all the time." She shrugged. "We did what we always did at the shelter. We made do. It wasn't until, I

242

think, the fourth or fifth day without power that things started getting weird. You know how it is. Nobody knows anything but that doesn't stop them from spreading stories. You know. 'It was worldwide. It was national. It was terrorists. It was space aliens.' Whatever it was, it wasn't getting fixed and even worse, it didn't look as if it would anytime soon."

Carol continued. "Then the hoarding started. The people with money and connections - they did okay at first. The rest of us, well, it was getting tight. Real tight. The Army was driving around in Humvees with loudspeakers telling everyone not to panic. They said, 'Food is on the way.' But it never came. At least not in our area." The last was delivered with bitter venom.

"The Army came and told me they were closing the shelter. They said everyone was going to be moved to Camp Victory. You know, the one out by Ft. Belvoir."

I nodded and said, "Yeah, I heard that one really sucked."

"Gardener," she said, exasperated, "they all sucked."

I laughed. "Yeah. Some sucked more than others, Carol."

She ignored me. I remembered her ability to do that and mentally sighed.

"So I told the girls if they had somewhere to go then they better go. Sometimes I think I could have done better by them. Sometimes, you know, I think I could have brought the ones with babies home with me. But I was worried. Worried about my family. So I told myself they would be okay and I left them."

She stopped talking and was crying for real now. Jesus, I hated the sound of that. One of the women glared at me as if it was my fault or I was supposed to be doing something. Hell, I never knew how to deal with this stuff.

I reached out and put my arm around her. I felt her move toward me, then stiffen, and pull back just a little. I awkwardly let my arm drop. She had her fist jammed into her mouth so hard that when she pulled it out I saw teeth marks on it.

"Sorry, Gardener. I don't like to be touched by...men anymore."

She took a deep breath and continued her story. "So, me and Bobby, we lived up on the mountain. We organized our neighbors and got as ready as we could. Bobby taught our two boys to shoot. Well, as much as he could with the time we had and the ammo shortage. I thought we would be all right, Gardener. I really did. Then the people came. We tried warning them off. At first I thought they would flow around us. There was just so many of them and they got to be such assholes as time went by. We had nothing to give them but they didn't believe us. We had the people and the mountain on our side at first."

Carol sighed. "We wore down, Gardener. They didn't beat us. They just wore us down. It was like, for some of them, they didn't care if we had nothing. It was what they wanted to do. Like it was a game. Overrunning us wasn't about food or anything. They just wanted to hurt us at the end I think. Bobby, he fought like a lion."

She paused, looked at me, and said, "You would have been proud of him. I know I was. It wasn't enough. We lived at the top on the west side of the mountain. It's woods until you come down on that side and then it's farmers' fields all the way to Front Royal just about. We didn't think we would have to run for it. We kept expecting the Army to come. I guess we were out of their goddamn zone."

One of the women behind her laughed mirthlessly and mumbled, "Fucking Zones."

Carol said, "They didn't come. We saw them overhead a few times. You know, helicopters. Once I saw a little plane. Bobby said it was probably a Cessna. I don't know. I just know they never came. We had radios. You know, AM and FM. Dakota John over on the next street had a short wave that he ran off a car battery. We heard that the government had the situation contained and relief was being dispatched. I don't know where

244

the hell they sent it but it wasn't where we lived." That wasn't surprising to hear.

"We started running, no, make that we had run out of food. It was getting cold and it was getting really obvious we were not going to be able hold the line. I think if it had been just Bobby he would have stayed until they killed him. It wasn't just him but he was still bothered about going. He called it 'bugging out.' He did it anyway. He was worried about the boys and me. We were hearing some ugly things. Sometimes people would scream at us, 'We're going to eat you!' I thought they were kidding. The funny thing is they were not as bad off as some of the people we ran across later." She shuddered.

"So we bailed. Bobby said if we planned on eating we were going to have to go while we still had some ammunition to shoot. Our plan was to head for Front Royal. We had friends there. And the radio said the government had a processing center and a camp there. We didn't want to go into one but my kids were hungry." She looked at me and said, "You know I had two boys, right?"

"Yeah." I searched my mind. I had seen the drawings in her office and the photographs. Names, crap, what were their names? Then I saw an image of stick figures of a family and a dog done in magic marker. The name at the bottom was Kyle.

I blurted, "Kyle!" Then I thought, *Oh hell, please don't let that be the dog's name.*

She smiled. That was nice to see. "Kyle. He was my youngest. He was six." The smile disappeared. "He didn't make it. His brother, Zane, he's eight."

I hadn't seen any kids with her. I had a feeling that I wasn't going to. No sign of Bobby either. Her voice, which had been almost animated, well, at least it sounded alive, changed to a flat monotone. She looked around and seemed briefly startled.

Then she said, "I'm sorry, Gardener. Please bear with me. I will try and speed it up."

I held up my hand. "Take as long as you want, Carol. I'm not going anywhere." Loco didn't know it yet but he might be on watch longer than he planned.

"Bobby died right after my youngest. I almost lost it, Gardener." She laughed. Well, she might have thought it was a laugh. It sounded like a harsh croaking. Actually she wouldn't have to work very hard at talking to the crows if she could make that sound whenever she wanted.

"Maybe I did. It was a hard time." She looked at me. "You know how it was. Anybody who is still alive knows how it was." The women behind her grunted and said a chorus of "Amens" behind her.

"Yeah, Carol. I know." What else was I going to say? It was tough beating Freya to all the cinnamon desserts?

"Me and Zane did it. Nobody ate my kid! We were lucky for a while. We hooked up with a road crew that had some good people in it. Yeah, we did things, but we survived. If there is a God I know he will understand." She didn't sound real positive about that though.

I wanted to tell her she needed a new god but, like everything else I wanted to say, this wasn't the time or the place.

"Then things went to hell again. We jacked the wrong convoy and the Army finally showed up. I guess we were getting too good at it. It was the Army police, except they sure weren't armed or acting like police. They chewed through us like a buzzsaw. No arrests were made either." She shook her head. "So what was left of us, which wasn't much, ran for it. We ran right into the arms of the Brethren."

"The Brethren. May they rot in the Hell they so love to talk about." She paused and once again her chorus seated behind her sung their affirmations of her righteousness. "You know anything about them, Gardener?"

I shook my head and said, "I could make some guesses."

She cawed again. "I doubt it. They are special. You know my Bobby was black, right?"

246

"Yeah," I replied. "More like tan. As if anyone cares."

"Yeah. Some people care. The Brethren especially. I mean not all of them, but enough to matter. They also believe women, especially unbaptized and unsealed ones, are second class citizens." Yeah, the chorus agreed with that. "I could live with that. Hell, I did. What I can't live with is they took my boy from me."

She reached out, grabbed my arm in a grip of steel tendons and ceramic bone, focused those eyes directly on me, and said, "You have got to get my boy back. Please!"

Everyone but me held their breath. I just looked at her. She whispered, "Please..."

I didn't think it through. I didn't worry about the ramifications. I just said, "Sure."

Her grin and the hug that followed were nice. Almost nice enough to silence the voice in my head that told me I was an idiot.

She pulled back, looked at me, and said, "I wasn't sure if you would."

I shrugged, and said, "Hell, Carol. It's what I do." The chorus was making a big deal of it and they were all grinning from ear to ear. Dental hygiene had slipped badly since PowerDown. I was glad when they turned it down a notch or two.

"So, Carol. Where is he?" I asked. I don't know why but I figured he was in the next town over.

"I don't know."

"Oh. Okay. You have a rough idea?"

"Sort of. I think he is east of here." She paused. "About a hundred miles." She was starting to look a little anxious.

"Okay. You got a picture?" I asked her. She looked down. Her hair fell forward and I wanted to brush it back.

She said, "No. I lost all my pictures."

I thought, *Well, this is going to be a little more difficult than I thought.* I was also getting a little bit irritated. I fought to keep it out of my voice and asked calmly, "Can you describe him? Does he have any distinguishing marks? Scars?"

She must have heard the irritation in my voice because she said, defensively, "I will recognize him!"

I thought about that for a couple of seconds, and then I said quietly, "You are not going. If I do this, I'll do it alone. Think about it. He has to have a scar or something. Do you have anything of his he would recognize?"

She stared at me with her eyes welling up. Damn. Maybe she was right. Maybe she had lost it.

I stood up and said, "I have to relieve Loco. Think about it, Carol. Give me something to work with." Then I turned away and went to find Loco.

CHAPTER TWENTY-NINE

Loco was surprised to see me. I was early. I guess he saw the look on my face because he didn't argue. He just went. I wasn't thrilled with our location. It was too damn close to the town. I would have pushed us on through the night but despite what Carol and her friends had seen and done I doubted night marches were one of them. My night version was outstanding compared to someone from pre-PowerDown times. Now I was finding it was damn near miraculous. Vitamin deficiency had really taken its toll on most people's night vision.

I took up my position, relaxed, and let myself drift out into the fields surrounding us. I was looking for anomalies. I am not sure how to describe it. I was good at it, almost as good as Max, who had taught me how to do it. He was still far better at moving in the woods though. Part of that ability can be taught, part of it is mental, and another part is just a gift that you either have or don't have. I didn't have it and I had accepted that I didn't. I don't think I was mentally wired for it. I liked to roll out and go too much.

Carol was quiet, but nowhere near the level she would have to be now to run with us. I heard her pause about twenty feet from me and whisper, "Gardener..." I fought back the flash of anger I felt. This was really stupid of her on so many different levels.

I slipped over to where she was and said, "What?" just before she called my name again. I startled the hell out of her, which I have to admit I enjoyed.

"Damn, Gardener...you" I cut her off by holding my finger up to my lips.

Then I said, "Try being a little quieter, Carol." She nodded her head, and I whispered, "What?" She looked at a loss for words, something I had never seen before. She looked good in the moonlight. I doubt if she could see me as well as I could her. This was good. I could stare at her breasts more openly, especially as she had her blouse open a couple extra buttons, which was strange. I thought, *Maybe the buttons fell off or she doesn't realize it.*

While I was hoping she would drop something she said, "I have one of his t-shirts. He would recognize that. Plus, I can give you a good description. He has a scar on his left arm that is very noticeable."

Okay, fine, I thought. She could have told me this later. I was getting ready to wave her back and whisper "Later" when she hit me with the high beams.

She opened her blouse, cupped the twin delights, and said, "Can you see these, Gardener? They're yours to have." She hesitated, then added, "And much more."

They were beautiful. She was beautiful. Not all that long ago I would have been a happy man moving rapidly toward being ecstatic. Not now. Instead all I felt was sadness. Well, mostly sadness.

I sighed and said, "No, Carol. Not like this. I'll find the boy but...no. Please go."

What made it worse was the relief I saw in her eyes. If she had pushed it I probably would have gone for it. The expression of relief I saw, though, was like a knife in my heart. I turned and slipped back to where I had been and listened to her snap sticks all the way back to where the others were.

I watched, rather I attempted to watch, but my focus was gone. I relived the moment over and over. I came up with different things I could have said. I sure thought about different things I could have done. Yet, behind them all was the look I had seen in her eyes.

Then I started thinking about Night. I realized that perhaps my going off to find Carol's kid might not go over very well. I began to get angry. Angry at myself. Angry at how complicated everything had to be. Angry at Carol. Why was there relief in her eyes? Was I that unappealing? Was something hanging out of my nose?

The night went far too fast. I was feeling as reluctant to face the dawn as I used to when I was coming off a night spent getting wasted. *Oh well,* I told myself. *Shit happens.* It wasn't comforting.

I reached out mentally for Freya, half hoping I wouldn't get her. Of course I did. Nice and clear, too. The Horde had rolled some distance since the last time we had talked. As usual she appeared in a window inside my head, my webcam goddess. She was in a good mood. As usual we dispensed with formalities.

"Hey, Freya."

"My! My! I like the artwork. Couldn't you have cut off some heads?" She flashed me an image of what the main Horde had done earlier to a village. Heads on poles and burning houses.

"Yeah, well, I was in a bit of a hurry." I sent her my images.

"Too clean, Gardener. I understand the rush but you need to find the time to leave our trademark."

"I got it, Freya. Heads on poles and 'Freya' written in blood."

"Yes. I like the blood part especially. So what's up? You want to talk to Max and Night?" I could hear the amusement in her voice. "Or just Night?"

I realized that I had better lock away the images of last night's unveiling. This was going to be complicated enough as it was.

"No. I need all three of you on. Can you do that right now?"

"Sure! Hang on." Damn, she was chipper. I guess getting your name written in blood was a good thing when you were a goddess. I was going to have to check her teeth next time I saw her. Maybe she had vampire in her. My musing was interrupted as Night and Max came on line.

"G!" The blast of affection, hell, love, from Night was so focused that it literally rocked me back a step.

"Hi, Night. Hey, Max."

Night knew right away. "What's wrong?"

Well, this was going to fun for Max, too, I thought. I felt his eyes narrow. Damn, he must have caught that. Then I started sending images. As soon as Carol flashed by I felt Night mentally stiffen and become more guarded.

Max, that asshole, didn't act as if it was a big deal. All he said was, "Nice work."

Night knew something was up. I have no clue how she did since I didn't send the part where Carol had asked me to find her kid. I had wanted to do that "live" so to speak, but now I had to explain what Carol had asked of me and how I had agreed to look for her son. Then I waited for the storm.

It didn't come the way I expected. Freya was unreadable which she could do. An unfair advantage I always thought. Max was amused but underneath that was anger. He was doing a good job of masking it, but I still felt and heard it.

Night wasn't angry. She was livid. "That worthless, cheating, no good bitch. I am going to cut her fucking throat and pull her tongue out through the slit. She fucking played you but she sure as hell isn't going to play me." All this was as cold as steel and empty of anything but the desire to do exactly what she said she was going to do. Then she switched to Chinese. I really wished I had a mute button then. She flipped back to English and I could feel her eyes boring into me.

"Did you fuck her?"

I opened up. I hoped I was doing it just for her. It wasn't where I had wanted to go but I realized if I didn't I would lose her. It stopped her dead. I heard her whisper, "Oh, G..." I waited. I knew there was going to be more.

"Keep her out of my sight, Max!" Then Night was gone. Everyone was silent for a couple of seconds.

Then I said, "Well, that went over nicely." Only Max laughed and that wasn't for very long or very loud.

Freya stayed silent. After about forty seconds she said, "Fine. This can work to our benefit. I see possibilities forming already." I felt her attention focus on me. I mean, really focus.

She said, "Do you two realize yet what I expect of you?" I'm glad it was a rhetorical question and she kept going because I was getting ready to answer, "Good personal hygiene?"

"Max, you will be a General and you will lead the Horde in battle. And such a battle it will be - one that will be spoken of for a thousand years. You, Gardener. You will never lead an army. Yet you will also be known," she paused, and then said, "as my Champion. You are Fire and Steel." She paused, and then said, "I would expect nothing less of you, Gardener. You would no longer be you if you had answered her in any other way."

Her words rang in the space between us. My first thought was to say, "Thanks, Coach." Instead I said, "Send me the dogs, Freya. I want Woof."

Her reply was what I wanted to hear. "It will be done."

We did the usual predawn stand up with everyone awake. Carol wasn't meeting my eyes I noticed. Fine. I didn't really need the distraction right now. I pulled Loco aside and told him the new plan.

"You're going to be leading the ladies back to the Horde. They're about thirty-two miles east of us and headed our way. You will probably meet them in less than ten miles. Max will tell you what's up after that."

He raised an eyebrow and said, "What about you?"

"I'm going with you until we are about five miles out from them. Then I'm splitting off on a secret mission."

He grinned. "Going to look for Carol's kid, huh?"

I should have known. Nothing stays secret. "Yeah. Until then we're going to loop around the town and stay off the roads. I am going to get a view hopefully in the next few minutes of what is between us and the Horde. I want to avoid trouble. If we have to sit down and shut up for awhile, that's what we'll do. I'll take point. I want you on drag. Put whoever you think has a clue behind me. We leave in ten minutes."

I headed away. I wanted to take a leak and hook up with the goddess cam away from everyone when Loco said, "Hey, G."

"Yeah?"

"Two might be better than one..."

I was surprised, maybe even touched. I walked back to him, put out my hand so I could shake his, and then let him pull me in for quick embrace. "Thanks. If I was going to take anyone, it would be you." Then I went off I to find my spot. I finished, zipped up, and put in the call. She was there within a second.

"Hey, Freya."

"Hey, Gardener. Guess what?"

"What?"

She said excitedly, "We found some chocolate!"

"Really?"

"Yeah! And I ate almost all of it!" She laughed delightedly.

"Thanks for sharing that with me," I replied dryly.

"No problem," she replied. She laughed again and then asked, "You want a bird?"

"Yeah. From where I am back to you in sweeps. Ya'll made a contact lately?"

"Nothing major." She sent a few images of a fire-blackened truck. "Someone tried to push past the point." She didn't add anything else. "Okay. I'm going to have to use a couple birds.

254

I'll send you what I can see in your area now and whatever I can do as you move." Then she was gone.

CHAPTER THIRTY

Moving everyone went about how I expected. The women were used to hardship and they knew where they were going was better than where they had been so their spirits were good. They were better at moving in the woods than most people were prior to PowerDown but they had no idea how to move as soldiers. They didn't have their eyes where they needed to be. They were wary rather than watchful.

When we stopped to take a break, Carol sought me out. Everyone knew something was going on between us. That was obvious from the way their eyes followed the both of us. That was probably the biggest problem I had with living in close quarters with people. Everything became amplified. Emotions echoed and ricocheted. It was annoying.

She sat down next to me and said, "I'm sorry."

I told her, "Not a problem," and smiled.

She looked at me, searching for clues, I suppose, on how to play it. Then with the directness I always admired in her, she dug into her bag of belongings, well, mostly other people's belongings she had looted on our way out. She dug out a small t-shirt and handed it to me. "This is Zane's." Then she began reciting her facts: "He is four foot five, and he is skinny. He has blondish brown hair and he always looks tan."

No kidding, I thought.

She continued. "He has a four-inch scar on his right arm from when we were crossing all those fields. Damn farmers love their barbed wire. I was lucky. We still had some Neosporin left. And he was healthier then. I am pretty sure he is in West Virginia now. Some Army Colonel has his own private kingdom out there. He has ties to the Brethren and a few other groups including what is left of the government. He supposedly isn't a slaver or a racist. He just wants young men like my son to raise. I heard talk that he wants to build a new Sparta, whatever the hell that means."

She stopped. I assumed she was done so I got up. As I did she grabbed my arm and then let it go just as quickly. It was daytime and she could see my eyes now. The anger left me when I saw the need in hers.

"Find my boy, Gardener. Please."

I bit back what I wanted to say and instead gave her what I hoped was a reassuring grin. "Sure." Then I told everyone else, "Let's move."

We moved on. Freya hit me with a quick update at one point. I was glad she did. I wasn't focusing the way I needed to be. I kept going back and forth between the problem of returning to the land of the Colonel and how the hell I was going to pull that one off, and the problem of Carol herself. The only way I could see that working was to return with her son, then take them both and split off from the Horde.

I knew that was bullshit. I saw the look in her eyes. I had also felt the rush of Night's love when she was online. I finally did what I do best with problems like this. I made my mind go still, led the Carol image into a room, and shut the door on it. I had a lot of rooms like that. Some I hadn't visited in years.

I wasn't going all the way in to meet the Horde. I figured we would bump into the Horde screening element and I would turn it over to Loco and head to West Virginia. Perhaps detour into Brethren country to see if I could pick up a trail. There had to be some kind of network or formalized way of trading surplus kids for whatever the Colonel was paying that week.

I picked up the screening team about an hour later. Actually the bird picked them up earlier and I had guessed where they would be based on our rate of travel. I saw them before they saw me, which gave me the advantage. I wasn't going in for a kill but I didn't mind patting myself on the back sometimes either, especially when it came to my skill in sneaking around in the woods.

I stopped about fifty feet from where they were laid out and said, "Okay. Ya'll can come out now." Ninja rose up from a clump of bushes about fifteen feet from where I stood. I stopped patting myself on the back.

"Ninja!" I was happy to see him. It felt as if it had been forever. We embraced and I held up my fist and flashed the "hold in place" sign, which I belatedly realized none of the new people would understand. Someone must have understood it behind me as no one pushed forward. Ninja and I stepped under the canopy of the oak trees growing along the edge of the streambed I had been following. No sense in standing out in the open.

"Hey, G! Damn. How's life? I missed the connection the other day." He grinned. "I was busy."

"Busy? Oh yeah. How are you and she doing?" Damn if I could remember the name of the girl he had picked up at the bridge coming into Ohio.

"Oh. Not her. I moved on." He grinned again.

I laughed, shook my head, and said, " So, Ninj has discovered sex...finally."

"Yeah." He laughed. "Life is good. We have some catching up to do. So the people you're bringing in, they behind you?"

"I hope so," I told him.

He lowered his voice. "I hear Carol is with them." It wasn't a question. He knew and was fishing for my reaction while watching my eyes as he did.

"Yeah. She is. How's Night?"

He laughed, tried to choke it down, and didn't succeed. "Oh brother. She is trying so hard to be an iron ass about it."

I interrupted him. "What? Does the entire world know?"

Ninja almost stopped laughing and held his hand in a placating gesture. "No. Just the people that were linked and me." He added, "Night told me. Shelli has no clue unless Max told her, which I doubt, because she asked me what Night's problem was."

He laughed again. "My sister thinks she is being so calm and cool. If she had a half a brain she would realize that everyone knows she is really pissed about something and they are staying as far away from her as possible."

I shook my head. "Ninja, life is just too fucking complicated sometimes."

He was still grinning. "Yeah. Let me help you out on that." He whistled, and Night stepped from behind the tree that had hidden her.

I looked at him and said, "You know, you're an asshole," but I was grinning and moving toward her at the same time.

She dropped her daypack and met me halfway. I caught her as she leaped and wrapped her legs around me. A few minutes later she broke lip contact to look over my shoulder. I didn't have to ask or turn around to know who had come into view.

She unclamped, then dropped off me as if I was a horse and she had reached her destination. I turned around and saw that she had already covered half the distance to Carol and wasn't slowing down.

Carol, to her credit, didn't cower or even look nervous. She stood there and waited. She didn't have to wait long. Night was in her face in a couple blinks of the eye.

I tensed up and got ready to move. I wasn't going to let Night cut her down. Give her hell, yes. Cut her throat? No. I had noticed she was carrying her fillet knife. Not a good sign. Night stood there for a couple of seconds.

Then she said quietly, in a steely monotone, "Hello, Carol."

Total ice was in Carol's reply. "Hello, Night. Long time no see."

If this had been me and someone else going to head to head I would have been stripping the body by now. I was never going to understand women. This I knew without a doubt.

Night broke off the staring contest by telling Carol slowly, as if she was addressing a retard or a child, "Gardener will go look for your child. You will come with us. If he isn't back in a month I will kill you. If he comes back within a month - with or without your child - you will live but not amongst the people of Freya. Do you understand this and accept?"

Carol swallowed, the first sign that Night had gotten to her, and said quietly, "Yes."

Night didn't say another word. She turned, and marched up to me, stopping only long enough to hook her arm around my waist and say, "Let's go." We stopped so she could pick up her daypack and then kept going. I had an idea, actually a rapidly growing hope, that I knew what was coming next. I was right.

About two hours later we caught up with the team working drag security for the Horde. Ninja was with them. He greeted Night as she walked past him smiling. When she had covered enough distance, he waved the rest of the team on to escort her in while he waited.

He looked at me, shook her his head, and said, "Damn, Bro. She's smiling. All is well?"

"I suppose."

He continued. "I asked Max if I could go with you. He said it was your call."

I thought, *Thanks, Max.* I looked at him. We had come a long way together. I almost said yes, but then I changed my mind.

260

"It wouldn't be right, Ninj. They need you. If me and you go, that's two thirds of the real warriors missing." I saw the disappointment in his eyes. "Plus, I need you to keep Night alive for me," and grinned.

"Yeah. Be careful, Bro." Then he was gone.

I watched him move at a trot until I lost sight of him and then I went and found a log to sit down on. I was suddenly tired and I felt more than a little empty, maybe even stupid, and very alone.

13546118R00156

Made in the USA
Lexington, KY
06 February 2012